TWEAKING THE DREAM:
A CRYSTAL METH TRUE STORY

CLEA   MYERS

I dedicate this book to the life and memory of
Grannie, Constance Munro Reid Ryves Lieberman

NAM MYOHO RENGE KYO

CHAPTER 1

Seeking Greener Grass

Coelum non animum mutant qui trans mare currant.
(Those who cross the sea change the sky above
them, but not their souls.) Horace

This ain't no disco it ain't no country club either this is LA . . .
Cheryl Crow *All I Wanna Do*

The west-bound plane climbs into the night sky of
Boston and the sensation hits: a mix of robust glee,
anticipation and pure joy. I have no idea what my new life in
Los Angeles offers, yet I am consumed with hope as if I have
been given an irrefutable psychic prediction. The promise of a
new life, alongside a reinvention of myself because no one
knows me in LA, swells me with lightness and fresh
determination that I will be a huge success. I know little about
LA except what the Beach Boys and the Mamas and the
Papas sang, as well as images from films that I'd grown up on.
My favourite childhood memory is of my mother closing the
drawing room curtains on a Sunday afternoon to cosy up
together on the sofa, with tea and biscuits, watching black and
white American movies like *Casablanca* and *Double Indemnity*,
clasping wads of tissue. Also, I feel some compunction to go
there that I cannot explain, but I keep this to myself.

A large middle-aged woman, with an almost-black mole
under her nose that needs a pluck, sits in the window seat. Her
forehead shines with beads of sweat and her eyes are closed.

"Excuse me mam, but please don't worry. There's no
way this plane is going to crash-"

"Oh yeah! How's that honey?"

"Because I have a date with destiny." I whisper. Inwardly

I cringe at the absurdity of this remark while the woman chuckles and gives my thigh a friendly slap.

"Honey, I'm real happy to hear that. Now let's get us a drink."

Last night my Russian-American cousins, the Vronskys, held a farewell dinner for me at their beautiful house in Providence, Rhode Island. It is due to them that I'd attended Brown University, the prestigious liberal arts college that I'd recently graduated from, with honours.

Boris Vronsky, and his brilliant wife Tess, a Modern Languages Professor who heads her department at Brown, had taken me under their wing when I was a teenager. On visits to the UK they had witnessed my floundering potential and determined to set me on the right track, having discussed matters- academic, not personal- with my father, while I was still boarding at Heathfield, an all-girls school in Ascot in the Home Counties. I think they realised I was a late bloomer who needed a boost, while my parents were preoccupied with their own problems.

"Hey kid!" My neighbour nudges me just as the fasten seat-belt sign blinks off. I had talked her ear off for the first two hours of the flight and then collapsed into myself, worried about my skittish cat Jezebel stashed in the undercarriage of the plane.

"Oh my god, this is it! The beginning of my whole new life!" I jump up, butterflies whirring in my stomach.

"Honey, may you get what you want and want what you get."

In the cab from LAX to Hollywood, I stare at people in their cars, moving in rush-hour swarms, isolated in their own public privacy within their individual rubber and metal cases on the wide, unattractive roads. Cement seems to be everywhere. As the cab crosses the narrow residential streets of West Hollywood I am surprised by the neat rows of bungalows. Their fairytale quaintness reminds me of the pink and white Wendy house I received on my sixth birthday: my hideaway where I hid my favourite Bourbon biscuits in a pale blue tin up on the pretend rafter.

I find the key Walter, my new landlord, has hidden for me and let myself in to the small bungalow. There's a message for me by the phone:

Welcome to La La Land!
Call Zoe (212) 243-7824 ASAP
<u>**Important- about Ryan**</u>

Oh no- what has happened now? I dread thinking about him- my good friend Ryan had made it back for my graduation a couple of months ago, but he was not the charismatic, brilliant, fun Ryan he had been only the year before. He was a broken young man. His mind was addled and shot to pieces because of some drug I had never heard of called crystal meth.

He had moved out here to LA a year ago, following his graduation, and got a good job at Georgio Fashion and Fragrance in Beverly Hills. To start with he had loved it- dealing with celebrities, organising promotions and events, getting lots of freebies- but not as much as the thriving gay scene in West Hollywood, known for its full-on parties and drug scene: a place where a handsome, young man like Ryan would be very welcome. I had tried to find out what exactly had happened over the phone and then when he came back to Brown to visit. Each time he got a glassy look in his eyes and changed the subject to something completely unrelated and bizarre- the price of airmail postage, Danish Restaurants in NYC, Reagan's policy on tuna farming. And then when I had told him I was moving to LA, I expected him to join in with my excitement. Instead he took both my hands and looked really sad: he kept repeating quietly, more to himself than to me:

"Please be careful, please be careful. . ." over and over again. After what seemed an age I grabbed my hands away, demanding to know what he meant. He gazed off into the middle distance and I became peeved. I was determined that my new life in LA was to be a mega success story and his negativity infringes upon my dreams. Besides, nothing could be worse than the week before my arrival at Brown, three

7

years ago, when I received the news that I needed laser treatment for the early stages of cervical cancer. Fear short-circuited the excitement and anticipation of the new start I craved. Arranging appointments and waiting for test results was hardly the start I'd envisioned, but I'd learned stoicism through my uncomplaining father. As soon as I underwent my final check-up six months later I banished the incident from my memory. New friends like Ryan, who loved to party, helped me to forget.

At seven, the morning before my graduation, Ryan quietly knocked on my bedroom door: "Sorry to wake you but I've gotta go home."

I flick the switch on my bedside lamp. I cannot believe what I'm hearing because he had only arrived in Providence two days ago.

"Home? What? Where do you mean 'home'?"

"Back to Nevada."

"Nevada! But you hate Nevada!"

"That's where I'm going. I haven't actually got any choice about it." He gives me a 'that's life' half-smile.

"Why didn't you tell me?!" I jump out of bed and almost tear the blinds yanking them open.

"I thought we were supposed to be close friends and you were staying for my graduation!? What the fuck is going on? How are you going to get to Nevada without any money?"

"I borrowed some money for the ticket- I gotta be at the airport by 10am."

"I don't understand. Why didn't you say?"

"Sorry- I forgot."

He really does look sorry and I realise in that moment that Ryan is not who he'd been; clearly he needed to do whatever it was that could help him repair the damage and get him back to his old self.

"I'll take you to the airport- I just need to find a car to get us there. Can you put on some coffee?"

"Thanks Clea- I didn't really wanna take the bus."

Ryan was originally from Nevada, so it sort of made sense that he wanted to go back there for a while to piece his life together. At least he could stay at his parents' rent-free, although I was suspicious of how good an idea it was

8

considering how strained his relations with his folks were; in fact his father had still not accepted that Ryan was gay. The truth was that Ryan had outstayed his welcome with all his friends, bar me, but I am in transit myself. He also has no job or money, so was borrowing whenever he could. I reasoned that maybe a trip back home was the answer, at least while Ryan got back on his feet.

"Maybe this is a chance to sort stuff out, once and for all," I remark hopefully.

He nods in a non-committal kind of way. I really care about him, but he's become so distant and cryptic that I find myself impatient and irritable.

Later, while I wave him off at the small airport, I'm secretly pleased and relieved to see the back of him. Vulnerable people make me nervous and I am perplexed as to how things had gone so wrong for him, in the space of only one year in LA. But then, who am I to judge because I have also suffered from severe delusions: I'd equated getting to Brown with reaching nirvana. Whatever my expectations had been, they were impossible to meet because I had based them on fantasies that my college life would be perfect. Instead I have to make a whole new set of friends (I'd transferred from Pine Manor College in Boston where I'd gone for a year to get my grades up), work really hard to maintain decent grades and not let my cousins down who are paying for me to be here.

Near my graduation I decide that the east coast is the wrong setting for my life to pan out happily and successfully, just as the UK has also been not-quite-right. The answer is Los Angeles, but my plans certainly meet with resistance from both my parents and the Vronskys. Aunty Tess looked at me askance: "Clea dear, who do you actually know in Los Angeles?"

"A couple of people from Brown and Mia, our cousin." I replied confidently.

"I have to be honest and say I really think you'd be much better off in New York City. At least to start with- then you'll have us around some of the time, as well as a bunch of Brown friends all finding apartments and jobs together in the city."

Of course she's right. But how can I explain that I

actually want to get away from family and people from Brown because I've never really fitted in? I would have sounded incredibly ungrateful. My adventure of getting to Brown and graduating has left me with strongly mixed feelings. Besides my difficulties making new friends, the sharpened intellect of my contemporaries, particularly within the Modern Culture and Media department that I majored in, rumbled me. My small, non-academic British public school had not prepared me for this, and I feel unformed, clumsy and out of my depth. I think I give off the impression of being relatively together and I do make friends, but something still does not fit. A dalliance with cocaine during my final year suggests otherwise- there's a scent of desperation in my 'party use' that has my friends concerned for me. Part of me recognises I am unhappy, but I figure a new location will fix this.

Hollywood beckons- the great intellectual desert- because it will be better suited to who I am. I need to make it on my own and on my own terms.

Inside my new, West Hollywood bungalow, on Lexington Avenue by Plummer Park, I admire the wooden floors throughout, compact bedroom, bathroom and kitchen. It is adorable, with heaps of potential. Finding furniture to fill the space will not be difficult. A certain promise of cosiness strikes me.

Breaking the silence, the phone rings and I excitedly pick it up for the first time.

"Clea?" A gravelly female voice asks.

"Yes. Hello."

"This is Zoë." The cogs reel as I assume it is the native New Yorker with bouncy corkscrew blonde curls. We had been in a film class in junior year and she had used Ryan in her final project, deconstructing sexual stereotypes.

"Hello, how are you doing? I just got here- to LA I mean. I heard on the grapevine that you got a great job at MTV in New York?- That's fantastic." I ease up, realising I am gabbling.

"Thanks. Are you able to make it then- Thursday week?"

"Sorry, what? Make what?"

"Next week in Nevada- the funeral." A long silence.

"Shit! You don't know, do you?"

"Know what? My new land-lord left a note; I just got in from the airport"-

"It's Ryan."

"How is he doing? I've been meaning to call him; everything has been so bloody hectic and-".

Zoë cuts in: "Ryan's dead- I'm sorry to be abrupt but I have a lot of calls to make."

"Oh no, oh God! How?"

"He had a car crash on the freeway."

"But he didn't have a car, did he?" I stupidly ask.

"I'm not sure. Look I'm sorry. It would have been quick- that's what the doctor told his parents. I'm sorry but I need to make some more calls-"

"Yes, yes, of course. Sorry. How stupid of me." My mind is racing- 'No way' it keeps saying. Not Ryan- alive, vibrant, weird Ryan; the gorgeous, kind Ryan I'd made plans for the future with. This cannot be happening; it is not part of the master plan and my friends do not die like this, out of the blue, in ridiculous accidents.

Zoë's voice echoes down the phone; I find a pen and paper and take down the time, date and location of the funeral service. I do so as if in a trance.

I cannot remember hanging up. I collapse onto the dusty, wooden floor; the gritty coolness comforts me while Jezebel nudges my calves impatiently, wanting to be fed.

I have no idea how long I lie there, wishing the phone would ring again and I would answer it and they would tell me it was someone's idea of a sick joke.

When I gather my strength to stand it is pitch black in the backyard and for a second I wish I were anywhere but here in this completely strange city.

I stumble about looking for a light switch, finding one by the front door that gives off an overhead glare. A slew of moths appear as if from nowhere. I absolutely hate moths; they remind me of my father's sad derelict house in London that is covered in twenty years of dust. A rage erupts inside me and I start yelling: "Where the fuck is that bottle of Freixenet?"- I'd

11

had the cab stop at a liquor store- even while I clutch it in my hand. I'm tempted to smash it.

Grappling with the metal and foil cage, I rip the cork out, spilling the fizzy wine across the floor. I remember hungry Jezebel who cowers under a chair. I find my cigarettes and light one, inhaling deeply. The bastard! This was not in the plan: Ryan was supposed to go home to Nevada for a couple of months, get better and then return to LA and start up his life again, with me. And now here I am in a new home, in a fresh city full of ripe hope, optimism and enthusiasm and Ryan crashes his car and kills himself. The whole picture that had been crystal clear in my mind is now hopelessly out of focus. How can I accept that this has happened? What is really going on? I gulp down the fizzy acidic wine, lighting cigarette after cigarette.

Eventually I collapse on top of the unmade bed in the otherwise unfurnished bedroom, too drunk and tired to undress.

Even though Nevada borders California and I could drive straight there, I do not make it to Ryan's funeral. Outwardly I go through the motions as if my intention is to attend- calling various friends all over the US, writing to his parents, sending flowers in advance- but then I find myself leaving a message on Zoë's machine. I am relieved that she doesn't pick up. I make up a lie that I just got this fantastic job as a production assistant on a commercial and I have to start filming tomorrow and I really need the experience and the money and how I know Ryan would want me to do it etc. I will never admit to anyone that this was a lie. All along I knew I could not go because deep down I am a coward. The finality of death is not part of my dream and I need to keep my dream alive. Acknowledging Ryan's death will only diminish it and I am secure that his spirit has long left his body and is somewhere like Thailand now, sipping cocktails on the beach in a parallel world.

I push Ryan's death out of my mind because it's such an incredible waste: a young man who had such a gentle soul, sharp brain and huge potential. As my mother, over the telephone put it in her fake Yankee twang: "Clea- life ain't fair darlin'. Sooner ya learn that, the better!"

This was her way of showing sympathy and maybe she realized I was not quite as tough as I encouraged others to believe. I suppose it was drugs that killed Ryan; if he had never got involved with them I doubt he would have veered into the freeway centre-divide, in small-dick-fat-knucklesville, Nevada (Ryan's description) at ninety miles an hour with no other vehicles involved. Something snapped in him; that I am sure of, and I lament my inability to recognise how seriously unhappy and unsettled he had been the last time I had been with him.

I know I am not heartless. It is just that I do not know what to do with the mass of feelings that his predicament silently spoke of. It is easier to ignore them, or bury them rather than actually allow them to take me over. Two years ago at Brown, a female student had drowned herself in the Providence River. She had been in the same 'transfer' group as me into Brown in 1989. On the morning of her memorial service I awoke with leaden legs and could not leave my off-campus apartment, instead curling up in bed for the day with *Brideshead Revisited*. I perceive this as a strong sense of self-preservation. Occasionally I slip into speculation about how my excuse was received by those who attended Ryan's funeral; I quickly screen out the recriminations. Don't most people have short memories anyway?

I investigate the local streets of Hollywood where I live. Although officially the bungalow is in the smarter West Hollywood zip code, the area seems more like Hollywood with grimy side streets and cheap fast-food restaurants like Astro Burger and Denny's.

Few people walk here except for the homeless, prostitutes and a few elderly Poles who spend hours in Plummer Park playing chess and cards. The main boulevard of Santa Monica is the nearest to my bungalow.

On my walk I head into a 7-11 to buy some cigarettes. I am desperate for the loo so I ask the teenager with lanky blonde hair at the counter if I can use their toilet. He fumbles in his pocket and slides the key over to me, with my change: "It's gross- enter at your peril lady."

He is not joking! Inside the facility there is an exit door that I fling open because of the horrific stench. To my surprise there is a small bungalow not dissimilar to mine, bar the peeling paint and broken windows, set in a small patch of wasteland, invisible from the row of shop fronts on Santa Monica. The bungalow has a poorly made wooden cross nailed to the front eave of the roof. I am intrigued because it looks like a secret, makeshift chapel. I try the mosquito net door, which opens with an angry squeak, and then ease open the warped front door. It smells damp. I wedge a brick at the entrance to allow some air in.

I flick my lighter and in the flame see a rustic pew made of planks of wood with space for about six people, set before a simple altar that has cigarette burns on the top. I examine a broken statue of Christ, with chipped paint, standing about three feet high. He is missing one arm and half a foot. I carefully lift him up onto the altar.

"Hey lady- what the hell ya doin'?" The teenager from 7-11 pokes his head through the door.

I jump and feel my face redden with embarrassment.

"Sorry- I didn't expect to find a chapel in the back of a 7-11."

"I thought you'd done a runner!"

"A runner? Of course not."

"I need my keys-"

"I'm sorry. What is this place?" I hand him the keys.

"Some weirdoes were renting it- they fixed it up like this. And then one day they packed up n'split. Left this stuff behind. I think they were in some weird cult."

"Can I stay in here for a little bit?" He looks amazed at my request, shrugging:

"Sure, but flick the door catch on your way out. Don't want no street scum movin' in coz my manager'll get pissed with me."

I cannot remember when I was last in a church but now I want to pray for Ryan. I kneel in the dark and close my eyes. A few minutes pass and I feel very cold, as if a strong wind has blown through but the door is almost closed. I am strangely happy, almost uplifted. A car pulls into the strip mall with Madonna on its stereo, full blast:

> *Life is a mystery, everyone must stand alone*
> *I hear you call my name and it feels like home. . . .*
> *when you call my name it's like a little prayer. . .*

It's Ryan's and my theme song. I run out into the sun bursting with renewed hope.

CHAPTER 2

Crazy Gordon

To the highly-sensitive a touch is a blow, a sound is
a noise, a misfortune is a tragedy, a joy is an ecstasy,
a friend is a lover, a lover is a God and failure is death.
                                                    Pearl S. Buck

I suspect and hope that it is a matter of time before
things go further with my neighbour, Gordon. Our friendship
has been developing and the chemistry is there, plain and
simple. Also, I am new in LA with only my cousin Mia who I
barely know and Roxanne- whom I'd recently met through
work- as friends. Conveniently, Gordon lives directly across the
street in his 'studio', a shack surrounded by a plethora of junk-
furniture, car parts, hunks of metal- that he collects on a daily
basis, so far as I can tell.

Our initial meeting had set an unusual tone: I had been
out looking for my cat near his shack, when he had snuck up
behind and then leaped round in front of me while shoving a
camera in my face and taking a photo.

"Now I've got the proof I need! Ha ha!" His handsome
face declares.

"What are you talking about?- I'm looking for my tabby
cat, Jezebel-"

"You're a snooper for them! I know it!" His wide mouth
permeates into a Cheshire-grin.

"Them? Who's them? Please. I live across the street-"

"I'll be watching you!" His smooth tone hints of seduction
and knowing.

Later that evening he comes over with some beers to

17

apologise for his 'weirdness', claiming it was all part of his artistic temperament.

"By the way, what is a snooper?" I demand, cracking open a beer.

"What 'dya think?"

"A busy body."

"Nooo- An undercover cop."

"You thought I was a cop?!"

"Yeah. Why not."

I smart at this; somehow it strikes me as an insult.

"Why'd a cop be snooping round outside your studio?"

"Coz that's what cops do."

His struggling artist persona, living in his garret, increases his appeal for me; he was nothing like the boys I had dated at Brown and his derision of conventional living makes him all the more attractive. The fact that everyone I know would disapprove adds to his intriguing aura.

I am thrilled when Gordon knocks on my door, a week later, to invite me to a party on a Saturday evening.

He will not tell me where we are heading; he wants it to be a surprise and I know it will be fresh and different. I drive us over to some place in the valley- he haphazardly directs and I have no idea where we are going except that it involves swerving off and on various freeways, with little warning from Gordon.

"I think we're being followed- pull over."

"What are you talking about- why on earth would we be followed?" Gordon says nothing, but seems needlessly on edge. He then leans in close to me, whispering:

"Any car with an Enterprise sticker on it- on the right hand side of the back bumper-is an undercover cop car."

"What?" I cannot believe my ears and start to laugh; I had hired an Enterprise car myself when I first arrived- there are thousands bombing about LA. Catching a glimpse of his face I do not dare mention this.

We park outside what looks like a partly burnt-out building; some dim light emanates from a basement area. There is no way I would usually enter a place like this.

"I don't want to get in trouble with the cops, or anything." He nods his head in a 'don't you know anything' kind of way. I decide to shut up and go with the flow. I had wanted adventure and excitement and now I am getting it.

I follow him down some steps where the smell of urine is dampened with disinfectant, along a dark winding corridor that ends at a makeshift entrance draped in heavy, dark velveteen fabric. Finding our way between it we enter a large space partly filled with mattresses. Candles and tea lights are scattered across the floor while bodies recline on the mattresses chatting or fondling each other, while others mill about in an energised and goggle-eyed fashion. There are some paintings up on the walls and a projector goes in a corner, emitting grainy black and white images on the white wall. A couple of men peer suspiciously at me and Gordon grabs my arm protectively. They have a look in their eyes like Gordon's when he had freaked out at me over the 'snooper' business.

Gordon indicates a female propped up on a more elevated mattress
which has two columns at the far end draped in silks and satins, some velvet and even European flags. Bizarre.

"That's Valencia- they had to carry her in. She can't walk."

"Oh that's terrible. What happened?"

"I think she fell down the stairs, or something. Or someone pushed her. But she likes it coz she's always the centre of attention."

"What's she doing here? Her bed is fancier than the others."

"She's psychic- otherwise known as the Queen of Truth. She's also a hermaphrodite."

"What?" My head reels.

"I'm sure she'll do you a reading- as long as you give off the right energy."

"That would be great. Let's open the wine I bought."

I drink some white wine out of the bottle because there are no glasses or plastic cups around. Gordon brings out a baggy and starts emptying a pile of tiny white crystals onto the back of a magazine that lies on the booze table.

"I didn't know you did coke-"

"I don't. This is crystal- it's a different world."

"What does it do? You don't trip, or hallucinate or anything?"

"Nah- try it. Burns a bit the first time. It's pretty harmless stuff but makes you very creative."

I am in a quandary because how can it be 'harmless stuff' after what happened to Ryan, but then I look at Gordon and he seems on the level, although rather different to the go-getter Ivy Leaguers I have been around for the past few years. Surely he would not want to cause me harm. I decide one small line should be okay, for the sake of experimentation and experience.

He hands me a broken off plastic tube from a Bic biro and cuts the proffered line in half. People around us appear oblivious and unconcerned about us openly taking drugs, with no sense of judgement whatsoever. Maybe they are anarchists. I feel like I have time-travelled back to the 60s- an era I had always wanted to be part of.

"Better take it easy- don't want you flying too close to the clouds."

I insert the plastic tube and inhale-Owwww! This stuff burns like a hot torch searing the insides of my nostril. The sensation is acute but short-lived; within minutes a magnanimous pull exerts itself over my being. Everyone and everything takes on a hue of interest and uniqueness all of its own- whether it be visible in their beautiful hair, delicate hands, original attire or through their unusual, thrilling conversation. Gordon appears to glow. His long chestnut wavy hair, tied back in a loose ponytail, emphasises his aristocratic features with chiselled nose and chin, while he holds court like he was born to, discussing his 'found object' sculptures.

Apparently MOMA in New York has expressed interest in mounting an exhibition of his work. I romanticise our developing relationship as akin to that between my heroine Leonora Carrington, a surrealist artist and writer, and Max Ernst. I had written my thesis about her work, having become transfixed by her self-portrait: *The Inn of the Dawn Horse* (1936-37). The wild haired woman glaring out of the painting was talking to me, egging me on: "Grasp life now, devour it before it devours you!" Never before had a painting provoked such a strong reaction in me and not through lack of trying: I had sat for hours in the Rothko Room at the Tate waiting for my Art History teacher's promise that I would be transported to a new place- or back to a place like the womb- but I had felt very little, except stiffness.

Throughout the long evening Gordon occasionally sends me coy looks from under his camel eyelashes and I know that we are destined for each other.

I feel like I have entered some modern-day salon, full of fascinating people who want to be my friend and lover.

I speak with Virgil, a man of indeterminate years, who has a thick python called Angel wrapped about his neck like a woolly scarf. I have to re-direct my smoke as Angel is allergic to cigarette fumes and burnt toast. A thin blonde girl in a tight fuchsia dress approaches and throws her arms about Virgil's tiny waist. Her face is streaked with dark tears.

"She's lying- she doesn't like me!" She looks over at Valencia who has moved on to somebody else. He hands her his drink which she slugs down.

"Virgil, she said I'll never have a baby- never!" I find it hard to believe this frail and pale girl- she looks maybe sixteen- would even be thinking about babies and motherhood. In response he starts to lick the tears from off her face while I watch, moved by their plight. I feel part of their private dilemma, even though I have just met them. Virgil takes her hand to the snake caressingly:

"Angel's our baby- she's enough for us."

"No she is not! I want my own baby!"

"You seemed to like Angel fine last night- In fact Angel seems to satisfy you better than I ever can."

I am hanging on their every word, although they now seem oblivious to me, when Gordon re-directs me across the sticky floor to Valencia, sprawled out on the haphazard bed with her eyes closed in what I presume to be spirit meditation. Or maybe she is half drunk and wired like me?

"I don't want to disturb her." Her thin features are witch-like and her cold blue eyes intimidating.

"You're not- it's a favour to me."

"Are you having your Tarot read?"

"No- I don't believe in it."

"Oh go on, just for fun." I give him my most sexy 'come

hither' look.

"I don't have fun with things I don't understand."

"Oh how wise- well I'm game."

A hush has descended on the basement; very few people remain and those that do huddle close together. It is cold and you can see your breath. Hours have passed in what feels like minutes. Most of the candles have burnt out while the light of approaching dawn seeps through cracks in the walls. I still feel energised but ready to give over my attention to Gordon. Maybe Valencia can help me with this because I can feel my heart swelling in my chest in anticipation of our lovemaking.

"Someone died recently didn't they- not in your family, a close friend?" An ice cloak envelopes me- I thought this was meant to be a lark, not anything verging on reality.

"Why do you say that?"

"Because your friend has a message for you. Wanna hear it?"

"Errrr. . . I don't know."

"I'm getting Robin, Robbie, Ryan-"

"Yes! Ryan! Oh my god- what does he say? Where is he? Is he okay?" I am bursting with excitement; I almost expect Ryan to appear from the ether.

I look around for Gordon, wanting him to join me and be part of my experience, but he is deep in conversation with one of his cronies; they are snorting more stuff off the end of a penknife.

Valencia takes my hand and holds it loosely. I grab it back, not at all comfortable with her touching me.

"There's no need to be afraid- your friend and his spirit group are looking out for you. He just wants you to be careful. Think before you jump in, head first. And keep dancing."

"Oh, yes! . . I'm new here in LA."

"I know. Right now you're living and thriving on the emotional. That's okay, but you need to trust yourself more, trust your intuition. I feel some waves but eventually things will work out. You have a willingness in your soul to learn- that's a gift and you should treat it as such."

"Can you tell me when I'm going to get a decent job?"

"Soon enough. You need to live in the present and stop

chasing the future; it arrives as we speak. A job is not necessarily the answer for you, ya know."

Later on Gordon and I lie in my bed. Time is disjointed- I giggle to myself thinking it is teatime back home in England, whereas here in my little pink bungalow in West Hollywood, Gordon still has his bag of goodies on the go. He has cut out lines on the back cover of a book by my bed. In the shadowy light he looks older, his hair dirty and his clothes lie on the floor heavy with grime and sweat. His lack of vanity does not turn me off. Instead, I find it appealing. He genuinely does not care and that is sexy in spades. I have decided to keep him as my secret.

I have taken a tiny bit more of the crystal meth and all my mundane concerns- finding work, visa sponsorship, making enough money- have drifted elsewhere, detached from my conscience.

We have sex over and over again- clearly this drug prolongs erection and ejaculation and explains why it's so popular within the gay community.

"You'll never need me, will you?" As usual, I want some form of guarantee, a sign that this magical realm we have entered is not only for this moment.

"I'll always like you."

"Hardly the same thing, is it?"

"Clea- we come from nothing and we will return to nothing; either you require a lot or you're happy to stick with nothing."

"How do you define nothing?"

"Nothing. . .is nothing. It is how it sounds. It is complete by itself, like a circle."

"So all you need is the circle, magic man?"

"I am the circle, and yes- that is all I need."

Having made some calls I realise that on the West coast, or at least in LA in the Entertainment Industry, potential employers are not duly impressed by academic achievement. On the few occasions I cold-call production companies, I detect snorts of derision down the phone, following my usual preamble: "I recently graduated from Brown University with honours and-" this is the point where they cut me off with 'we'll call you if something opens up'.

I take up an unpaid internship with Chanticleer Films as a production assistant in order to gain experience. One evening, I join Gordon sitting on the curb smoking a cigarette, across the street from my bungalow, where he's waiting for a friend- I have never known a person with so many friends- to show up.

Exhaling, he takes a ring off his little finger. Holding it up above his head in the diminishing sunlight I see it is gold and platinum, in a knot design.

"This is for you." He takes my hand and slips it onto my index finger.

"What for? - I mean . . . where did you get it?"

"I got it from a friend- it was part of a deal." His studied casualness makes me think that maybe it is not just a throwaway gesture. I want to believe I am special to him, hence the ring, but his vagueness about where he got it – and the absence of a box- makes me suspicious. We have not even been to the cinema together, so a sincere love token is hardly in the equation. But I like the ring and I can live with illusions.

"What kind of a deal?" I enquire.

He jumps up.

"It's yours if you like it- take it or leave it." I grab his arm and give him a kiss on the lips.

CHAPTER 3

My Brilliant Career

The only thing that makes life possible is permanent,
intolerable uncertainty. Ursula LeGuin

Anxiety creeps in. I wake up most mornings with a jolt
and cold with damp sweat. I need a proper paid job and I also
have my work permit and legal status to consider. At present I
have an extended Student Visa that will last a year out of
Brown. I have no time to waste if I want to stay in the US-
legally that is.

It is Thursday lunchtime in early September and
seriously hot. I am sunbathing when Walter, my landlord,
enters the small ornate gate that connects the yards looking
purposeful. I assume he is pissed off about something to do
with the bungalow. I quickly pull on my T-shirt that I had been
using as a headrest, and wipe off the shine I can feel on my
forehead.

"Hiya!" I give him my most friendly smile.

"Can we have a talk?"

"Of course." Walter is gay and dresses like a classic
preppie in chinos and button down shirt; he looks at his Oyster
Rolex. I assume that he is in a hurry, but then I catch him
giving me this hopeful look. He takes the pose of some one
about to make a speech.

"You see- well actually- I have a proposition for you. I
mean I guess you aren't working right now?"

"Not since my Internship ended. I'm looking, but I guess
it takes time." I omit that I left my internship after Chanticleer
Films refused to start paying me, after two months of free
labour; granted I picked up valuable work experience but I

need paid work.

"The thing is I need someone to cover for me while my boss Amory is away and I thought of you."

Amory Dorset is one of the most respected independent producers working in LA. I cannot believe my luck.

"Brilliant! Yes, I'd love to work for him."

"Amory likes you English girls for some reason. I'll call ya later okay and explain everything."

"Good morning Clea. What a pleasure to finally meet you".

A face fits the telephone voice from the past two weeks, but not the one I had envisioned. I am surprised by Amory's pale skin– almost anemic- evenly speckled with freckles and his strawberry blonde hair. Offering my hand I hope I cover up my disappointment; in my mind I had conjured up this image of a dark, dashing Clark Gable-type. Looks aside, he immediately puts me at ease and he bursts with quiet charm, thanking me for stepping in for Walter.

Amory is from old money in Huston, Texas. His lilt is divine and a welcome contrast to the clipped businesslike East coast rhythm I had become used to. When he asks: "How are you doing today?" I actually take time to respond because he sounds genuine, unlike the customary American greeting: "Hi-how-are-ya!" that sounds like a question, but is really a clipped acknowledgement-in-passing. Back on campus at Brown, I had paused to reflect only to find myself speaking into thin air.

I suspect Amory is not like other Americans, at least most of the ones I have met, and his choice of office backs this up: a Spanish hacienda-style ground-level apartment on Havenhurst Avenue, off Sunset- directly across from the junction leading up to the Chateau Marmont, where Jim Belushi had spent his final hours. In the kitchen there is an Arreggi Cappuccino maker like they have in restaurants and all the furniture is the genuine Arts and Crafts that Amory collects.

The next morning I arrive early, which is nothing short of a miracle for me. My plan is to make such a positive difference that he takes me on full time, now that he is back from his summer break in Maine. He rents a duplex in the same building as the office and each time I enter the lush courtyard, the bright colours and aromas overwhelm me.

I notice a pile of books and scripts on the large cedar table by the window.

"Good morning Miss. Clea- how are you doing today?" booms over the intercom; I quickly turn the volume down before it melts my eardrums. I love the way he calls me Miss; it makes me sound so dignified and proper. He mentions the selection of books and scripts.

"What shall I do with them?"

"I'd like you to read the stuff, see if it's got any kind of potential for further development- stories and characters for a movie- that kind of thing. Do you know how to do script coverage?"

"Yes I do. I've already worked freelance for The Producer Circle Company in New York and Bedford Falls in Santa Monica. I started over a year ago when I interned a couple of summers ago in New York for an Entertainment Lawyer."

"That's great. Let's have lunch at one and we can talk it all over."

Over a macrobiotic lunch, Amory explains his on-going slate (a list of projects at different levels of development). The range includes an adventure-horror story to smaller stories of interesting lives- like that of a 19th Century female photographer overcoming the odds in the Montana outback- to an adaptation of a literary classic.

We get on really well and I am thrilled when he offers to keep me on. Beyond some correspondence and phone enquiries my job is to look for material and read material that either Amory, or myself has found. What a great job!

Letting myself in after work, a rusty, yellow Beetle pulls up on my street- hitting the curb in its haste- with a sweaty-faced black guy at the wheel. Next to him sits a buxom bleach blonde with fine features and the kind of button nose that Beverly Hills girls pay plastic surgeons for. She is already out of the car before the driver has time to pull up the hand brake.

She runs across to Gordon's shack. She bangs on the

door and Gordon appears; there is no mistaking his glee.

"Twister! - You're out." He embraces her. She is pale and almost frail, but her hard eyes and angular features say 'Don't fuck with me'. Her immense breasts are barely shaded by shiny pink lycra and she wears tight black jeans with scuffed gold platform heels; every thing about her seems slightly worn and faded- dated in fashion terms- except her eyes that are bright as glistening white paint in the sun.

Gordon envelopes her possessively in his thick, muscular arms- something he has never done to me- while I force myself to cross the threshold of the bungalow, before he catches me jealously watching them.

I know they are more than just friends. A blind man a couple of blocks away would smell their attraction for each other.

I have no choice but to retire gracefully, because making a scene seems pointless. I am humiliated. This guy is no more interested in me than I would have been in him a couple of years back, when I was running after uninterested preppie college boys. What the hell have I done? Why did he give me the ring? As an apology in advance? I need to forget about him because I am certainly not on his mind.

Clearly an affair with one's neighbour is risky, especially if the neighbour lives in a shack- a tool shed for Christ's sake- with no loo, or shower. Then the reality hits me: that's why he bothered with me- because I have a loo and shower that I would let him use, throughout the day and night. We have 'our secret code' of knocks on my bedroom window and I obediently leap out of bed to let him in. I believed him when he said he had just returned from the Valley, or Long Beach or wherever he claimed he'd been, because I had no reason not to and when I rushed out to work his white van would be laden down by stuff- bed frames, banisters, barrels, plants, planks- tied onto the dented old roof that backed up his claims. I was awed by the old van's stoicism.

His night visits came with a pay-off for me: Once he had scrubbed and showered he would join me in bed. He had sexual endurance I have never experienced before; in fact, sometimes I wished he would get on with it. Once he gamely admitted he wanted to outdo his own personal record. I found

28

his primitive delight in his own manliness endearing, although I often wished we could behave like a normal couple- outings to restaurants, the cinema, shops, watch videos in bed, have sex before midnight- but it never happened.

One day Amory questioned me outright:

"Ya know what Clea? I don't mean to pry, or anything, but I've been noticing you look really tired."

"Do I?" I feign surprise.

"Perhaps a case of burning the candle at both ends?"

"Not really. I don't always sleep very well." I am hardly going to lapse into the details over my midnight cowboy-lover who I rarely see in the daylight.

"Ya know Clea- LA can be a very dangerous place. There are heaps of weirdoes here; for some reason, they all gravitate to LA. You need to be careful." Amory is dead serious.

"Oh yeah, I know. I pass them everyday on Sunset, on my way here."

"You just take good care; there're a lot of wolves in sheep's clothing around."

"I only mix with friends from Brown really. I haven't met that many other people yet. . . but I'll be careful."

He looks at me in a way I had not noticed before- resignation almost.

A ringing phone saves me from further discomfort. I like him caring about me, but on the other hand it is weird when he openly voices it and I find myself lying. Sometimes I think he sees right through me.

I replace the handset on the phone in my bedroom. I had just filled my Aunt Tess in on all the progress I was making with my new job with Amory, setting up the bungalow and making new friends. She sounded genuinely thrilled for me.

Walter knocks urgently on my bedroom window.

I amble outside the backdoor, presuming it must be some detail he wants to iron out in his usual anal manner regarding the bungalow- he is a very meticulous landlord- or it's something to do with Amory, but somehow I doubt that. He rubs his hands together nervously and will not meet my eye.

"I have some very bad news-"

"Okaaay. You might as well fire."

"Oh God. . ." He looks skyward for inspiration.

"What's happened?"

"Your cat got hit by a car- she's lying out on my front lawn."

I want to respond tartly: "Is she catching some rays?" hoping that would make it all a joke. Instead I just stand there nodding my head in disbelief. Not Jezebel, my faithful friend who'd weathered the transition from east to west coast even after her ordeal in the airplane luggage hold.

Walter puts his hand on my shoulder; the only thing we have in common, besides Amory, is a love of cats:

"D'ya want me to take care of her? I can have her taken away."

"By who?"

"There's a City Animal Disposal Unit-"

"No, thank you. I'll take care of it."

Jezebel looks peaceful lying there on the yellowed grass, like an abandoned rag-doll. I kneel down by my beautiful dead cat that could be sleeping if there was not a sharp red gash above her eye. The dry, thick clot of blood dabbed above her brow reminds me of dressing up our beige pug dog with my mother's eye shadow, when I was a girl. She must have been hit with incredible force- one sharp blow to the head.

Gordon: I want to see Gordon- he is the only one who can comfort and help me bury her. I need Gordon.

I hear light footsteps approach: it is Walter who puts his arm round me, but I gently shrug him off. I do not want a hug and besides I hate the huggy American thing. I tell him I would prefer to be left alone.

Now more angry than sad, I stomp across to Gordon's shack and bang on the door. No answer. I bang, I holler. I continue to bang chaffing the edge of my hand on the rough wood of the door. Steam begins to erupt inside me and I feel like my head is about to explode . . . with frustration, anger, hurt.

No response. I weep in sobbing gasps, leaning my full body weight against the door when I hear faint echo-like giggles. I cannot believe it. Twister is in there with him, again.

How dare he flirt and enjoy himself, while I am emotionally marooned with a dead cat to bury. The reality of what I have just heard prompts me to creep away, desperate and humiliated, but also not wanting to be discovered suddenly when I am looking such a mess and feeling so vulnerable. Obviously Gordon is not to be counted on, even as a friend. This realisation serves to deepen the empty sorrow- the hole inside- I already feel; a growing hollowness that I am becoming more and more aware of.

Months later, when I look back on my experience with Gordon, I realize that I must have been deluded, or slightly out-of-my-mind, to actually take anything he said seriously. But at the time, I had placed him upon a pedestal. I had even written a short film script entitled 'Homage to a Genius' all about him.

I believed him when he claimed that MOMA was interested in his artwork, because it backed up my naïve, gullible concept of Gordon- the great artist- slaving away in his garret. When the LAPD swooped down and took him away I was completely shocked and a little scared. If I were honest with myself- not an easy thing for me- I would have to admit that all the signs of manic lunacy were there: furtiveness, grandiosity, ego, and unkemptness. Apparently he had been building a bomb, inside the shack, but I find this hard to believe because he never brought up politics with me. But then he never gave away any of his history either, except that he originated from Vancouver.

One evening a police officer comes to my door:
"Did ya know that guy from across the street?"
"Only in passing, Officer," I lie.
And that's how it should have been.

I cannot go into work. I lack the physical will and desire. This feeling- a massive hole inside me- is familiar (memories of dismal grey mornings at college, even when they were sunny, I experienced them as grey), but this feels more ominous and frightening, possibly because there is more at stake- my income and reputation, for starters. There is a part of me that truly cares, but right now that part is the weaker part.

I know I have to call work. Amory has been so good to

31

me: he has sponsored my H-1 Visa without blinking an eyelid, tolerated my tardiness, mediocre secretarial skills and bought me countless lunches. He even walked in when I was surreptitiously speaking to 'Drug-Line' about Gordon, right before he was arrested:

"How can I help him quit crystal meth?" I asked the counsellor.

"You can't, unless he wants help. Has he gone as low as he can go?"

I have no idea about this- how low can anyone go? Only that morning he'd announced himself 'King of Hollywood', standing high upon a big, black dumpster on our street. I had not known whether to laugh, or cry.

Catching a glimpse of Amory approaching through the crack in the door, I'd quickly ended the conversation and hung up. I suspect he overheard because that afternoon he handed me a pile of scripts, "to keep me out of harm's way."

I find my phone hidden under a pile of clothes. I dial, hoping that Walter is out of the office, on errands, because his supercilious tones are more than I can cope with today. I know he will come up with some dry, snappy comment like:

"Have you been dumped again Clea, arrrrh."

Amory answers. His familiar drawl somehow gives me confidence.

"What's up?"

"I'm not sure." I try to sound normal. A long silence. Amory is a decent man, but I can sense he is feeling uncomfortable and wants to get off the phone.

"I don't feel very well. I don't think . . ." Uncontrollable sobs squeeze their way out of me. I cannot suppress them any further, but I try to continue speaking. It is no good. It is impossible for me to stop crying once I start, especially as I have been suppressing tears for so long. My guts explode like a pressure cooker. I can always count on it happening without warning.

"Look Clea, I think you need to see a professional. I can't help you with this stuff."

"I-I-I was thinking that myself-"I manage to whisper.

"Do you have anyone in mind? Or do you want me to make some calls."

"Errrr- Well there was this woman at Brown- she's a psychologist. I could give her a call. Try to get some recommendations for therapists in LA."

"Are you sure?"

"Yes- I'll be fine tomorrow."

"Do what you need to do Clea- I'll see you tomorrow. Now take care."

Is it surprising that I am falling for my boss because he is such a truly caring man? I call the Psychological Services at Brown and they tell me to call some Board of something for a list of registered psychiatrists in LA. The conversation with the operator at Brown is so abrupt that I recoil from the whole idea. This is exacerbated by the fact that when I mention my past sessions with Dr Johnson, it makes no difference because I am no longer a fee-paying student with health insurance. I really believe that an extended talk with her might get me back onto a more level ground, but clearly this is not to be the case. I never call the Registry and Amory never mentions the embarrassing episode again. I suppose he assumes that I am now in some form of therapy. He has certainly been compassionate, beyond what I would ever expect from a boss.

I am his employee, not his friend, lover or surrogate daughter, although I want to be all three.

Working in development, for Amory, helps me understand that I will never feel satisfied working on other people's projects, at the lower end of the ladder. If I want to move up, I need to write my own screenplay. So in between coverage and research for him I write a screenplay based on the life of Leonora Carrington, the subject of my undergrad thesis.

Having recently completed a re-write workshop at AFI, I need to re-write my first draft of *Surrealists in Love*, but I feel uninspired, lonely and sad.

Hours of computer dead-time agonisingly pass while I mull, drink red wine and realise what I really need is a boost of confidence. Alongside my fragile ego and 'stuck-ness', I hit on the idea of scoring some crystal meth. I'd not taken any since that night with Gordon, almost a year ago, but I know where he'd gone to get it because he had me drive him there on several occasions to meet up with a black dealer called Harold.

Anticipation of that euphoric sense of heightened awareness, brightness and intense energy propels me out the door. I justify it as an 'emergency measure' to kick-start me out of the doldrums and to inspire and motivate this re-write. After all, occasional use is relatively harmless.

I drive to the end of Cahuanga, just by the Hollywood freeway exit, and park besides a condemned building, remembering Gordon's instructions:

"The people who live in this building are desperate- they're on the edge- and I'm real serious. Don't eyeball anyone okay, they'll probably take it the wrong way."

Nothing's changed. A momentary glance at the huddled bodies lining the corridor, with their skinny hunched frames, weeping sores spotting their faces and parts of their undernourished bodies visible, not to mention the absence of women prove this is not a safe place for anyone- man, woman or junkie, on their own- but now I really want to score. I leap the stairs- what's left of them- and bang on number 69- now 666 in thick maroon graffiti.

I yell: "It's Clea- Gordon's friend, you remember, I'm cool. . . please let me in." I plead.

Eventually, a skinny black guy undoes a cacophony of locks. Once I remind him of our connection he is happy to see me, confiding: 'Yeah that scum bag Gordon's in the pan'. He sorts me out with a gram and agrees to walk me out after I voice my very real fears, especially as now the junkies outside will all know I am holding. Harold grabs a funny looking gun from a shoe box under his sheet-less, stained single bed and shoves it in the waistband of his worn sweat pants. He wears no shirt and his ribs stick out like nails in a shiny brown plastic bag. He tells me cockily:

"It's a replica but this lot don't know the difference."

"But isn't that asking for trouble- having a gun on you, replica or not- just being armed- I mean doesn't it put them on the defensive?" I am terrified that Harold will be jumped, the gun not go off and then myself floored by the hungry and desperate pack. Not feeling at all confident – or even much safer- I am desperate to get back to my car and away from this dark (of course there is no electricity although exposed wires hang out of all the walls), damp, putrid half erect building.

"No way babe- it's all about the power dynamic. Anyway I'm the man round these parts. A little lesson babe- it's usually not the smartest idea to bite the hand that feeds ya, know what I mean babe?" Harold smugly informs me and from the suggestive look in his eye I really want to get away from him too. What am I doing here? The palpitations in my chest are ready to burst out.

Even Harold is King of his castle, even if the castle is a hazardous wreck. We get to my car that I had parked out of sight- another helpful tip from Gordon- and I jump in and lock the door. Harold continues his gabble so I unwind the window:

"Smart move- they'd have got it otherwise- stripped it bare. Hey can you do me a massive favour and take me up to Hollywood and Vine?"

I should have known that the only reason he walked me out was because he wanted something. It seems that tweakers never, ever do something for nothing but hey, quid pro quo.

Fuelled on crystal meth, I re-write the screenplay over a twenty-hour stretch and to my glazed, bloodshot eye it hits the right note.

Still buzzing, I meet up with Roxanne at the Bourgeois Pig, on Franklin. She's an actress who also works reception at Propaganda Films. She has delicate features, wispy blonde hair and a South African twang she can't lose, hence the day job.

Looking at me aghast, she tells me blatantly:

"You are soooo asking for trouble!"

In between burning her tongue on her skinny latte, she regales me with the story of a childhood friend who had ended up on the streets, through drugs.

"Crystal meth is an entirely different thing." I shrug my shoulders, not in the right frame of mind for a lecture.

"Is it?"

"Of course! For a start it's not a daily routine- like, say, my morning coffee, and to be honest it makes me feel alive, more on the ball, confident-"

"God you're naïve- all drugs are the same." Roxanne bangs her tiny fist on the table, irritated now.

"It's more than that- it's like I wasn't really feeling anything before and now I am. I suddenly feel positive again. Life's exciting, the colours around me are bright, I have energy and enthusiasm; I guess I'm not . . . numb anymore and everything isn't so scary and alien."

"I don't want to be rude Clea, but that's kind of extreme. I think you should see someone."

"What do you mean 'see someone'?"

"You know, go and talk to someone- an analyst, or a psychotherapist."

"Charming! Thanks a bunch- you're supposed to be my friend and now you're telling me to save it for a fucking shrink!" My raised voice propels some looks from other tables.

"Whoa! Sorry! I didn't mean to upset you, but I really don't want you to become a tweaker. . . "

"Don't be ridiculous!"

"Well from the way you're talking. . Look I'm sorry, but you do seem to have some . . . issues. I think that someone objective, a professional, could really help you."

"You Americans are all the bloody same- the slightest sniff of a problem and I'm on the couch."

"Actually I'm South African, but that's not the point. Did it ever occur to you that listening to you and your endless litany of dramas and problems is downright exhausting?"

"But I thought we were friends- good friends?"

"Yeah, we are. So lay off the crystal meth- it doesn't suit you."

Natasha, my best friend from boarding school, calls me from London:

"I'm getting married!"

"Oh my God- to who? And when?"

I am genuinely thrilled for her; Marcus sounds like a decent guy and she deserves a happy life. The only problem is she is getting married in seven weeks time in London and she wants me to be her maid of honour. Yikes! It does not cross my mind not to go- that would seem like the ultimate betrayal.

36

My instructions were to look fabulous (thankfully no scary dress supplied) and to read 'The Owl and the Pussycat' at the service. I am thrilled. The only problem was finding the cash to fly back home to London.

Amory has quit LA for the summer, spending it in Maine, so I am working for him on a freelance basis. I also have sporadic PA work with Asymmetrical Productions, David Lynch's company and I have recently learned Script Supervising/Continuity at UCLA Extension. My plan is to finance my new writing career through continuity work.

I re-organise my resume fabricating a couple of continuity jobs and distribute it to everyone who has anything to do with production.

I receive a phone call a week later.

"Hi Clea. It's Rob Bierman- remember I hired you as a PA on that Adidas commercial."

"Yes, of course, how are you?"

"Look, the thing is, I see you've moved into continuity and I have this job in White Sands, New Mexico for a week- Ali Mc Graw's making a yoga video. Can you do it? We leave on the 7th."

"Just checking my schedule (flicking pages of Elle so as not to sound too desperate) . . . Yeah I can do that. "

"I can only pay you $250 per day. Is that okay?"

Is that okay? It's fantastic. I suspect he knows I have never had a real continuity job before but is willing to give me a chance.

I love LA! Enthusiasm combined with ambition count for something here.

And just like that my pessimism evaporates and I experience that thrill I'd had when I boarded the plane from Boston to Los Angeles.

Having sent off the finished screenplay to numerous agents, I receive numerous thick brown envelopes in the return post, clipped with a polite rejection slip. On the verge of giving up all hope, I receive a phone call from Deborah White at the William Morris Agency suggesting I come in for a meeting.

I am both thrilled and terrified at this prospect and start

rehearsing my 'pitches'. The image of the verbose and eccentric character played by Richard E. Grant in 'The Player' invades my mind, while I bore Roxanne rigid running through them.

Deborah White rises to greet me warmly and my nerves subside. She is a diminutive, attractive brunette on the verge of marriage, judging by the hefty rock on her finger and the circled florists on the tear sheet by her telephone. Her office is one of many within a glass-domed office building on El Camino in Beverly Hills.

"Here's the coverage for *Surrealists in Love* - I thought you might like to see it."

It feels weird to be in this position of turned tables where now I am the one to be judged; I skim the evaluation trying to focus on the positive:

> This script is well written, the characters grow and change throughout, and the story itself has a certain power to it. This could be an interesting project-

"The biggest problem with your screenplay is the time period it's set in and the fact that the two leads are not very sympathetic-" Deborah remarks.

"They're based on Max Ernst, the German Dada and Surrealist artist and Leonora Carrington, an aristocratic British artist who loses her mind when Ernst is interned during World War 2. Her English Nanny goes by submarine to find her in Spain and Leonora ends up in Mexico City-"

"Look it's an interesting story but the bottom line is that it just isn't commercial enough. Period dramas are costly and this time-period has already been quite well-covered with no commercial success, to speak of."

"Okay, well. . ." I'm at a loss and wondering why she suggested we meet.

"But I like your writing style and I think it's well-written with strong characterisation so I will pass it onto someone at Miramax. But please don't get your hopes up- it's definitely a long shot."

"Fantastic."

"So what other projects are you working on?"

"Okay. . .The Rise and Fall of Aleister Crowley, focusing on the time he spent in Cefalu, on the Southern Italian coast, where he set up a Sex Magic Colony with a coterie of British Society ladies. This was well documented in the British tabloids of the period, (c.1920-30's) and I have loads of genuine research material from the British Newspaper Library. Plot-wise I'm unsure whether to have an undercover journalist infiltrate Crowley's colony, or a possible kidnap scenario/victim escape."

'Rather you than me- who in their right mind would want to make a film about a truly evil man?" Deborah makes a face. My spirits dampen momentarily, but I forge ahead.

"Actually I'm not convinced he is evil- misguided perhaps- and most people are fascinated by the lives of truly evil men and women- Hitler, Stalin, Mussolini, Manson, Genghis Kahn, Pol Pot, Lizzie Borden to name a few- and I can always write it from an undercover journalist's point-of-view-"

"Interesting idea but to be frank with you it's not commercial enough for Hollywood. Fine if you're talking small art-house features and that kind of thing, but that's not what we're about."

"I see- well I'll just have to come up with something else then."

"For starters, let's get this off to Miramax and we can take it from there, okay."

CHAPTER 4

Trip Home

Blaming mother is just a negative way of clinging to her still.
Nancy Friday

My mother, who now lives in the Charente region in France, arranges a trip to London to coincide with mine. I meet up with her at her friend Sylvie's house in Fulham. As always, things get off to an enthusiastic start.

I excitedly explain about my script- the characters and story- and how it has gone to Miramax, but that gets short shift. In fact, I get the distinct impression that I'm boring her. She has never had much interest in the arts so I imagine it is as tedious for her as it would be for me if I had to politely listen to a golfing fanatic.

Over dinner at La Bersagliera on the Kings Road, she asks me:

"Why don't you have a boyfriend, darling?"

"Haven't met the right person I guess-"

"It's just that what with Natasha getting married and all my girlfriends' daughters have lovely young men in their lives. I met Jessica's beau a couple of weeks ago and he was divine . . . so handsome, charming-"

"Well, that's great but I'm very different to Jessica." I pull back from adding that I actually cannot stand her.

My mother takes a studied sip of her gin and tonic, lightly rocking the ice.

"Is there something wrong with you?"

"Like what?" She means I'm not like her.

"I don't know, darling but-"

"But what?" I demand loudly.

41

"There's no need to shred the table-cloth to bits, darling." I look down and witness a tiny mass of shredded paper.

A lengthy pause ensues in which I can hear my own seething, loud and clear, although mummy seems oblivious that anything is awry.

"I suppose you care more about your career- you're a modern woman."

I'd forgotten what a love junkie my mother is: romantic love easily surpassed friendship, family, education, career; it is her raison d'etre. I have consciously determined- and been deliberately contrary- in my efforts to be as different to her as humanly possible, not because she is wrong or bad but because I have always sensed something inherently undignified in her attitude to men.

"I thought you'd be happy that I'd made some progress with my script!"

"I am . . . it's just a shame you're so far away. You know full well that I hate the US."

"Well sorry, but I like it."

The next day Mummy and I head over to Marks and Spencer's, on Oxford Street, where she always likes to visit when she's in London. In between shopping we stop into a wine bar for a snack. She orders some white wine.

"Why do you always have to drink?" I ask, immediately regretting it when I see the flash of indignation in her eyes.

"At least I've never had an abortion!" She leans in and hisses at me.

I cannot actually believe she's brought this up after five years as if she's been storing it up, waiting for the right moment. Thus far I'd successfully banished it from my memory. Before I had gone travelling to India, on my gap year, I'd had an abortion. I became pregnant through a drunken escapade with an old Harrovian I had met on a visit to Edinburgh. He was not particularly nice and it was a mistake. I had been comatose with shame when my mother had eventually guessed what was wrong with me. I never gave the foetus a thought- somehow it just did not seem possible or even alive- and in my denial all I desired was to banish this intrusion out of me.

An abortion was arranged at a private clinic and a friend took me because my mother and stepfather had already booked a holiday and there was no way I wanted them to cancel, on account of my stupidity.

"Either you apologise right now, or I'm leaving." I tell her calmly, teeth gritted.

"Oh go on, leave. See if I care." An impenetrable glaze covers her face.

I do not see her for the rest of the trip.

Relations with my mother had been strained for quite a few years, so I was upset, but not that surprised by yet another rift. After our showdown in the wine bar, I spend that evening drawing up a chart of all the men I have been involved with in my life to see what the truth is about my relationships, if a chart is capable of showing that. In the chart I list in columns all my boyfriends and flings- a fling being anything longer than one night- and how long each one lasted and who ended it and why. Lots of ticks and more crosses, but as a representation of my dating history it is not as dire as I had imagined. In fact the ticks and crosses were fairly even and I was honest because no one was ever going to see it.

From it I realise that whenever anyone had actually liked me I had gotten rid of them and the men I desired were serial womanisers, with either a drinking and/or drug problem. But it had all started off promisingly with a gorgeous first boyfriend who had treated me well until he started two-timing me. It seems that things went from bad to worse during my three years at Brown, but then that was after the abortion and cervical cancer scare. Perhaps things will start to fall into place now that my dating history is clearer in my own mind. I deduce that I am not as big a failure in the relationship stakes as my mother's comments suggest.

My three week trip to the UK is a social whirl with Natasha and Marcus' wedding, seeing my parents- separately because they are divorced- and lots of fun invitations from other friends. The night after having done my 'chart' I attend an

43

art opening in Camberwell where I meet a German sculptor, called Max whose charms I easily fall for. We embark on a holiday fling that bucks up my flagging adrenaline; he also gives me an alternate focus point to stop me dwelling on the sad and difficult confusion that always follows a rift with my mother.

Natasha glows with happiness. On the one hand I want to spend time with her- even though stories of wonderful Marcus are beginning to wear me down- because we have been close since we met at Heathfield, age twelve. On the other hand I am jealous that she is getting married. I certainly did not anticipate this and the feelings I have are very uncomfortable. I am in constant fear of revealing my darkness in an unguarded moment.

She also has no concept of what I do, or at least am trying to do out in LA, because she has never worked in the film business or lived in LA. I know it must sound somewhat 'up in the air' (echoes of 'pipe dream' I hear my mother proclaim loudly), but why can't they just accept it, rather than ask my wholly dreaded question: "What are you going to do if it doesn't work out?"

"That isn't a fucking option, okay!" I feel like shouting back in their face. Of course I would never say that because I hate confrontation.

I am almost out my father's front door in Parsons Green in Fulham when the ringing phone stops me. It is Marcus calling from Bath where Natasha and he are setting up home.

"Clea, this is really awkward, but there's something I want to talk to you about-"

"Yeah sure- is everything alright?" Suddenly that empty pit in my stomach erupts in anticipation of tragedy.

"Where's Natasha?"

"She's at work. She has no idea I'm calling you-"

"What is it?" My curiosity peaks.

"Well- God this is really difficult- well. . ."

Now I am reeling: "Please Marcus. Just say it!"

"Alright. The thing is Natasha is really upset with you-"

"What are you talking about? I don't understand-"

44

"She feels like you came over here and took part really grudgingly and sped off to be with that bloke, Max, every opportunity you had."

Indignant, heat rises in my chest.

"That is total bullshit. I'm sorry Marcus but I had to bust a gut to get the money to come over for your wedding, which I might add I was more than happy to do. It was lovely, the ceremony was beautiful-"

"Clea, we offered to pay your flight."

"Huh?"

"You do remember, don't you?"

I scale my memory and a ghost of vague suggestion comes to mind. As if I would have accepted knowing they were struggling, with Marcus having just set up his own architects' practice and taken out huge loans to do so. Natasha works for a Cancer Charity so she is hardly flush.

"Yes- well that was out of the question."

"The thing is, well there's something else."

"Great- go on, continue the character assassination."

"Look, this is because we're concerned about you-"

"Thanks a bunch- People always say that when they're about to really nail the coffin down!"

"The thing is- well there were a few things- like when you took the milk-"

"What the hell are you talking about- took the milk?"

"When you took our milk over to that bloke's flat because he asked you to pick up some milk on your way over and you took ours."

I hazily remember the incident a week ago. The three of us had had dinner at Marcus' flat that he had finally sold so the mood was celebratory with corks popping and as usual they were all over each other. The bloke was Max, the sculptor I'd met on this trip at an art opening, and he had called me at about eleven on the off-chance that I'd like to go over. Like Max Ernst he was German and divorced. I figured he'd help to wash away the bad taste of Gordon still lingering in my mouth, not to mention my mother's suggestion that I was somehow unlovable.

During the phone call at Marcus', Max had mentioned he was dying for a cup of tea, but had run out of milk and could

I pick some up on the way? I called for a taxi and grabbed their carton of milk out the fridge and put it in my handbag. Okay it was somewhat inconsiderate and a bit rude leaving them with no milk for the morning, but in my excitement I was not thinking.

"Well I'm sorry- I didn't think it was a big deal. If it's any consolation the bloody thing spilt all over my favourite handbag and now the suede emits a rather sour smell that I can't get rid of so what goes around comes around. Right?"

"Clea, it's not the milk that we care about- it's you. Natasha thinks you've really changed since you've been in LA. She says you wouldn't have dreamed of doing something like that a couple of years ago. She spoke to Vanessa as well and she told us what happened the night of our wedding."

Now my heart is pounding; I am furious that they have been conferring about me. After the wedding dinner at Borsch n'Tears on Beauchamp Place, Vanessa and I had gone to Flix, a seedy basement club on Ledbury Road in Notting Hill. Vanessa, a Heathfield friend who had flown over from Toronto for the weekend, was set on jamming in as much as humanly possible. We walked downstairs where diner-like seating lined nicotine stained walls.

"It's kind of gross in here!" said Vanessa who deplores smoke.

"I warned you that it wasn't exactly Annabel's- but it's great fun I promise you. And you said earlier that you wanted to go somewhere different."

"Yeah well . . . Oh what the hell! I'm on vacation!"

I scrutinized the sea of unfamiliar faces and recognised Billy, a big black man with dreadlocks down to his knees, who is a record producer with a small label. He waves us over to his table. I am in no doubt as to why. Vanessa is stunning and a dead ringer for Michelle Pfeiffer. He goes off to get a round of drinks and we chat with his two friends, Simon and Johnny. I can tell they both really fancy her because Johnny has straightened his slumped shoulders and comatose Simon has somehow managed to maintain direct eye contact and small talk with her since we sat down.

This always happens with Vanessa. Dressed in a figure-hugging strapless cream brocade number, gold leather strappy, Ferragamo stilettos with a light chocolate wrap casually slung about her tanned shoulders, along with her Chanel evening purse she looks quite simply stunning, epitomising everything I wish I could have- perfect skin, fine features and slim with curves and boobs. I had felt clumsy all day- I had tripped in the church on my way up to read 'The Owl and the Pussycat' but, worse than that, 'shit' had slipped from my lips and echoed through the ancient church walls in true megaphone style. By the time I reached the podium I was beetroot red; I read the poem and quite frankly messed it up by stuttering on words and generally wanting to get it over as quickly as possible. Thankfully Natasha and Marcus were so full of joy that they deemed it hysterical, but I was clearly left with egg on my face. I made a conscious point to guzzle down as much champagne as possible.

By the evening Vanessa is glazed and content, but I am on a mission to find some drugs- preferably crystal meth, or coke. My dire need overtakes my dignity and I corner Billy at the bar, whispering:

"Who can I score some crystal meth from in here?"

"No way love- you won't find that shit over 'ere. That's yankie speed and it sure as hell ain't over here in London- not yet anyway. Charlie's the thing 'ere; Simon's usually holding."

I console myself that soon I'll have some coke racing through me and shake off this empty edge of a mood that's not allowing me to focus on anything, bar finding drugs.

I wait for Vanessa to go to the loo and then ask Johnny and Simon who has some coke. I can feel the pleading my eyes communicate because Simon hesitates, for a mere split moment, and then goes into his wallet under the table and hands across a small but recognizable plastic baggy into my sweaty paw. It feels divine.

"Take a line with your friend but no more okay- that's got to last."

I give him that look that says 'my God you are my saviour and of course I will only take an incy-wincy bit'. I do not mention that Vanessa would never touch the stuff because that leaves more for me. I go to the toilets and pass Vanessa on the way back to the table; she glides by unperturbed, keen to return to her adoring attendants. I cut out the powder on top of

47

my Filofax and hoof it up my nose with a rolled up piece of cardboard that I break off from the empty loo roll. This place is rudimentary and the toilets bear that out- no mirrors, no loo paper and one bare light bulb for three wobbly cubicles; the smell is bad, but I do not care because all I need is privacy. I do not stop at the two lines; after all what is the rush? I sit for what feels like ages and then hold the baggy up to the light and figure he won't miss a little bit more . . . and a little bit more. . . and a little bit more.

My heart pounds fast, intensity bursting out of my chest and I take deep breaths. I stagger back to the table relieved to see Simon at the bar, talking to a straggly longhaired, pale guy who has clearly seen better days. It dawns on me that I have actually nicked all his gear; I panic. I grab Vanessa, urgently whispering:

"We have got to get out of here, now! I just heard there's going to be a drugs bust. We've got to go!" Vanessa looks shell-shocked, but follows me.

We run out and she starts to laugh when we are far enough away to know we are safe. I cannot laugh because I feel ashamed- how could I do that to that nice guy Simon? Vanessa takes both my hands and looks directly into my eyes:

"What the hell is wrong with you?"

"Nothing. I'm fine- that was a close call, that's all."

"Well something fishy was going on in there but I don't think it's what you just made up."

"What do you mean? I swear I overheard this girl in the loos saying the cops were on their way- there had been some tip off, or something-"

"Look, I wasn't born yesterday. When you walked out the loo you had white powder stuck at the side of your nose."

How gross! I cannot believe it; my worse nightmare is to give myself away through abject stupidity and then I remember the absence of mirrors in the club's loos. I am mortified.

"I'm really worried about you- you were fine all day but things just got weirder and weirder at that club. I know that it's drugs, isn't it? They don't suit you at all, you know- you go weird- kind of far away and spaced out. Please just stop now while you can."

"Look Vanessa," I tell her, feeling buoyed by the coke:

48

"Something was going down and I had a little bit of coke that one of those guys gave me- offered me I should add- and that's it. I was really knackered and I just wanted a little pick-me-up. Nothing more than that- it's hardly a big deal."

"I flew in from Canada yesterday and I'm okay without bloody drugs to keep me going. Please do something about this because it's not normal- I'm really serious."

By now we are in a taxi back to my house. The next morning I wave her off to the airport after three hours sleep, having mentioned nothing about what had happened the previous evening. I assume, wrongly, that will be the last I'll hear of it. The idea that my old friends Natasha and Vanessa are concerned about me just makes me feel humiliated and angered- I wish they would mind their own business.

"Well Marcus that was a misunderstanding between Vanessa and me. I don't see why you're all talking about it, anyway-"

"Clea, for exactly the same reason I'm calling you up. We are all very concerned." The exactness of his pronunciation makes him sound like a cross teacher.

I am really fuming. Who the hell do they think they are- my parents?

"Well, thank you Marcus for your concern, but let me tell you it is completely unfounded and on another note, if Natasha is so fucking concerned, then why the hell does she have you doing her fucking dirty work?"

"I've already told you that Natasha doesn't know I'm calling you. But I thought as we're all close friends it was important to get these misunderstandings out in the open-"

"Errr, yes. I agree. . . And I apologise. I wasn't thinking and. . . I need to slow down, think before I jump in and do stupid things."

"I'm saying this because we care. There's no hidden agenda, or anything."

"Thank you, Marcus. I'll try and take what you've said on board." I catch sight of the Grandfather clock in the hall.

"Oh my God is that the time! I have to go!

I slam down the phone and grab my bags. I run up to New Kings Road where I flag down a taxi to take me to Heathrow, thrilled to be on my way back to Los Angeles.

CHAPTER 5

Marnie

Her name was Magill, she called herself Lil/
But ev'ryone knew her as Nancy.
Rocky Racoon Lennon/McCartney

As much as I loved my old public school friends back home and my clever Brown friends, Roxanne and Marnie's crew were seriously 'hip.' To me they seemed capable of taking risks in a way that well-educated, conservative people do not. They used drugs seemingly without regret and guilt and a couple had enjoyed some level of fame, as artists, actors and musicians.

None of the new posse has regular jobs. They work in bars or restaurants and live mainly on hope that they will realise their dreams. And every so often they get a professional gig that sustains that dream. I find this utterly novel and liberating. Vague plans are made, but they go about it in their own fashion without making you feel inadequate or insecure about what you are doing. It dawns on me that my friendships from Brown had threatened me with their normality. I feel different now because I am part of a whole new scene where unusual and bohemian lifestyles are commonplace. I also like the idea of an older female friend- Marnie is in her late 30s- who can give me guidance and encouragement, because she has the air of experience about her. I am really pleased when she suggests I move into her apartment with her because the annual lease on my bungalow is almost over and I do not want to live alone anymore. Besides, I'd been spending all my free time at her place.

So I move in with Marnie, seduced both by the fairytale gardens of Normandy Towers in the heart of Hollywood and her unusual personality. Her apartment complex is an amazing kitsch, downscaled replica based on a Bavarian castle built by Walt Disney for his studio employees during the 1930s.

Marnie's apartment is decorated in an understated but classic chic- a cross between Ralph Lauren and a neat, hippy witch's coven. The serenity is hardly in keeping with the amount of drugs ingested on the premises. Rich polished mahogany floors dotted with Kilim rugs and spare beautiful objets d'art from all corners of the earth, from New Mexico-via-Brixton to Kilimanjaro. She has the innate ability to balance space and objects so that the calm and serenity stays intact. I know she has lived all over the States but she will not be drawn out on the subject of her life- "It's complicated." This is something I have heard before from similarly dramatic women- with her somehow, I believe it.

My burgeoning friendship with Marnie is a curious mix. On the one hand her creative chutzpah and spirit have been of incredible value to me- she has helped me consolidate and strengthen my ideas, but on the other hand she does imbibe vast quantities of chemicals- alcohol, opium and pills. The thing with her is that she is consistently off the wall- in turn cocky, cutesy, dry and wholly liberated sexually- and she stays abreast of this bizarre mix of characteristics like a finely tuned actress. To my mind a woman who can keep it all together- rent, car and be involved in a plethora of creative ventures- must be doing something right, or at least she looks as if she is totally in control from the outside. After all, good self-presentation seems half the battle and she pulls this off with panache.

She fascinates me. It feels almost like a crush, whereas she can be strangely maternal towards me. Most noticeable is her personal aroma- sweet, musky and vaguely antiseptic- that wafts around her. Whether it emanates from perfume, her self or a combination of both, I can't tell but it is seductive and repellent at the same time. She has all sorts of different ventures on the go- some really outrageous like selling soiled panties to perverts by mail order to less alarming projects that include tie-dying kiddies' clothes and selling them to a funky store on Venice Beach. Even this, though, she comes at from a new slant by shrinking adult clothes first before dyeing them. She does not cook, or seem to eat for that matter, but huge pots of garments stew on the cooker for hours. She claims that a buyer for Saks is interested, but she needs to expand her output, which means hiring help. The apartment is undeniably a hive of industry

I am juggling work for Amory on a freelance basis, looking for more script continuity work, plotting the Crowley screenplay and applying to the UCLA screenwriting masters program. I feel overwhelmed, until I chance upon an unexpected surprise in the bathroom, when I'm hunting for a tampon.

Sliding open the bathroom cabinet, a shiny blue tile falls away to reveal a fist-sized recess, where a couple of lines are laid out on a small compact mirror, with a cut-off straw and a transparent baggy with clumps of tiny crystals inside. The tiny crystals catch the morning light like magic diamonds and I feel like a naughty child that has discovered hidden sweeties. The portable radio by the bath purrs with the news that Kurt Cobain has been found dead, followed by *Smells like Teen Spirit* and during those first few bars it makes perfect sense to start this day by snorting a fat line of crystal meth- to commiserate, commemorate, connect, vibe with. The blast of sharp burning pain inside my nostril makes me gag. I had forgotten how strong crystal meth is, having not taken it since I'd done the script re-write about six months ago.

Even though the sensation is hardly pleasant, it is strangely gratifying at the same time- you know it's the real Mc Coy- if nothing else.

Since that morning, I have got into the habit of taking about half a line before I head off for work. Just like a coffee, but more powerful and a lot more fun.

"Clea, I think you've changed recently," Amory surveys me from the doorway.

"For the better I hope?"

"Oh yeah, definitely." He quickly adds:

"Not that there was anything wrong with you before, you catch my drift, right?" I suspect he is recalling the time I called in sick and collapsed into sobs down the phone, but thankfully he has the sensitivity, good grace or both not to mention it. My grin spreads from ear to ear- I am a total sucker for praise.

"What's different about me then?"

"You're. . . perkier, for want of a better word. Yeah, more perky."

"Was I a rather morose individual before then?" He searches for an inoffensive response, probably regretting that he had ever mentioned anything.

"No. You just seem more cheery and certainly a lot more efficient- in fact I would describe you now as super efficient!"

"Thank you- I'm glad to oblige."

"Have you been working out more, because you're looking really good too?" I am hardly going to admit that I have a diamond geezer of a new friend in crystal meth, so I just nod in thanks.

No sooner had I gone back to typing up some comments for coverage on a particularly dire script, than Amory appears in the doorway again, looking pleased with himself.

"I almost forgot-"

"Yes, what is it?"

"I had a great idea about your car-"

"My car? What about it?" I know he hates my old Rabbit convertible.

"If you're gonna be working for me on 'Sketch' then you will really need a larger, better car. Ya know- for generally work, ferrying Joan Corres around, helping with pre-production- that sort of thing."

This does not inspire much interest in me because I am happy enough with the Rabbit, rumbling about with the roof down soaking up the rays and breezy pollution; the only drawback is the manual gear shift which becomes tedious when you spend as many hours in the car as I do.

"Okay, I'll think about it."

"Actually I have a suggestion-"

"Oh yes. What?"

"I know this halfway decent Mercedes Dealership in

North Hollywood that has some very good deals."

"On a Mercedes?" He cannot be serious.

"You'd look great bombing about in a shiny, new Merc."

"Maybe, but there's one problem there- how do I actually pay for it?"

"Well! That's where I come in." Is he going to buy me a car as part of my job? He'd bought an ex-girlfriend a Mercedes Sports Convertible, that she'd duly crashed before she had got around to insuring it, but I am only a humble employee. A promotion perhaps? My mind buzzes with possibilities.

"I'll underwrite the loan for the car. At this Dealership you don't even need a down payment- just monthly instalments over a fixed period of time."

"So you're offering to be my guarantor." I am lost for words. Amory hands me a business card- 'Lankershim Mercedes'- with Ray written on it, in blue felt tip.

"This guy Ray knows all about it, so give him a call."

I am curious as to where Marnie disappears to, for what seems like days on end. Sometimes she will return home with random goodies- kitsch china ornaments, bags of clothes, boxes of gorgeous fur coats, stoles and hats. When relaxing at home she has a penchant for draping fur about herself, often with nothing else on; initially I found this quite startling, but have grown used to it, alongside her other idiosyncrasies. I draw the line at the fox fur triangle and pearl thong she has created 'especially for me' because she found the fur in a dumpster that also had a pile of old-peoples' nappies inside it and the vague pong of old people's poo still seems to hang around, even though she claims it was sitting at the other end. Another time she found a beautiful set of crystal glasses and decanters- two with silver trims- and numerous other items including a working stereo, books, pots, toaster oven, microwave, tableware- in fact the majority of her household has come out of a dumpster, a fact that she does not share with me until I have been there over a month.

I am in the bathroom rummaging about when a sharp knock interrupts me.

"What are you looking for?" Marnie asks coolly.

"Nothing."

"Can you open the door please- I really need to pee!"

I open it and she holds up the little mirror that has become familiar to me.

"I thought you might be a little lost without your faithful little friend-"

"What are you talking about? I've never seen that thing before-"

Now stern, Marnie eyeballs me: "Clea, please do not do me the grave injustice of lying to my face. I know you've been helping yourself to my emergency stash and it's okay- what's mine is yours- you just need to contribute because this stuff is not cheap. I only get the seriously pure stuff."

"I'm sorry, I feel such an idiot. I've been meaning to talk to you about it. Can I buy some off you?"

"I'll give you some. So what are you up to today?"

"Not sure- writing, I suppose. I also need to work on my UCLA Application."

"Wanna go dumpster-diving instead?"

"Well, I really should . . . Oh what the hell, yeah okay!"

"Baptism by fire!" Marnie squeals with delight.

In between snatches of Public Image Limited and Ice T on her car stereo Marnie explains the rules of Dumpster Diving in daylight, on our way to Beverly Hills:

"Rule numero uno- no diving if the owner is about- they get nervous about what you might find and it's their property. And don't let them see you go in their garage either because they can legally shoot you for trespassing. Number two- always get kitted out- I have the right gear in the trunk and number three if you find something good, grab it and get out quickly because chances are it has been left there for a reason and someone is probably on their way back to pick it up."

"Like what kind of stuff?" This is getting better and better.

"With any luck you'll see!" Marnie gives me a wink.

"Serious cloak and dagger stuff! I always thought it was street people that were collecting cans and looking for food."

"That's what it looks like on the outside, but that's only a tiny percentage of the divers- that lot are just looking for 5 cent cans to survive- but the rest of us are on a mission."

With that Marnie turns up Ice T and we head down the back alleys of Beverly Hills. We had taken some crystal before we left the apartment so I am pumped, focused and ready; it sure makes a change from poring over screenplays and sitting at my desk, writing.

"Hey, check out those deflated balloons outside that mammoth monstrosity of a house." We drive by a neo-colonial style house where a plump Hispanic woman yanks them down off the gatepost.

"What does that mean?"

"That'll mean they just had a kiddies party and their dumpster will be full of cool kid's stuff which I'm gonna need for the party I'm organizin' for my friend's twins next Saturday" (Party planning is another one of Marnie's 'professions'). She heads round the back where there are several cars and delivery vans lining the alley. Marnie jumps out and starts rustling around in the trunk. She hands me a pair of green rubber over-trouser galoshes.

"You have to be kidding! I'm not wearing that insult to fashion!"

"Initiation Ritual- you have to, no question about it-"

"And what if I don't?"

"You can't dive, simple as that."

"How are you gonna stop me?"

"I'll drive away and call the cops- anonymously of course- and say I think I've witnessed a robbery." A sense of uneasiness pervades the whole escapade, because suddenly Marnie seems quite alien and sinister.

"For god's sake I'm having you on! You are seriously gullible man!!" She grabs the trousers and throws them back in the trunk that is already jam packed with boxes and clothes.

Not one to fear the unknown, I climb into the dumpster which has conveniently positioned metal ridges on which to balance and wedge your way over the top. A fair amount of poking and sifting takes place with a split poker cue before I take the plunge, feet first. Once I am in the dumpster there is not much to worry about, except what you could possibly come across, because no one knows you are in there, unless they saw you get in. That first dive we find enough discarded toys- Barbie dolls and outfits, crayons, Gameboy etc- boxed and brand new- to throw several kiddie parties, not to mention balloons, hats and party paraphernalia. But Marnie is very bossy. I cannot wait to go out on my own with no one barking instructions at me.

I glean snippets of information regarding Marnie's past: she was married and served in Guru Mai's Ashram in upstate New York for five years until she got thrown out for 'unruly conduct', the definition of which she declined to elucidate, but I gathered it had something to do with her discovering her husband's affair with Guru Mai's secretary. She also spent time with Deepak Chopra- assisting him in some capacity- although she is uninterested in divulging what, where or when. I am naturally curious, but with her I know when to stop because she has extreme mood swings that I dare not set off. I have witnessed her wrath and it is not pretty.

One summer evening, I sit on the sofa threading some beads onto a piece of wire- found in a dumpster full of reams of fabric, braid, buttons, trims, beads and sewing miscellany outside a recently closed haberdashery, in Sherman Oaks- when she walks in and sits down in the rocking chair across from me, fixing me with her green serpent eyes. A month ago I would have felt uncomfortable, but I have quickly grown used to her peculiarities, or so I thought.

"So who the fuck is doin' fat fuck-head over there?" Her habitual drawl now has a sharp, sassy authoritarian edge to it, as she looks off into the distance at something I cannot see. She starts to fondle her left breast while undoing the pearl buttons on her '50's floral patterned blouse.

"Psssssss-" Marnie hisses at me, her chin indicating something somewhere, just not in our sitting room. I giggle because I have no idea what else to do. Maintaining her gaze at the phantom person she methodically fondles her right breast in time with her left, like she is performing for someone standing in close proximity to her.

"What are you doing, Marnie?" I enquire as casually as I can, because she is freaking me out.

"Who the fuck's Marnie?- I'm Mary-Lou and you sure as hell know that so don't start pissing me about you bitch!" Her eyes are glazed over, almost trance- like.

"Have you smoked some opium tonight?" I innocently ask, while she continues with the breast fondling, but now her right hand moves down to her nether regions. Oh no, I cannot cope with this.

"I need to go to 7-11 to buy some fags-"

"Oh nooo you don't- I'm not gonna let you get away with that. We're both doin' the fat fuck-head together. We made a deal. I'm not gonna let you screw me over, after all the shit I've gone through for ya, d'ya understand?!" She spits this at me and I acquiesce out of fear. A few moments pass and cars headlamps from outside bounce off the far wall, while I wait to hazard a getaway move.

Marnie's head drops momentarily and shudders. Then she looks up and all around the room.

"Why are you sitting here in the dark, Clea? Don't you find it kind of depressing? You silly nut-head."

"Errr, Marnie?"

"Yeah, what honey?"

"What was that all about? I'm really freaked out, I mean..."

"Oh yeah. . . well, sorry."

"But I don't understand. What was going on?"

"I switched personalities-"

"Oh. . . what? Like Sybil?"

"Ya got it honey- and you're the only friend I've ever done it in front of, so make what you want of that."

"Okay. . . I need some fags. I'll see you later."

Perplexed I go for a long drive. I'm beginning to understand what Marnie means by complicated.

I finish up some coverage for Amory and call Walter to arrange to drop it off. Walter's familiar cackle pierces the cool air; I enter the office and greet them both.

"Who does that hideous monstrosity belong to- please tell me it is not yours Clea?" Walter exclaims in horror.

"Yeah it is- what's wrong with it? You drive a Volvo for Christ's sake."

"There are Volvos and there are insults to humanity-what colour do you call that- ugh! There's no name for that colour!" He snorts with derision. Granted, the paintwork looks like someone attempted to re-spray it and got caught in acid rain, but it runs okay.

Amory is looking at me in a way that is distinctly hostile.

"Looks like you decided against the Mercedes then."

I had completely forgotten about his offer because the plan had seemed so pointless to me, primarily because of the expense. It was decent of Amory to offer to guarantee the car loan, but I was the one who was going to be locked into years of steep payments. Judging by the look on his face, he does not understand my position- well how can he?- he was born rich in a world where he can pick and choose his fleet of cars. I take a deep breath in preparation to stave off his subtle manipulation techniques:

"Right, the thing is I really appreciate the offer of the loan, Amory. It was very kind and generous of you but for me, right now, a smart car is just not a priority."

"Fine," he snarls and swivels on his handmade boot heel, leaving the door wide open, something he only ever does when he is incensed. Instinctively I knew there was something final in that one word- and all because of an overpriced, second-hand Mercedes.

"Hi Walter." A pregnant pause follows, rich with possibility. I forge ahead:

"I haven't heard from Amory for weeks now and I left a couple of messages-" I can feel some strange atmosphere at the end of the phone and can just see Walter going into his 'I'm in charge and this is the situation' mode that I have witnessed so many times before, when I have not been on the receiving end.

"This is kind of awkward, but I need to be honest because you know I don't have anything against you (Walter is loving this) - but he's hired another girl to work on 'Sketch'."

I cannot believe what I am hearing, while my legs seem to float up about my ears and my stomach vanishes into thin air.

"What? Why? What have I done, or not done?"

"Think about it, Clea. When he offered to guarantee that Mercedes for you- he went to quite a lot of trouble you know- finding a dealer and all that." I snaffle myself from blurting out: You mean he had you do it.

"Because I exchanged my Rabbit for a Volvo I'm off the film? That is insane."

"Right at the beginning I warned you he runs very hot and cold."

"Telling me!"

"Well, to be honest Clea I don't understand why you didn't take him up on his offer."

"Because I'm struggling enough already, trying to make it as a writer and pay the rent by working in production-"

"Yeah, well don't you just want it all- sometimes you have to make compromises in life you know- didn't your little English Mommy and Daddy ever tell you that?"

I am shocked by the mean tone that he classes as humour, but at least I am finding out what the real deal is, because if anybody is Amory's right hand man, it is Walter.

"Please be serious- I can't afford it and I didn't even like the bloody car!"

"And you actually like that death trap monstrosity you're currently insulting the roads with?. . . Look, the bottom line is you could have done the smart thing- bought the car that looks good and isn't a death-trap and be working on 'Sketch'."

"I'm not interested in working for anyone under those terms- quite honestly the whole thing is bang out of order! I can't believe how manipulative he's been and where people's priorities seem to lie."

"Welcome to the real world-"

"Well it's a world I want no part of, thank you very much."

I am knocked out cold from my woolly and deceptive comfort zone; I got it really wrong. I had naively believed that my freelance work for Amory was safe, a sure bet and that we had some form of unwritten, but somehow understood contract. I miscalculated rather poorly, but then wasn't Amory the one who ironically warned me about 'slippery Hollywood folk'? He had even been embarrassingly free with praise about my overall improvement and newfound versatility. If he had caught me snorting crystal in the office then it would all be fully understandable, but being 'dismissed' figuratively and in reality over a car was downright ridiculous.

I refuse to dwell on what could have been and think how I can make the most of what I have now. I really have no choice, but to embrace these unplanned changes- regardless of my blue-in-the-face fury- and take what little work I still have available to me: freelance PA and continuity jobs, which I will now really need to hustle for.

Perversely, though, I feel relieved, as if let off the hook because I am no longer beholden to anyone. No one I like and respect, and hence want to impress is expecting anything of me, besides my family, but they are thousands of miles away. I can truly be 'me', whoever that is. I can let the rules go and see where that takes me, at least for a short while as I sort out my application for the UCLA Screenwriting Graduate Program. I hope to enrol for the next academic year, in ten months.

I feel like the true bohemian I am now convinced I am predestined to be, following in the steps of my heroine, Leonora Carrington. Even my new friendships gel effortlessly and are testament to the new me, alongside the relative ease with which I moved in with Marnie and her weird community. Their liberal approach to drug-taking redeems it, restoring it to its original value and purpose: true self-discovery. I want to travel somewhere else, somewhere nihilistic, anarchic and unknown.

CHAPTER 6

Crystal Methamphetamine

My name is Crystal Amphetamine and what I gave to___
was euphoria-oblivion. What I took way from _____ was
his health, his conscience, his rationality, his discretion,
his sense of accountability, and responsibility to other
people. I warped and distorted his values and sense of
morality.

Cover *Los Angeles Times Magazine* 1999

"When an inner situation is not made conscious, it appears outside as fate."
C.G.Jung

Crystal meth is my perfect drug because it erases my over-active mind: I now live permanently within the present.

Crystal is my perfect lover because he never lets me down.

Crystal makes me feel good, exceptionally good. I've been searching for this release all my life and crystal gives it to me.

Crystal has alerted my senses in a way I have never experienced before. Technicolor rules instead of grey-beige with fuzzy edges. Blurriness has become crystal clear.

My energy levels stun me.

My new body thrills me.

My bad skin has miraculously disappeared.

I like to be looked at again.

My stamina for life is empowering. I have broken through my own limitations.

Crystal, crank, Tina-girl, go fast, ice. . . is made by cooking up a wide range of substances- including farm fertiliser, lye, ammonia, ephedrine. Anyone with some knowledge of chemistry can cook it if they have the recipe, although it is a risky endeavour because of the high levels of heat needed. The recipe tends to be guarded closely, like a rare alchemical transmutation. It was first synthesised in the 1880s and was used by Germany and Japan in World War 2 to improve soldiers' performances.

Once crystal meth is coursing through me and stimulating my nervous system I am not conscious of the 'need more and more now' obsession that coke instigates. Instead I can revel in the suspended sensation of total focus, freedom from emotional conflicts and an expansive desire to create. It really does transform my sense of self from a minor earthbound woman into a superhuman, where all things are possible; I have not felt this enthused and excited since I was a small child.

It also stops me from questioning and instead gets me 'doing'. Activity is paramount and I understand now what was happening with Gordon and his friends when they were pulling apart and/or constructing various objects- they were 'tweaking'. And we all spend days collecting things from dumpsters, abandoned buildings and the side of the road in order to be able to tweak them.

The euphoric state and intense energy is akin to extreme sports- parachuting, bungee jumping, sky diving- done over and over again, but with apparently no risk. You get high energy, adrenaline and happiness, almost for free, or so it insidiously appears, before the crash and burn cycle has ingrained itself upon my brain receptors and taken over my soul. Paranoia increases over time: you hear voices and think you're being watched and followed but this only adds to the fiery, adrenaline rush.

Following my fall-out with Amory- if one could call it that- I had little interest in Propaganda anymore, perceiving the employees there as a herd of sheep, like those at any other corporate enterprise, and I wanted none of it.

I was of a different species now.

It was with this daredevil bravado that I challenge my limits: 'How far am I willing to go?'

The downside of this new lifestyle is horrific time-keeping, which has always been a problem for me. My father claims I inherited it from his Russian mother, married to the British Commissioner of Customs in Shanghai, who'd had no qualms about holding up the Shanghai express train for hours, because her husband had some clout. That my father found her behaviour embarrassing I could never understand; I secretly find it a fabulous idea that a train can be held up for you.

I now stay up four days in a row, followed by about 25 hours dead-dodo sleep. I had tried going to sleep normally, and had partly succeeded, while I was still working for Amory but now there seemed little point. And the perversely winsome sight of my double bed, cool sheets within, had proved altogether unappealing- my new lover was prompting action, not slumber. It just seemed that there were so many more exciting things to do, rather than sleep.

The steady interchange of a baby's routine between feeding and sleeping is akin to the rotational lifestyle of snorting and sleeping and snorting again. That steady sequence, along with the warm Californian climate and long daylight hours, provides the perfect conditions for tweaking.

The basic routine is so all-encompassing that we tweakers create our own colony, separate to regular life: sleep versus tweak.

By pushing myself to the limit I stave off the crash, so that I am either high, or asleep: the crash is prevented and euphoria is restored upon waking and snorting up again.

Living with Marnie makes it impossible not to use crystal meth. At first I had made efforts to continue as before, with the occasional crystal use- a high-days and holidays mentality- but as soon as I set about my writing, either editing, research or coming up with a treatment plan for a new screenplay, Marnie knocks on my door and entices me out to play. Once when I declined her offer, I ended up with my ear pinned against the wall eavesdropping, desperate to be part of it all. After an hour, I gave up and joined them.

Once you have sampled the nectar it is rather dull returning to water. And having it right under my nose- literally- was a recipe for high times.

Even though writing is harder, actually impossible, because I am too energised to stay still for long stretches of time, the ideas flow. Occasionally I remember to jot these down, making future plans to see them come to fruition. My screenplay is still doing the rounds, although Miramax rejected it.

Expectant, I feel positive that my life has clicked right into place.

CHAPTER 7

Dumpster Diving

I try to empty myself of images that have made me blind.
Leonora Carrington

Crystal meth and dumpster diving go together in an unholy alliance: neither of these activities could survive without the other. Part of me recognises this, but I also perceive it as part of my last fling, or adventure that would come to a natural end, either when I sell my screenplay, or I start at UCLA in the graduate program. I do not consider the reality that I could fail both of these options.

When dumpster-diving I am on a mission, in search of the Holy Grail. It resonates deep inside me, in a wholly regressive and child-like way. In fact, the activity is not dissimilar to the many afternoons I spent as a child rummaging in the attic at Gravesend Farm where I had lived in with my mother and stepfather. She had inherited it from her elderly guardian who was an avid collector of everything. The stash was almost impenetrable in all its haphazard glory and I would carry down items- fabric, beaded scarves, satin trimmed boxes, baubly costume jewellery, buttons, old postcards and photos- to ask my mother meekly if I could keep them. Usually she said yes, unless it was something she took a shine to herself, and then she would say: 'Sweetie, that's too grown up for you'.

I have trailed up, down and across every alley within the LA grid of streets- from grotty Western Avenue to the Salvation Army Dumpster behind Fairfax to mansions in Brentwood to the UCLA campus.

Undeniably, there is always something of value to be resurrected from the dump. The growing concern for me is that the longer I partake of this lifestyle the less discerning my eye becomes. Almost every box I break apart has something- a trinket, a toy, a bag of buttons, a bunch of Polaroids of people I do not know, books, paintbrushes, videos, personal letters, ancient newspapers- that I believe I can make use of in an art work, in a screenplay or for props for my short film.

All these projects I mentally plan out and prepare for, but then I have forgotten the next day- mislaid my idea- for why or what I wanted that particular set of self-heating rollers, or the stack of back catalogues from Sears, but I am convinced there is a truly valid reason, if and when I can remember.

Besides the hygiene factor there is also the growing need for space. When Marnie took me on that first dive with her, she certainly did not expect me to take to it like I have. She has wagged her finger many a time at me, but now she is really putting her elegant foot down- no more dived stuff in the apartment. The result of her playing mother has me storing it all up in the Volvo, which has led to strange looks from passers-by- one pasty middle-aged buffoon tartly informed me that living in my car on his street was an illegal offence and could I please park my sorry ass somewhere else. His eyes came out on storks when I waved my keys at him and unlocked the entry gate to Normandy Towers, while I yelled back at him about the perils of judging books by their cover.

Not entirely immune to how people are responding to me, I jump in the shower and try to get out the tiny splinters of glass that have become part of my fingertips and nails. They are extremely painful and I need to use tweezers to remove them, while the hot water helps to soften the skin. The heat is total bliss after days of scavenging and occasionally I nod off only to be roused by Marnie's fishwife yell: "Get the fuck out of the shower! You're using up all the hot water! Get out now!"

Naked, I walk around my room looking for some clean clothes; Marnie stands in the doorway, concern flooding her pale face.

"Oh my God, Clea- You are way too thin!"

"Oh come on, I think I look great."

"You look like an Auschtwitz victim!"

"Gimme a break- that's absurd."

"You're not seeing yourself properly- you're losing the plot big time!"

"What are you talking about?" I feel my cheeks redden with indignation.

"Clea, you look ill- not slim and certainly not sexy."

"Thanks a lot Marnie- obviously you're jealous! You're jealous because now I look better than you and you don't like it."

A total renegade, Jeremiah is one of Marnie's many lovers. I visit him on my own, unbeknownst to her, because he's teaching me all these new skills and techniques- French polishing, cane webbing, and the myriad uses of the staple gun- that are helping me turnaround a profit on my dumpster-dived finds. Extended tweaking makes it hard to actually finish a project and Jeremiah helps me focus.

Jeremiah resembles an eccentric professor with shaggy grey shoulder-length hair and very pale skin; his paleness and the subtle smell of Imperial Leather soap reminds me of my own sweet father, whom I rarely speak with nowadays. Back in the 70s, Jeremiah directed and presented a hugely successful TV show- totally revolutionary for its time- but it had all gone very wrong, following the unsolved murder of the producer. He was not implicated in any way, but is convinced of a conspiracy.

He lives in a cave, literally. It is in a back alley, parallel to Fairfax and about 5 minutes walk from Kanter's. You walk down four steps and there's a narrow door that looks like a back door to a storage space. Once inside you walk down more steps- wider now- and you are in a basement. The walls are lined with books, TVs and other technology that flashes and burps intermittently. It is rather like a bizarre set for a film about a madman. He is also a Conspiracy Theorist of the Highest Order.

I suspect that Marnie is jealous of me spending time with Jeremiah. She likes to be in control, like a chief puppeteer, but when we get our own ideas about how things should be, she becomes defensive and insecure. She locked me out of our apartment once when I spent two days in a row with him. She peeked out to see me standing there, brick in hand and deadly serious about breaking the window to get in, before she threw open the front door in surrender, head bowed in self-pity, and announced:

"I've been lonely."

"Well, you could've come over. We were putting that chaise-lounge back together. Jeremiah reckons I can ask $1600 for it! We lacquered it in gold and black using this lace transfer effect and I staple-gunned a thick aubergine velvet over some polystyrene cushion we ripped off a piss ugly sofa left outside a duplex on Doheny."

"Hold yer horses Miss Steptoe! I was the one that saw that chaise first!"

"You have to be kidding- I saw it weeks ago and I told you about it and then you went to try to take it, but it was too big for your car. And how do I know? Because I followed you! - So there; two can play at that game, Nancy Drew!" My newly strident tone takes me by surprise.

I notice Marnie looks completely different, like a little girl who has been caught with her hand in the cookie jar. Her body language is childlike and even her posture has become small and crouched- only four feet tall- which has to be an optical illusion, unless she is a genuine shape shifter.

"I need to go to my special place." Her usual husky tone of voice is light and punctuated with staccato, like a scared young girl's. She refers to the deep but narrow walk-in closet in my room that she still keeps most of her clothes in. She creeps by me- eyes downcast. I wait a few minutes, even though my curiosity is killing me, and then tiptoe along the corridor to listen at the door. I can barely hear her; she repeats the same thing over and over again:

"I'm sorry, Daddy, I've been a very naughty girl, I'm sorry, Daddy, I've been a very naughty girl. . ." interspersed with, "Daddy's always right, Daddy's always right."

Spooked, I decide I am better off with Jeremiah,

breathing new life into wrecked furniture.

"Did I freak you out?" Marnie asks, back to her usual brassy and forthright persona.

"No more than usual." I want to make light of the situation because, in a strange way, I feel a mixture of embarrassment and pity for her.

"Have you heard of Multiple Personality Disorder?"

"Vaguely- is that what your weird behaviour is all about?" By now she is inhaling a line of crystal, through a silver straw. She wrinkles her face up in evident pain.

"Shit! This stuff really burns."

"That means it's good shit."

"Please don't change the subject."

"Sorry- I don't know what to say really. It's happened twice right? That time when you called yourself Mary Lou and got your tits out and then yesterday when you disappeared in the cupboard for hours on end. I was really worried about you, but somehow I thought interrupting wouldn't have been the right thing to do. I had no idea what to do and it kind of scared me."

"I have much more control over it now than I used to. It used to happen every day- I have two dominant personalities- the two you witnessed and three others."

"I don't really understand how it happens 'coz you just suddenly switched and everything about you changed- your voice, your posture, gestures- it was like you had become a completely different person. Have you ever attacked anyone, or hurt them?"

"It's not like that- it's my way of protecting myself. These different personalities are where I go to hide. You're the first person, since my ex-husband that I've switched in front of-"

"I feel honoured . . ." I smile uneasily.

"So I'm crazy- you're pretty crazy too! The thing is my dad abused me when I was a kid and this is how I learned to respond, to survive it."

"I'm really sorry-"

"It's okay. I forgave him- I held his hand when he was dying of cancer. It took some time but I forgave him- he was

71

just doing what he'd had done to him as a little boy so . . .
you move on, ya know."

Clearly she has not entirely moved on, but maybe you
never do fully recover from something like that.

"Actually that's how I got caught up with drugs again-
we'd had all this therapy- my Dad and I- and then he went and
got cancer and was on all this pain medication. I'd steal it and
the nurse must have known, but no one ever said anything so I
got a really bad painkiller habit."

"I'm sorry about your Dad."

"So am I- I took his body from the hospital to this
amazing Native American Burial Ground in New Mexico, in that
car outside. That's why I don't want anything to happen to that
car 'coz he spent his last time on earth in it. He had an eighth
Kiowan in him, ya know. I think that's where my wild streak
comes from."

"So what do I do when you 'switch'?"

"What you did was perfect: act normal, play along if you
want, just don't confront me over it. They usually only last
about ten minutes max. Yesterday was a bit different 'coz I got
a card from my mother and I haven't heard from her in seven
years."

I sense there is a whole other story there, but Marnie is
not forthcoming and I am grateful for that, for the time being
anyway.

Someone is pulling my toes viciously, and it is Roxanne
who is red in the face, her blonde hair in rollers, yelling at me:

"Time to get up, you crazy tweaker bitch! Come on-
we've got to be at the club by 9:00 and you need to look hot so
get your ass out of bed and clean yourself up 'coz you stink!"

"Huh- what are you talking about?"

"'One Eyed Jacks' is opening tonight, or had you
forgotten?! We haven't got time now to get into it- I've gotta get
my hair finished- but you looked a total sight getting out of your
car, not to mention the pile of junk you've loaded it down with. I
mean, what are you thinking?"

"I found some really cool stuff dumpster-diving and I lost
track of time-"

"Again! Well there's a surprise- you know what? You're turning into a fucking tweaker just like I knew you would if you moved in with Marnie!"

I inwardly cringe; to be labelled a tweaker was my worst nightmare because to everyone else, tweakers look like spooked freaks who never sleep or eat, but just hoard. I guess that sums me up! But I'm not really like those weirdoes, because I still work (occasionally), I still have a car and pay my rent. I decide she's just very angry with me because I have been less and less reliable.

"All I care about right now is that you make it to the club on time, otherwise I will never talk to you again."

The stony expression on her face backs up her fierce demand, and I drag myself up. For the first time in my life I take a cold shower.

The club venture had come about through Roxanne, who'd named 'One Eyed Jacks' after a little-known Marlon Brando film; she hopes this will serve as a subtle wink to the seriously cool and hip brigade in LA. I helped to compile the guest-list and send out invitations. Opening night I am supposed to take the money on the door, but I am so zoned out I keep dropping it and miscalculating so Roxanne furiously takes over, while I skulk around the darkened bar. A surf band, The Blue Hawaiians warm up in the background.

"Shit, she's so skinny!" I recognise the acerbic, husky tones of Mia, my second cousin whom I had invited. Mia and I had met up a few times since I'd moved to LA- we were relatives after all- but had never developed a genuine rapport.

"Yeah she is, but you've gotta admit she looks great." Mia's boyfriend, Jake actually spits out something good about me.

"Yeah but she's acting pretty weird, don't you think?"

"We never got on, so how would I know- she was always opinionated and obnoxious as far as I recall- so what's so different now?"

"Well for starters, she's dressed up like something between a transsexual vamp and a hooker-"

"Sexy look girl! Maybe you should try it?" Jake interjects.

73

"Yeah, yeah whatever- she's just like a totally different person."

"Maybe that's a good thing, Mia?" Thanks a lot Jake, I can count on you.

"She must have lost at least twenty pounds and she's all wide-eyed and nervy. And what's with the black patent leather thigh boots? She would never have worn that outfit a year ago."

"Give the kid a break- she's just trying something a bit different."

"Kid!! She's only six years younger than me. No, she's on something- I know it."

"It's a club opening for fuck's sake Mia! I would guess quite a few people in here are on something."

"No, really hooked on something."

"Well, you should have a word with her." Even from five feet behind her, I can sense Mia's sudden bristling.

"I can try, but she's not the easiest of people to get through to."

CHAPTER 8

Crowley Cult

I met a Californian who would / Talk
California – a state so blessed, / He said,
In climate, none had ever died there / A
Natural death.
> Robert Frost *New Hampshire*

We had been in Marnie's car for what seemed hours. I
have the map spread across my lap, but I have absolutely no
idea where we are, so I can hardly contribute to her repetitive
demands: 'When's the turn-off, for fuck's sake?'

Finally the exit appears and Marnie swerves into the slip
road, like she had been caught off-guard and not waiting for its
appearance for the last two hours. This is typical of her.

We are on our way to a Crowley Full Moon Ritual in the
San Fernando Forest area and she is over-excited,
undoubtedly not helped by her hourly stops for crystal
refreshment in the toilets of Denny's and a service station toilet
whose reek of urine still hangs in the recycled air of the car.

"Okay Clea, you are here purely as an observer. I want
you to sit quietly and don't do anything weird, or say anything
out of place."

Her tone of voice is patronising and I let her know:

"Like what, for fuck's sake- what do you take me for?- A
fucking imbecile, or what?!"

"You really freak people out, you know- your energy's
really weird and you fixate on things and it's kinda

disconcerting."

"I apologise for being such an embarrassment."

"All I'm saying is that if they knew you were working on a screenplay and you weren't genuinely interested in joining, they could get nasty. They don't just allow anyone with a passing interest come and hang out on the eve of Baltane, ya know."

"Marnie, you know I really appreciate this. I know you went out on a limb for me and I'll repay you. I'm not quite sure how yet, but I will."

"Finishing the screenplay and getting it to your agent will be reward enough. Now look out for signs to Lake Mearo."

I hand over total trust to Marnie because there seems little other choice; whenever I leave the safe limits of Los Angeles County I enter meltdown mode. She also seems to know exactly where we need to go, now that we're off the highway.

"So was it Jeremiah that drove you out here in the first instance?"

"No . . . it was my Dad."

"Your Dad? What? You're kidding!?"

Her pursed lips tell me otherwise. I am stumped; our fun and interesting adventure has morphed into something verging on the inexplicable and decidedly strange.

"I should have mentioned it I guess, but I kinda forgot in the excitement."

"What the hell was your Dad doing taking you to one of these rituals in the middle of a forest in God knows where?"

"My Dad was very active in the order- that's how I know all about it."

"So Jeremiah has nothing to do with it?"

"Kind of, but only through me-"

"Shit! I don't know what to think anymore."

"Don't think then." She gives me a wry smile. We pull over onto a wooded-over track that's unrecognisable from the road, unless you already know of its existence. Marnie is even more manic than usual and that is saying something. She barks instructions about how to camouflage the car, after we have deposited it in a huge furrow; she even has a greenish grey tarpaulin for this purpose that she drapes across the

Honda, while I forage for moss and a couple of rocks to hold the tarpaulin down.

I usually find her manic-ness tolerable and vaguely humorous, but today she is like a woman possessed. I regret the whole trip now and find the thick trees with snatches of moonlit grey overhead ominous and spooky.

"Follow me and keep quiet- Oh yeah, you don't speak English by the way. You're from Poland."

"Am I?- Right, always helps to know where you're from."

"Don't be a smartass. It was the only way they'd let you come."

We continue to walk and for once I am grateful that I took Marnie's advice to dress in plenty of layers and wear my stiff hiking boots. I had bought them upon arrival in LA- for hiking in the hills and other such wholesome activities- but this was only their second outing. It seems like hours that we are walking, what with stopping for toots and the iced tea Marnie carries in her backpack (she adds a couple of miniature vodkas to her helping). I do not say anything- why should I? - but it makes me even more nervous, like she is in preparation for something that she does not want to share with me. Her manner is controlling and girl-guide like, except of course for the toots and vodka.

A hazy orange hue breaks up the near darkness and we arrive in a clearing with small campfires set out in an arc, welcoming us, almost. Huddles of bodies- sex indiscernible- turn to see who we are. An imposing figure with wispy longish brown hair and a crinkled face, dressed in full-length black velvet robe with flared sleeves and a large gold pentagon on the chest, approaches us.

"Good, you made it. Now go and cleanse. Then we can talk." He does not greet, smile, cajole or even acknowledge me; clearly social niceties are foreign in this arena.

"Where's Jeremiah?" Marnie asks.

"Who? Ohhhhh him- he won't be coming back."

"What 'dya mean? He's meeting me here!"

"No he's not! Now go and clean yourself up; you've already held us up enough!" The man demands belligerently. I take a serious dislike to this obnoxious dictator.

Turning to Marnie to take my cue, I can see that she has

taken on the same stooped, childlike posture that had taken her into solitary confinement in the cupboard in my bedroom; I deduce this is a bad sign.

Unease enters my whole body. The faces lit by the glow of the campfires look mean and pinched- especially one woman whose black eyes look positively devilish while a skinny, naked young man of about twenty lies on his back, holding his erect member and staring at us in a kind of trance state, like they are waiting to claim something they believe is rightfully theirs. All around, I sense they are calmly, but eagerly, waiting to pounce. Their eye-lines seem to converge on Marnie, which makes me doubly suspicious. What role is she destined to play here? And more importantly what are they planning to do to her, or with her?

Marnie takes my hand and leads me off to the south side of the camp, where there is a yurt-like tent. She instructs me to sit and wait, but I am pumped with adrenaline.

"It's really just a sick excuse for an orgy with some spells thrown in-" she whispers through the crack in the canvas.

Suddenly, I jump up and grab Marnie.

"We have to go," I whisper.

"What? Are ya kiddin'?"

"No- I am deadly serious. Please!"

I drag her until she also starts to run with me. And then to my surprise, she bursts out laughing, overtaking me with huge leaps until we get back to her car.

"I always wanted to run out on those sick bastards!" She hollers, jubilantly flinging off the moss and tarpaulin from her car.

"Please can we get out of here! I'm scared they'll come after us-"

"Are you really that scared?" She looks at me in disbelief.

"Yes!"

Once we are on the highway back to LA, I demand an explanation; I am angry because she'd placed me in jeopardy. The eerie atmosphere of unfulfilled promise had genuinely terrified me.

Pulling over into the lay-by for a toot, Marnie explains

that she maintained contact with the cult group because she'd wanted to prove to herself that she'd mastered the childhood abuse from her father. And she had dragged Jeremiah along once before, but he had not wanted to be part of Marnie's self-destructive mission and had caused a bit of an uproar. In fact, Derek and three of his younger cronies had beaten him up and flung him out. Jeremiah suffered two broken ribs and a black eye.

"No wonder Jeremiah didn't come back-"

"But he was goin' to blow their brains out." I look over at Marnie and see her hands shaking.

"What?!. Well, thank god he came to his senses; that lot are not worth the bullets . . . What exactly is it that you want to prove? I mean how can taking part actually make you feel you've won?" I'm stunned by her warped logic.

"I'm the one in control. I've risen up through the ranks and now they pay homage to me. I can choose who touches and who doesn't-"

"But won't you still have to have sexual relations with some of them?"

"Only Derek, the one in black-"

"Oh god, no- how horrific."

"Ya know, my Dad begged me to let it drop when we were in therapy together- I kept saying I wanted to go back and change the entrenched memories- but the therapist said it was too late for that. I only could've gone there tonight completely loaded up to my eyeballs."

"Why did you want to take me?"

"I wanted someone else- a friend- to see what it's really like. . . it seemed too much of a coincidence that you'd showed up in my life an' had this obsession with Crowley. . ."

Marnie's last comment sets me thinking about how she perceives me and how I've become a negative influence in her life. After all, it is through me- and my naïve enthusiasm- that we were at the cult meeting in the first place.

When will I learn to stop making the wrong moves, endangering myself as well as others, seemingly upon little more than a whim. Even my agent had been unenthused by my ideas for the Crowley script.

Marnie cradles the phone in her hand and refers to a piece of scrap paper furtively:

"Right Clea, I'm gonna call your mother. I think she needs to know what's really goin' on with you."

I half smile: "You're kidding, right?"

She cannot be serious. For a start, how did she get the number because even I do not know where my address book has disappeared to and secondly, she wouldn't dare bring my mother into this, would she? While my mind zigzags through the possibilities I realize that she is actually dialling a number.

I leap across the room and grab the phone out of her hand. She steps back, pleased with herself, crossing her arms in a told-you-so stance.

"That actually scared you! You really care about your mommy and what she'd think if she knew what you were up to."

"What the fuck are you playing at?"

"Look, you need help and I can't cope anymore- You disappear for days on end and I'm worried the whole time that something really bad has happened to you."

This all strikes me as a bit rich coming from Marnie, but then she is a bundle of infuriating contradictions.

"So what the fuck can my mother do about it over in France?"

"She's your mother! I think she would like to be told that her daughter is emaciated and spends her time climbing in and out of dumpsters, high as a mad fuckin' kite on crystal meth, rather than the pack of lies you've been spinning: 'Hi mummy, I've been working really hard. . .yes, I'm nearly finished with the second screenplay." She mimics a very bad English accent.

"It's none of your business."

"But it is, you see, because you live here, with me in my apartment."

How in this moment I wish I had stayed in my little bungalow where I could close my bedroom door and no one would bother or question me; the bottom line is that I cannot deal with confrontation and she knows this and is milking her power over me for all it's worth.

"Okay- I'll move out."

She nods in agreement like that was already decided.

"Before you go, I want you to take a look at this book." She hands me a dark blue hardback book with loads of scribbled messages on the inside cover- 'best of luck', 'hang in there', 'see you at our Tuesday Meeting'; it is the Alcoholics Anonymous Book.

"I'm not an alcoholic-" I am perplexed and as I turn the worn pages the words all stick together in an indecipherable dark blob.

"Maybe not, but you are an addict. This can help you understand your behaviour and-"

"So what the fuck did it do for you? You're as guilty as me on the drugs front."

"I know! I'm not saying I'm better, I'm just sharing something that can help you- I feel guilty about the whole situation. I should never have suggested you move in."

"You're right about that," I spit back. I am not interested in stupid Alcoholics Anonymous, or her pathetic guilt and I just want to pack my things up and leave.

"You can't keep running away, ya know."

"Oh really. Watch me!"

"Look Clea, the truth is when I met you I thought you could help me. You were really focused on your screenplay and all that writing stuff and I thought you were great- don't get me wrong I still do- but the crystal is out of hand. It's changed you. If I'd known I'd never have dealt to you."

"Save me the drug dealer with a heart speech!"

"You know I only deal to support my own use, not for profit-"

"Oh yeah, so you say. I can't believe anything about you now, it's. . ."

I am lost for words to describe how much I resent this idiosyncratic red head who is about to really land me in the shit.

"I think you need help before it's too late."

"Big fucking deal- Thanks for nothing, Marnie. Have a nice life." I storm out the door, making sure to grab the piece of paper with my mother's phone number on. I turn it over and there is nothing written on it.

Bluffing bitch.

CHAPTER 9

On My Own

Well some say life will beat you down
Break your heart, steal your crown
So I started out for God knows where
But I guess I'll know when I get there
I'm learning to fly but I ain't got wings
Comin' down is the hardest thing. . .
                    Tom Petty *Learning to Fly*

Lies: that's what I need for the apartment on Loma Linda in the bleeding heart of Hollywood central. Besides the appealing Spanish street name, it's the *No Deposit Needed,* printed on an ever-present banner hanging from the roof that clinches it. Finally: a room of my own where no one can find me, unless I want them to. And now Marnie and me are over I need a new dealer, although I know finding links to the chain will hardly be difficult.

I contact a scary bastard called Conrad, who I had met at Marnies'. He is sexy in a gangster-rap, baggy jeans and tight t-shirt way with thick biceps and puffed-out chest; he's part Barbadian, English and Irish and struts like a cockerel. He introduces me to Elsie Buyers, a crystal meth dealer who is the daughter of a famous comic actor, now deceased. Elsie and I easily fuse a druggie friendship.

I have not heard from Conrad in a few weeks although my relationship with Elsie has been growing and I have become more used to tweaking alone in my new studio on Loma Linda. I am scrambling through a collection of newly

acquired vintage clothes when the phone rings and I hear
Conrad' gruff voice, with his indiscernible accent, thrusting me
back into real time:

"Can you come and meet me- I'm down on 8670 Martin
Luther King, between Crenshaw and La Brea, apartment
number 16 on the 3rd floor. Okay? How long ya gonna be?"

"Well- let's see- I'll need an hour probably."

"Shit that long?"

"Sorry- what's the problem?"

"I just got outa the can- I'm a bit antsy."

"Shit- what happened?"

"Just get your cute ass down here and I'll tell y'all about
it, baby."

My heart briefly stirs at the prospect of intimacy, but I
am in the middle of customising an apricot, velvet hat. I'd
traded a set of art deco, leaded glass panel windows at Joe's
Antiques (more bric-a-brac than old world glory) for a tightly
packed garbage bag of vintage clothes, including hats, belts
and gloves in velvet and leather, corduroy jackets and jeans,
brocade bags, jersey wool dresses, satin and lace lingerie and
nightwear. I struggle with the feathers I am bunching up, and
have to cut my fingers apart where the adhesive has stuck
them together- luckily, it's a fat dollop so I don't tear my skin-
and I do have about fifty pairs of gloves to choose from, if my
hands are unsightly. I want to finish the hat so I can wear it to
go meet Conrad- it's a good rule of thumb to look your peachy
best to welcome your man out of jail. I know he is not 'my
man', but pretending is fun; it adds a certain dramatic quality to
the evening.

I head off down Western and drive towards Hoover
when it dawns on me that the address Conrad has given me is
in South Central. While this does not overly concern me, the
time midnight does because I'm unfamiliar with the area. I'm
already tweaking hard- it had taken me three hours to make it
into my car after I took his call- but I pull over anyway into a
strip mall car park and lean across to open the glove
compartment, where I always keep a loaded tile, to take
another toot for added courage. I am dressed casually in tight
black 501's, vintage leather Frye boots and a skimpy scarlet
top with a sky blue tailored jacket and of course the hat with

84

emerald green feathers and gold brocade band which made the ensemble pretty damn hot and unusual.

I park and take a deep breath. The street appears empty, but all the droopy eucalyptus trees hardly fill me with confidence. When I open my car door a dog barks and rattles an ominous sounding chain. I find the tall narrow building and fall onto the buzzer, praying it works. Conrad appears- he must have been waiting- and drags open the rickety glass fronted door. I notice how grey his skin looks; he has dark bruises on his wrists. Suddenly I am not so keen to be here.

"Where the fuck have you been- it's been fucking hours." He smells of whiskey. I think fast.

"I'm so sorry! I didn't have your number to call you back and Elsie called with an emergency- her pit bull Mumba got in a fight with her neighbour's dog and I had to take it to the vet." (This had actually happened about a week ago but he would not know that- I even had the bloody towel I had laid her out on in the boot of the car.)

"Come in but keep your voice down- what the fuck is that thing on your head?" His aggressive questioning throws me and I want to leave, but he is steering me towards a steep stairwell. The pungent smell of urine hits me, combined with a strange scent that suggests burning.

"Who are your friends?" I whisper as convivially as I can muster; I must not let the scent of fear slip out. I take note of the route we take, just in case I need to get away fast.

"He's my cousin and his wife." We enter a room in which there is a double bed, a cot and a worn loveseat sofa. I detect humps of varying sizes in the cot and the bed. A plastic garden table with brown burn marks sits by the only window that has no curtain, while a street lamp glares in. How on earth do they manage to sleep?

A black man, Freddy, sits at the table with a cigarette and an almost empty bottle. He tears at the label and barely lifts his eyes to acknowledge my arrival. I have never been into a place like this and I am unsure what to do. It seems entirely wrong to be here when they all live together and there is a baby and a toddler asleep in the same room, not to mention the bump in the bed that I assume is Freddy's wife.

"Get your gear out then!" Conrad demands.

I oblige, but am apprehensive about opening my wallet where I keep my stash in a rip within the lining, because I have about $80 cash on me and I do not want them to see it. I hand the plastic baggy to Conrad who does the necessary. I hope it will level him out because I am not enjoying this weird situation and I want to get out of there.

"I was in the lockup so I'm fucking freaked out."

"What's the lockup?" falls out of my mouth. Freddy and Conrad exchange a look that melts my confidence entirely. I am way out of my depth now, and my heart is starting to pound.

"The lock-up is where the pigs put ya if ya make trouble- I've been in for ten days."

"On your own?"

"You got it!"

"Shit. . ."

Freddy takes a line and then to my total surprise goes over to the bed, takes off his shoes and lies down.

"Hey that's our cue-"

"Okay- let's go." We get up and I grab my bag tightly to me- I had noticed Freddy eyeing it- and we close the door quietly behind us. Conrad eases up to my ear:

"Now he can give his bitch a good pounding- Hey wait a minute, I wanna show ya something- I gotta new tattoo." We are in the communal bathroom and my heart feels like it is about to lurch out of my chest. Conrad unzips his jeans, pulls them down while sitting heavily on the edge of the peeling bath. I stand statue still and he pulls me to him, pushing my head down onto his cock that is now almost fully erect and very large. I am for once pleased that I have little sense of smell left, because it looks crusty; I close my eyes and do my best.

"Stop holding back you bitch, I know you want it! Suck me baby, come on suck me baby!" I acquiesce because he is strong and there could be worse alternatives. I go through the motions, while I sense him giving over to the sensations, when a loud knock breaks the mood. A gruff voice demands:

"Get a fucking move on asshole or I'll beat your fucking head in!" I jump up and unlock the door in one sweeping gesture. And I run. Things drop from my trailing handbag, but I know the car keys are in the zipped pocket where I always

86

keep them. I never even see the man who issued the threat as I tear past. I know that I have only a matter of seconds before Conrad snaps to. I suspect he needs me more than I him- for drugs, money and of course, most important of all in LA, a car. I drive away fast; I do not look back once.

I drive for what seems hours. The sun is coming up and I do not want to go back to the shambles that awaits me at home; somehow I am scared Conrad might find his way over, even though I never told him my address.

I catch a glance at my face and I look like a maniacal ghost with streaky smudged eyes and a glimmer of red gloss that looks more like blood; I look more closely and see it is blood surrounding a small deep cut on my top lip that I had not even felt. Why had I gone running to that loser, Conrad? The poverty I witnessed has stunned me. I had driven down there blaring Public Image Limited thinking I was the coolest white chick in town hangin' out in the hood. Now I realise how ridiculous I am, while I root out a Brahms cassette to listen to while I drive the empty streets.

All I know is that I'm scared to be alone, but a visit to Marnie is out of the question even though her apartment is a safe haven compared to where I live now. The vibe between us is just too weird. I find myself on Vista and Melrose where Elsie, my new dealer and friend, lives. I see a couple of dim lights and decide to give it a go. She opens the door immediately as if she had been expecting me; a tear slides down my cheek and I lick the saltiness away.

"What's wrong babe?"

"Bad night," I mumble while I ease myself down onto her huge comfy sofa; the room is covered in crucifixes- there must be at least forty of them- and they offer protection. Her pinched features look soft in the dawn light. She goes into her bedroom and reappears proffering some diamond-shaped white pills.

"Here. Take these Xanax- they'll take the edge off." She flicks the TV remote control and settles on an old film that seems familiar, but my frazzled brain is having trouble placing it. Then I hear it: 'Chitty Chitty Bang Bang, Chitty Chitty Bang Bang, we love you. . .'- and the tears flow.

I close my eyes and I float back home to my childhood bedroom at Gravesend Farm with the feather eiderdown all cosy up round my ears and delicate pink and green flowered wallpaper, where I know I am safe.

CHAPTER 10

Rasta Jesus

She came from Providence. . .
Where the old world shadows hang. . .
She packed her hopes and dreams
like a refugee
And they called it paradise
I don't know why. . .
                    The Last Resort The Eagles

        I lie in my grimy bed, almost paralysed with inactivity
and a hazy brain. I have been asleep for at least thirty-five
hours and I am starving, but I have no energy or will to get up.
The TV at the end of my bed is on for company and that is how
I know Christmas day has arrived. The cheery, nauseating
sounds from the NYC Christmas Day Parade- the jolly beating
of drums and blowing of trumpets- start to chip away at my
enervated brain. I have always felt uneasy around the forced
gaiety of Christmas celebrations. This year there's no need to
worry. My only responsibility is Kiki, the small tortoiseshell cat I
recently adopted from an acquaintance who was moving to a
building that does not allow animals.
        I try to force myself back to sleep but my mind will not
shut off. The bed is full of grit but I am past caring about minor
discomforts. I am in LA, on Loma Linda Avenue- a cess-pit
street- renting a cruddy studio in Hollywood. Actually, the
studio has potential, but my collecting compulsion has meant
that I can barely wedge through the plethora of junk across the
main space and into the bathroom. Even the bath is
overflowing with a bunch of clothes. Elsie has a friend called

Gabe who owns a bunch of buildings in Hollywood and he stashes old tenants' belongings in an unused set of garages. Elsie and I have spent days going through other peoples' belongings like the tweaking magpies we are, inevitably winding up with an untenable pile of junk.

So what joyous festivity awaits me? The smell and squalor is propelling me to find a place to go. I always lay out a couple of lines before I crash, because it helps me feel more organized and in control, so I munch down some apple jacks with some cold milk- otherwise I will faint- and snort the crystal. The habitual burn precludes relief: normal again. I dig out some cat food and pour a big bowl of milk for Kiki. I have no idea when I last fed her.

I get on the phone and invite myself over to Elsie's, who has a few other orphans- Henry, Lissa, Gabe- dropping by. Henry and Lissa are a weird tweaker couple I've met a few times; neither fill me with inspiration and I really miss Marnie and Roxanne, but my pride stops me from calling up either one of them. They probably think I'm in jail by now, or turning tricks on Sunset.

I have never met Gabe, but I have heard all about him from other tweakers, on my circuit. He owns quite a few rundown properties in Hollywood and is rumoured to be very heavy handed with rent backsliders, but there are more sinister suggestions afoot that include murder and the making of snuff films, all of which I take with a pinch of salt knowing how imaginatively creative tweakers are. Elsie is 'kinda close' to him as she puts it and I suspect they'd been romantically involved at some point.

A short Hispanic called Henry opens the door. I walk in and see Elsie and Gabe together on the sofa laughing and canoodling, I sit down opposite and light a cigarette, nodding at Lissa who looks so stoned she could be on the verge of a coma.

Gabe stares straight at me and his eyes are black. He has a few wispy strands of hair over his shiny pate; he could be anywhere between 40 and 60 years old. With his average build and casual dress style, he seems altogether nondescript, which probably helps to disarm unsuspecting women. But what un-nerves me are his penetrating, unrelenting eyes that refuse to diffuse and seem to target me as 'his'.

Cold blasts all around me and I start shivering. Someone remarks that I look like I've seen a ghost. The atmosphere is completely unlike anything I have ever experienced, although everyone else appears oblivious. Or has he drugged them before I arrived? Questions start to arise second-by-second and my head feels like it might boil open and crack. There is something sinister at work and I am not invited to be part of it, or maybe this is my warning to get out before something happens that I'll regret.

I jump up; I have to leave. Elsie looks confused because I'd just arrived and we had all put in an order for xmas takeaway dinner from Jerry's Diner that's on its way. I mumble something about having forgotten to feed my cat and I grab my bag and leather jacket, chucking $20 on the table for the food. 'Feed it to the dogs' I tell a baffled Elsie.

I had been in the presence of evil and I need to cleanse myself. Gabe never really addressed me- I think he lifted his wrist in a mute welcoming gesture- but I just knew it from my sixth sense. Whatever he has done and will do he is incapable of repentance or remorse. Suffering and pain are his currency, as well as drugs, cars, houses and money. I contemplate driving back to my place to take a boiling hot shower, but then remember that the bath is packed to overflowing with clothes, ironically collected from Gabe's garages- clothes that initially I had been thrilled to rummage through and take- but now I wonder why and how he has such a huge collection of female clothing from the 50s onwards? I know he is a slumlord, but what else?

Instead I drive all night around the city and find myself on the wide, vacant streets that lead to Compton. In the back of my alert- but strangely relieved- mind, I am grateful to be away from Gabe- whether irrational, or not- he gave me the serious heevie-jeevies. Right now, I need a sign of protection, some sort of talisman to ward off evil: a Jesus statue. Ever since I had come across the stuck-back-together figurine, behind that 7-11 store on Santa Monica, right after Ryan's death, I have developed a desire for their presence, along with ones of the Virgin Mary.

I have never entered a Catholic shop in my life and a

pristine statue was not what I desired- it needed to carry a story to give it any value and purpose. Marnie had a similar preoccupation with these plaster objects and had tried to sidle away with my favourite Jesus statue- the one I found behind the 7-11 store- when she threw me out. She hid it in a cardboard box in a cupboard in the kitchen, scrunched up besides a burnt frying pan but I found it having learned some of her tricks by this point.

I must have been in my car for 5 hours solid when I realise I need to pee. Nothing will be open, but I need to find somewhere to pull over and go. By now I can feel out where the safe dumpsters are versus the places where a lone, white girl should not even contemplate. That might sound like common sense, but there are so many variables as to what makes an outdoors space desirable for a street person- proximity to street lights, traffic lights, foot traffic, entrance or exit to a home or business- and each has their disadvantages and plusses.

The fresh, new sun feels like melting wax on my shoulders as I make my way to the back of an old but well kept 6-storey apartment building. The bushy plants on the ground level balconies inform me that thieves do not profit here and I notice a couple of the sliding doors are ajar; a very unusual sight in this city. I squat behind a beaten up Buick hoping that the embarrassment of being caught in mid-flow will not infringe upon the unexpected, soft touch of this rather special morning. Quickly pulling my jeans back up undetected, I walk for about half a mile along a residential street with almost quaint detached houses with well-kept front yards and fences.

The buzz of early morning television emits from some windows and small heads bob in and out of view through others, kids eating their cereal, demanding something, snuggling up on the sofa to watch 'Sesame Street'. On foot, I head back to Crenshaw Boulevard where a tall, skinny black man lays out a large, pale blue blanket on the pavement. He carefully unwraps and methodically arranges a selection of figurines, taken from a large wooden crate. He places the ornaments strategically on the blanket in a design that he juggles about, stepping out into the empty road to assess his handiwork.

I walk up and smile. Eager, he jumps in between his pottery and shakes my hand, which freaks me out a little, but then I ask him if this is his usual pitch to which he responds with his hands and I realize he is deaf. Most of his wares are of a religious nature- lambs and shepherds, Madonnas, angels and . . . Jesus.

I see it. The thing I have been driving round all night searching for, desiring, needing- a Jesus statue, but this is no traditional figurine in light blue, fleshy soft pink and gold. This is a Rastapharian head of Jesus and it is one of the ugliest ornaments I have ever seen, but I love it and I know it must be mine- that he moulded this one and half foot monstrosity for me, and me alone. It is made from a plaster mould and painted in thick stripes of yellow, green, red and black. It costs $25 and I write him a cheque, which he gladly takes. His eyes tell me he thinks he made it for me too.

Gathering my purchase closely to my chest, I walk back in the direction of my car, hoping not to have lost it. My keys are attached to my belt on a thick, heavy chain following the run-in with Conrad and I jangle them for reassurance. I feel a tap on my shoulder and my heart jumps into my mouth; I turn and see it is the street vendor and he is pointing down the wide boulevard, gesticulating with fervour. I take a few steps back and see a 60s style, wooden church set back from the main road; it is unadorned except for a simple cross on the eave of the roof. I nod in agreement and mouth:

"Thank you! Thank you very much."

I walk across to it and try the door. To my surprise it glides open, with no sound. It is empty and dark, except for the sunlight shining through the four windows at each corner. I enter the back pew, kneel and say a prayer.

I replace the phone and search out all the items I think I may be able to flog; I am desperate for money. My Pentax camera, lens, and all my gold jewellery has long since hit the shelves of the Hollywood Pawn Shop. Rent is due, by over a week, and it's only my second month at Loma Linda where I have hardly endeared myself to the other tenants, what with my late night activities and stacked pyramids of dived 'trash', as they call it (How dare they?). I have also left things outside in the hallway and this has caused some friction, to say the least. I try to be considerate, but tweaking habitually takes over and invariably I lose track of time and forget.

I replenish my energy levels with a couple of fat lines, now feeling the over-riding need for action. I ferry the various items out to my car parked out back. Kiki mews plaintively; no doubt suspicious that once I leave she will not see me for days. At the back of the empty cupboard I find a lone tin of tuna, which I open and give to her quickly before my wavering guilt propels me back into the apartment to cuddle the lonely wee thing. I should never have taken her on, but I was too lonely to use my better judgement. No time for regrets . . . I just need to get to the shop as quickly as possible.

Because all this has taken longer than planned- as usual- once I am in the driver's seat I step on the accelerator while fiddling with the dials on the car stereo. Damn! Where is that 'Sly and the Family Stone' song I like? I head down Western and traffic is like syrup; in mounting frustration, I turn off onto a side street and lean back to feel about on the floor of the back seat where I lobbed a bunch of cassettes. Truly irritated now- crystal throbbing through my light bones and thinned blood- I look around for what registers as a split second: thump, smash, screech.

I lurch forward, hitting my forehead on the steering wheel. I taste blood in my mouth. An echo of thuds banging on glass. Out of the corner of my eye I see a clenched fist through my door window.

"You bitch- what fuck go do? No looking, you fuckin' bitch!" A short, plump Hispanic man yells at me through my window. I stall in my driving seat quickly feeling my legs and chest to assess damage and take a deep breath while I look up into the rear view mirror. There is a bloody gash half way across my forehead, my right eye clouding and swelling so that I will not be able to see within an hour probably and a cut bottom lip- minimal damage, thank God. But where am I? All I know is that I need a payphone.

When I stumble from my car, dazed and dripping blood, a posse of people stand and stare. No one comes forward to offer a hand, a Kleenex or an arm to lean on to steady me.

94

I make it to the edge of the road and sit there, while the crowd continues to grow. I get the sense that the man whom I have crashed into lives very near here and his friends and family have come out in a flood of support. I am too dazed to feel fear, but I can sense their active hostility towards me in their suspicious, unsympathetic eyes. I fumble inside my handbag because I need change for the payphone; I also need a tissue to wipe off the dripping blood.

A pretty little girl of about eight approaches me uncertainly; her face is blank and then she raises her small, thin arm and points at my gash. She emits a cackle incongruous with the size of her. I stand up in shock while she continues to point and laugh. I have never been ridiculed and held to attention by an eight year old ghetto girl before and I am now terrified. I quickly stand and step back further onto the pavement and my eyes dart around looking for an escape route. I start to move away.

A couple of men follow me as I move towards a payphone, a few hundred yards away, obviously dispatched by the rest of the group to make sure I don't try and do a runner. Where would I run to?

For the first time ever, I am thrilled when I spot a police car approaching the melee; on the payphone I order a tow truck to rescue my car and more importantly, me.

The police car has pulled over and one of the policemen approaches me.

"Hi there officer. . . I think it was my fault. He pulled out and I had the sun in my eyes. I have insurance- of course." I have not paid my car insurance for over four months, but I still have the relevant paperwork in the car. This, along with my Driver's Licence, placates them and they do not bother with any more questions.

The Hispanics continue to give me the evil eye as if I had deliberately gone out of my way to crash into them.

I never thought I would be so relieved to be sitting in a tow truck on my way back to my apartment, with a trashed Volvo on the back, jammed so full of junk that people think I am living out of it.

My relief at having escaped the Hispanic ghetto is short lived when the reality hits: I now have no car and no money.

95

CHAPTER 11

Tweaker In Trouble

She had expectations she could never make clear
Thinking that others must know what she wants
As if they were Gods and could see into her heart.
The Meeting Julia Casterton

Life in LA is impossible without a car: it is essential in this sprawling, suburban metropolis. Now I am without a car as well as the rent money. Quite a dilemma.

My lack of transport means total loss of independence; it makes me very nervous. Without a car I feel I am fast becoming part of an underclass that I have only ever glimpsed while driving by a bus stop. I've never experienced LA for longer than four days without a car. Now I have no choice but to rely on a mix of highly unreliable, flaky people, like Tony and Zed.

I meet Tony and Zed through Elsie who calls them 'the terrible twins'. We all have one thing in common- the obvious link of crystal meth. The only difference is degrees of longevity and commitment to the lifestyle. Whereas other friends, including Roxanne and Marnie had tried to spell out the danger signals ahead, this lot positively encourage them. They are further down the path than me, but I do not see it at the time; to me they seem more clued in and deserving of respect. They wear the t-shirt while I'm still in nappies.

I am still kidding myself that this is all a bit of a lark, a bit of mad fun that can easily be left behind once I put my mind to it. I do not understand addiction and all its convoluted mayhem.

Today, Tony and Zed show up together to release me from the prison that my apartment has become. I am desperate to get out. Each time I venture out on foot, the offers from men either on the street, or from cars pulling over, are constant. Now I wear a permanent scowl and don't-fuck-with-me look on my face. Initially I had walked across to a beckoning man in an aqua blue Trans Am, assuming he needed help with directions when he abruptly cut in with: "How much for a blowjob?" I scuttle off damn fast while he curb-crawls me, until I run into a Laundromat and escape through their emergency back door. Now I only go out when I am desperate for a pack of cigarettes or donuts, Oreos and Snapple iced tea- my basic diet, alongside crystal meth.

Hence, I am grateful to open the door to Zed's gaunt, chiselled but undeniably handsome Native American face.

"Hey babe- Tony's on his way. We need to talk to you about something."

"I hope it's about fixing my car?" I half jest.

"Huh? No, but something that can help you get fixed up."

"Anything's okay by me as long as it's legal, well- you know- fairly legal."

Tony appears, slamming the door behind him: "Who's the asshole in number 3? I nearly punched his ugly fucking face in."

"Oh fucking great Tony- there've been about 500 complaints since I moved in here two months ago!"

Tony and Zed exchange a look that says 'let's keep her sweet', or am I imagining it? Fucking tweakers- there's always a plan lurking.

On the other hand, I'm obliged to Tony that I'm not alone with Zed because the last time he brought me back, after we had been tweaking over at Elsie's, he'd come over all sexy and touchy feely, stripping off naked and lying on my bed with a hard on. I had locked myself in my bathroom, until he recovered his dignity and left.

Tony protectively places his arm around my shoulder and pulls me into his narrow chest, where I am pressed up against his pointy collarbone.

"Oh I'm okay- just bummed out about my car. I feel like

98

a fucking prisoner in my own home."

"You could clean it up a bit."

"Yeah come on Clea, it's kinda disgusting," Zed chips in.

Despondent, I look across the room that is squalid by even a hungry pig's standards. I grab a towel and rub the bar as a concession to my guests.

"Sorry guys. Housekeeping's not my strong point."

"She's not kidding. Hey, let's try some of this crank I got from Henry- and then we can tell you all about our little plan."

"Fantastic- I sure need a fucking plan!" The dark feeling passes and I see some light. I am trying to keep smart and stay out of trouble because a couple of weeks ago, Elsie had walked in when I was going through a garbage bag, stolen from the Bank of America dumpster and expressed total outrage:

"What the fuck are you doing?" She demanded, making no attempt to hide her disgust.

"Looking for cheques that Tony can wash and then we can get hold of some cash-" I proffer amicably.

"You make me sick!"

"Why?" I'm genuinely upset, "It's not going to hurt anyone coz they can report it stolen and . . ."

"I see. You're not content just to fuck up yer own life, you have to fuck up innocent people by going through their trash- the trash- for fuck's sake! What kind of sick animal are ya?"

"It was Tony's idea. I guess I didn't really think about it."

"No that's your excuse for everything, isn't it? 'I guess I didn't really think about it'," she whines in a high-pitched tone that I hope doesn't resemble me. I am ashamed and embarrassed. Maybe she is right. Suddenly the trash that I so eagerly pilfer feels like a violation of a stranger's welfare and privacy. What kind of woman have I become? And for the seriously-fucked Elsie to comment makes it even worse.

Things have now accelerated and Elsie's taunts have fallen from recent memory, although she'd bulls-eyed the only decent nerve left in me. But since I have written off my car I am in despair. There is no denying my heavy heart and I know these two pariahs are waiting to feed. What choice do I have?

Even a crumb would be welcome right now.

The tweaking trio huddle together in Zed's clapped-out maroon Buick, running through the procedure- same drill, different bank. Yesterday we made $400 in a Bank of America on Maple Drive in Beverly Hills, so why should today be any different?

Against my instincts we are parked outside the Wells Fargo on Willoughby and La Brea, the bank that is used by Propaganda Films employees. It feels too close to home. I step out of the car and wait at the traffic lights to cross. I am dressed casual-smart.

I join the queue and push down my ediginess; this bank has a different atmosphere or maybe it's me? I am getting closer- three people from the front- when I am knocked off my perch.

"Clea? Is that you?" a 40 something woman with short cropped blond hair asks. Oh my God- it is one of Amory's partners' secretaries, Linda.

"Yes. Hello, how are you?" My face creases into a rictus smile. Please move on quickly.

"I gather you're not working for Amory any more? How come?- I thought you guys got on really well?" I cannot believe this woman I barely know is grilling me, but then I realise it works in my favour because it will authenticate my standing as a genuine customer cashing a personal cheque, especially because Linda probably comes here all the time.

"Well I 'm waiting to hear about my screenplay- it's with Miramax at the moment. Conflicting interests I guess." I lie.

"Wow! That's great. Good luck, honey."

"Thanks- great to see you." She leaves and I step up to the counter. It is a youngish female teller with her hair scraped back and no make up. I hand over the cheque- more worn than the one I cashed yesterday- and she immediately holds it up to the light. She looks at me- a slow, methodical smile puckers her mouth and in that moment I should have run, but instead what do I do?

"Is there a problem, miss?"

"I'm not sure. . . Mrs. Wade? Can I see some ID please?" Mrs. Dawn F. Wade is the name on the forged

100

cheque.

"I'll check- I think I left my purse, with all that stuff, at home." As soon as I utter those words, her hand hits the button under the counter and a security guard appears on cue, blocking the only exit. I panic. What do I do? No one briefed me on what to do when it all went belly-up. Advancing police sirens punctuate the lulled hush that has fallen and customers stare. I hear someone whisper:

"She looks kinda normal- not like a down and out at all."

"Takes all types! She looks fucked up- look at her eyes." My suppressed paranoia leaks out, transforming into rabid fear; I make a dash for it. I run and claw past the security guard who grabs me just as I get hold of the thick metal door handle.

"Where 'dya think ya going? You're goin' downtown with the boys in blue," he tells me in a surprisingly affable manner.

"Babydoll, ya screwed up!" He states the obvious, while I crumple inside.

I am handcuffed by an officer and shoved into the back seat of a Z car, separated by a scratched, black metal grill from them in the front. I look for Tony and Zed parked at the corner, but they are gone. I am alone.

How could I have been so stupid?

I wait in the cell with eight women, all black or Hispanic-street prostitutes, junkies or both from what I can glean from the way they talk. A couple have track marks on their arms. I sit in the corner on the cold stone floor, back against the filthy wall, disgusted and appalled at myself.

The stench of the toilet that is in the cell with us- so we all have to take a shit in front of each other- makes me want to vomit and the facilities do not run to loo paper or running tap water. There is nothing more sobering than a night spent in the slammer. Sleep is out of the question because the four bunk beds are already taken, and the stench leaping off them is enough to make me heave, if the stink of shit and urine does not first.

The bitter truth is I know how I ended up in here: the simple fact is I broke the law and I got caught trying to do so. But what I have never considered- in my altered state, high as a kite on crystal meth- is that this was not actually a game, but a serious delusion that has real consequences. Of course,

101

there had been moments when I had glimpsed the gravity of my developing situation- say when Marnie kicked me out and threatened to call my mother- but somehow it had all felt like a 'fill-in' activity before I started at UCLA (MA in Screenwriting Program) in the Autumn. I just took it for granted that I had been accepted. But I had not. In reality what had that plan evaporated into? For starters, I had missed the deadline for my Brown Professor's recommendations- crucial for any Masters Program- and I doubt my overall application was up to scratch, considering I had thrown it together- literally- on the day it was due, racing over to West LA to drop it off by hand. I was living in a self-constructed fantasyland kept afloat by snorting copious and consistent amounts of crystal meth.

Crystal had done such a great job of erasing my memory- the good parts as well as the bad- that here I am now in a jail cell in disgusting, downtown LA locked up with a bunch of derelicts who did not have the good fortune to be born into a life of privilege that I had taken to be my birthright. No wonder these women eye me with disdain and suspicion. They intuit I am not one of them- I was not born into this way of life- in fact I am as far removed from their reality as is possible, yet here I am with them. I have a degree from an Ivy League University that I had been desperate to attend and within two years of graduating, I am sitting here amongst squalor. I had a choice but I bet these women did not- they were victims, or survivors, of economic necessity whereas I am. . . confused, shameful and full of self-hatred.

I had wanted to 'live life'- what exactly does that mean?- experiment, embrace the unknown, involve myself with danger and dangerous men, live on the edge. And look where it has landed me. I am incredibly stupid and misguided. In my teens, I had hankered after guidance and when I finally receive it from my Russian-American family I completely ignore their advice: when they had voiced their apprehension about my move to LA I paid lip service, but had no intention of really taking their concerns into consideration. Instinctively they knew this was the wrong city for a girl like me and now I have really proved it.

Dabbling with drugs at college is one thing, but taking it to this extreme so you end up in the slammer for the night is a step too far. And had not guardians appeared to warn me in the form of Ryan, who trod this path ahead of me? He bore testament to the ravages of crystal meth addiction. From Ivy League graduate to gabbling, non-sensible, paranoid wreck within a year of graduation and then he had died- in a car accident that I believe was not an accident, but his 'no way out' response to an HIV positive test result. And only a few months back I had been told of a school friend from Heathfield- a pretty, clever blonde full of potential, who had ended up dead in a cheap Thai hostel from an overdose. How had I responded to this sad news? Instead of stopping and taking some time to contemplate and readjust my thinking, I had barrelled on in fierce denial that people actually die from drugs, telling myself 'No, that could never happen to super-human moi'. How naïve and ridiculous I am. It could even be funny if it was not so pathetically sad, delusional and destructive.

I am released the next day after a brief court appearance, with a continuation date set for a couple weeks later. From Ramparts Division Station in downtown LA, I get the bus. When I am released and given back my property, I am informed that I get one free ride on the bus with my jail ID plastic bracelet- yippee.

I head back to the apartment with serious determination to end this crazed and depraved way of life. It is the first time in months that I have not been either high on crystal meth, or sleeping.

The smell of musty clothes now growing mould alongside the dirt, debris, and pervasive clutter appals me. Whereas a day and a half ago this seemed 'normal' to me, now it seems wholly insane. What actually am I planning to do with this bizarre collection of goods?

I awaken after sleeping about fifteen hours feeling spaced out, disoriented, famished and yet determined to change my situation. I know the only way forward is to come clean with my family and see what they suggest. I have no suggestions beyond my willingness to admit I have a serious drug problem that has landed me with a criminal charge of cheque theft, bank fraud and drug possession (I had left an empty baggy in my jacket pocket, lined with crystal residue).

I call-collect my cousin Sonia in New York and get her soft-spoken husband, Luc on the phone. I confess all, deciding to explain about the arrest and subsequent charge against me, so that he knows how serious my situation is.

To my complete and utter amazement he is unfazed, responding in his slow, deliberate speech pattern:

"Okaaaay . . . What we need to do is find a place where you can go and stay to get over this drug problem, right? I need to talk to Sonia about it when she gets home, but do not worry. Everything will be okay. Now give me the number where we can contact you."

And that was it. Suddenly a solution is in sight, because the Vronsky family leap into action to help me, as best they can. Sonia ropes in my other cousin Mia to organize everything on this end and the only thing I insist upon- probably my biggest mistake- is that I go to a rehab in LA, whereas Sonia wanted me to fly to New York to be nearer the Vronsky family. I am resistant to her plan and insist that I am not leaving LA.

Mia, who is very kind, does her homework. She books me into Promises in West Los Angeles (before it expanded and moved to Malibu) which has a solid reputation as a strict, but caring Residential Drug and Alcohol Rehabilitation Centre.

CHAPTER 12

Promises. . . Like Pie-Crust, Are Made To Be Broken

Then the day came when the risk to remain tight in a
bud was more painful than the risk to blossom.
                                                    Anais Nin

Pat, a large black woman who is the Matron, welcomes us and shows me my room, where I deposit my baggage, which now strikes me as rather excessive compared to what my roomie has with her.

"Planning on bein' here awhile I guess!" Pat jokes, and then I am taken into a consultation room where I am to sit and wait for a counsellor.

I wave Mia off, glad to see the back of her because the situation is so damned uncomfortable and I just end up feeling more guilty- if that is possible- and ashamed. I wriggle my bony ass into a comfy chair, trying to manoeuvre the padding to cushion my aching bones that jut, jar and grind painfully with every move I make.

"Hi there- Welcome to Promises! I'm your counsellor Panda, short for Pandora that I seldom use coz I don't like it. I'll be working with you during your stay here." She is an attractive brunette- all smiles- who offers me her ringed hand. She takes a pile of paperwork out of her briefcase and lays it out in front of me.

"How ya doing?" She asks caringly.

"Okay, I guess," I manage to stutter, feeling overwhelmed and dizzy.

"It's not easy doing what you're doing- God knows I know, but it'll be worth it when ya get your life back. That's what you want . . . Right?" She looks expectant, while I shrug.

"Yeah I guess so- I'm sitting here, aren't I?"

"It's not gonna be easy, ya know? You're gonna have to work hard and follow our suggestions and strict guidelines. All the staff here- all of them, minus Juanita, the cook- are recovered addicts and/or alcoholics. We know firsthand what you're going through."

"I doubt it- you're hardly in my head are you?" Her smugness grates.

"No, but I do understand what you're going through."

She oozes sincerity and I feel like punching her in the mouth.

"Oh fuck off, will you!" splurts out of my mouth and I jump up, highly agitated.

"Whoa! What's wrong? I'm not the enemy ya know, I wanna be your friend."

I look out the window at Barrington Avenue wishing I was in the car driving by. Panda crosses to me. I turn to face her down when she gently places her arms around me and pulls me to her.

And that is it. I crumple into her like a sodden sandcastle on the beach, heavy tears streaming down my cheeks, nose dripping.

All I can say, into her ample, warm bosom, over and over is:

"I want my mummy! I want my mummy! I just want my mummy. . ."

I have no idea how long I stay there in her embrace but I almost pass out with emotional exhaustion when she lifts my head up and gives me a kind smile.

"How about some dinner in the dining area? Or would you be happier going to your room and I'll bring you something on a tray?"

"I really don't want to see anyone right now. I'm no way ready to meet the others yet"-

"That's completely understandable and normal. Now quit worrying and stressing and remember that today is the start of the rest of your life. You can make it Clea; I know you

106

can and you will! Trust me- I've seen a lot of people come and go through these doors and I don't say that to everyone by any stretch, so count yourself lucky. You are one of the fortunate ones- and I mean it- who can leave all this shit behind and go on to lead a full, happy life."

I nod, too tired to speak anymore. She guides me back to my room and I see the other patients' rubberneck when I walk by the dining room window.

"It's been a long fucking day!" I mumble more to myself than to Panda.

"Take each day as it comes; I know this is gonna work for you Clea, so hang in there."

I have absolutely no other choice but to trust her, and in that moment I truly do.

I love Promises. I love the structured routine and quite frankly all the attention I receive. I know that they are being paid to look after me, but it almost feels like a family, albeit one that is riddled with tales of woe. But it is this reality, this thread in common, that almost lets me off the hook. I do not feel like a 'bad' person, but instead a 'sick' one. Amongst the daily aphorisms that are flung around, solace is to be found here, if only for the brief 28 day stay.

I also know that this is what I need to do in order to get back on the right side of the law. Never having been arrested before, I am duly frightened by what consequences lie in wait and I follow the advice of Edward French, an expensive lawyer hired by the Vronsky family, to get in a Program and prove I am staying off drugs. Of course I want to stay off crystal meth; I would be mad if I did not considering where it took me, but these are early, heady 'pink cloud' days.

They do not miss a trick here and I learn this, much to my indignation, in my first week when I am pulled up by Matron Pat and my counsellor Panda. When I arrived my eye had automatically been drawn to a tall, muscular Hispanic guy, Omar, with whom I flirt outrageously. A cocaine addict and dealer, he'd turned up with $20,000 in cash to cover his month's stay at Promises. There is a strict 'no sex or canoodling' policy between patients- if caught, patients are immediately expelled- and he seems keen to break it with me, grabbing me in the dimly-lit corridor on my way to the loo late at night. I gently remind him that he has a girlfriend and child and he shamefacedly backs off; I do not have any intention of doing anything with him- at least while here- but his evident desire feeds my self-esteem. This, however, does not stop me from wearing tight tops and short skirts, walking provocatively and wearing more make up than is necessary for rehab.

After a week Panda calls me into the office.

"I want to discuss something very important with you regarding the opposite sex," she eyeballs me.

"What about the bastards?" I query, with a singsong, 'I'm all ears' smile.

"This is not the time to be flirting and getting crushes on guys in the Program and the reason is because it will destroy your recovery."

"I'm not- I don't know what you're on about!"

"Yeah right! You can't bullshit a bull-shitter- I've seen the way you look at Omar and the way you flirt with everyone."

"I do not!- Okay I flirt with some of the guys, but not all of them."

"Same difference- Focus on your program and after a year clean and sober you can think about a relationship, but certainly not until then." She smiles kindly.

"What about you; you were using with your boyfriend and then you got clean together, you told me?" I demand sulkily.

Panda sighs, resigned:

"I knew I shouldn't have told you that but-"

"There's an exception to every rule, right?!" I chip in.

"Clea, keep thinking like that and you're in real trouble."

Part of our day is filled with group therapy sessions and every week, on a Friday, we all have to share with the group a realization we have had about ourselves, in terms of our recovery, and what we think may be standing in the way of it- like our pride, fears of not being part of the crowd, fitting in, uniqueness, repressed anger, ego. Because this is my first

time in this group session I am invited to introduce myself
and tell everyone a little about my background. I have prepared
a crib sheet, with a few notes on for reference, which I notice
gets a few amused looks from the keen and interested faces
sitting in the attentive circle.

"Hi, I'm Clea and I'm an addict."

"Hi Clea," the group intone.

"Let's see now: When I was eighteen I left my parents in
England for adventures in America- land of the just and the
free with fields full of dreams. I was here to attend Brown
University- part of the Ivy League-where I excelled in my Media
and Semiotics studies and collected an impressive number of
contacts that would help me forge the kind of successful career
in the media I was clearly destined to have." I pause for effect.

"Upon graduation I moved to New York City where I
started at an entry level job within the most hip and happening
Film Production Company in Tribeca. I rose quickly, through
the ranks and within a year was poached by a prestigious Los
Angeles film company- another hip Indie with two sleeper
surprise hits so far- who were willing to up my meagre salary
and crown me Associate Producer. Not bad for the first year
out of college, eh?" Faces are starting to look expectant while I
continue in my chipper, forthright tone:

"In my spare time I had penned a screenplay and was in
talks with Disney for an option- But I might hold out for a better
offer." Now I turn on what I hope is my most beatific and
alluring smile:

"Did I mention my fiancé Johnson Phillips 3rd? He and I
are part of a select coterie of Manhattan desirables who are
invited to every opening, premiere and party worth mentioning
(I should add we are quite picky); we are constantly to be seen
in the society pages and apparently I have become rather a
fashion icon of my time. We summer in the Hamptons and ski
in Aspen at Christmas. I have always moved smoothly and
swiftly from one relationship to the next- without ruffling too
many feathers- as I am a woman who seems to attract the
opposite sex without much effort and although I am forward-
thinking in terms of my career, I am a traditionalist at heart who
would no more be seen without a man as without my perfect,
but subtle make up-"

109

"Clea," Panda abruptly interrupts me: "What is this?"

"I'm telling everyone about how my life should be going" I say indignantly. Panda smiles and gets up and I realise she is going to give me a hug. Oh no, I cannot bear more hugs; they are too much and too many on an almost hourly basis! Yuck.

Panda realises this and instead addresses the group: "Thank you Clea, I think that was actually very instructive for the group, wasn't it everyone?"

"What the fuck are you talking about, Clea?" Sidney, my black lesbian roomie, asks.

"If your life is so fucking perfect what the fuck ya doin' this place?" Omar angrily interjects, while the rest look baffled. I suddenly feel totally stupid and humiliated.

"Sorry everyone. I guess it's a fiction, a fantasy. My problem has always been that I want my life to be free of struggle, like a fairy tale." In fact, I am afraid to grow up, but I decide to keep that thought to myself.

"You need to get fuckin' real girl- this ain't no fuckin' fantasy." Omar expostulates in his less-than-perfect English and storms out the room, leaving me to dwell upon what I have unwittingly revealed about myself, by attempting to do the complete opposite.

Talking, or rather 'sharing' with each other is the name of the game here. They really encourage digging deep, learning to let it all hang out and thereby identifying triggers and self-destructive behaviour patterns. In a way I am quite enjoying this self-shedding; peeling away the onion layers as the counsellors call it.

Today in my private session with Panda I had a strong familial realisation. Inevitably forced to abandon my fiction about how I would like to be perceived, I am instead forced to accept that I am the third generation in a line of females- Grannie, mummy and now me- afflicted with alcoholism and drug addiction, or as it is called here 'the disease' (read as dis-'ease'). I suppose now I can assign blame to my inherited genes: I have an uncontrollable predilection that forces me to take drugs as often and as much as possible. Panda pounces on me: "Watch out- There's a ton of self-pity crashing down on us!"

In truth, this knowledge had always been lurking somewhere in the background, but somehow it was 'there but not there' because no one really wanted to bring it out into the open and directly address it. The Vronsky family had brought it up with me once, but that was it. It certainly now serves to help me fathom and understand an aspect of the depths of my unexplained self-doubt, lack of fulfilment, shame, guilt and self-hatred. Maybe I absorbed it into my cells while in my mother's womb.

I recall Grannie, who I have not really thought about for ten years or so. I had conveniently pushed her out of my memory. I'd been on Easter holiday break- 'the hols'- from Heathfield, and Mummy was living in Gravesend Farm on a trial separation from my stepfather- he had actually thrown her out and would soon be filing for divorce, but I did not know this at the time.

I did know my mother felt obliged to visit her mother, even though she absolutely hated to confront Grannie's dire predicament. She had recently been allocated a one-bedroom council flat in Brighton. (Grannie had lived in various B&B's around Hove and Brighton, but invariably she was thrown out. In more affluent times she had lived all over the world, originally from Scotland to New York, Madeira, Nice on the French Riviera to Chelsea in London before her money from her last husband dried up.) The bottom line is she is a serious drunk, who causes chaos wherever she ends up. My mother has given up trying to help her now- Grannie has never, ever admitted she has a problem- although it has been going on since before my mother was born when she would disappear for days at a time from her rubber planter husband's colonial mansion in Kuala Lumpar, Malaya- as it was called then. My grandfather had disowned both Grannie and my mother, claiming that he had met Grannie on a 'date' he'd had to pay for (the insinuation was that she was a high class call girl). Whether this was true or not, my mother and I will never know because of course Grannie was indignant. But the fact remained that crude aspersions had been cast and one could not help wonder. Clearly this affected my mother deeply- in fact she herself only ever referred to it once- and the understanding was that it would never be spoken of again; this was not to be the case because I threw it back in her face as a teenager during one of our many combustible rows- "At least you're not a prostitute like your mother!" I taunted. Then I caught a glimpse of her deep-seated and rarely-accessed hurt and pain; it sent me off to my room with my tail between my legs.

While my mother has recounted few memories or incidents to me, she has relayed a few: How Grannie destroyed her wedding day to my father when she drunkenly ran after their going-away car, yelling: "I hate you Bill Myers, I hate you!" She ruined Mummy's day but she did not care, or probably she did not even know what she had done, so deep and entrenched was her denial. On another occasion Mummy had been called by the police who told her Grannie was in the lock-up ward at Belleview, a mental hospital in New York. Collecting her, she saw another patient stubbing a cigarette out on an already scarred arm while Grannie refused to recognise her own daughter and Mummy had to go home and fetch their passports to prove they were actually related.

To be fair, Grannie had always treated me like a little princess. Trips to Harrods were the norm and now they are a distant, wonderful memory from my childhood. How had a privileged, beautifully dressed, intelligent, witty, extremely thin and striking, rather attractive woman, ended up in Whitehawk Close on the worst estate in Brighton? I remember one lovely day like it was yesterday, because it involved Grannie, Mummy and myself; we were all in high spirits. They were both big fans of San Lorenzo's in Beauchamp Place and there we sat together having lunch with the sun beaming through the glass dome overhead. There was a buzz of excitement in the air, and the waiter conspiratorially told us that Rod Stewart and his entourage were over in the corner. I had no idea who this person was, but before I knew it my mother had ripped a grey strip of paper from the back of her cheque book, fished out a biro and pointed me over in the general direction:

"Go on Clee! Please, get his autograph for me. Remember to say please and thank you", she urged.

Happy to be pleasing Mum I approached a round, shiny-faced Japanese man with wire rimmed glasses:

"Please sir, may I have your autograph (I almost added:

for my mother but felt this would be a betrayal)." Whoops of laughter went up all around me, and at first, I had no idea they were laughing at me. The waiter approached, telling me quietly I had got the wrong person and led me over to a whippet-faced man with long spiky, white hair and a wide smile. Rod Stewart graciously scrawled his signature and I returned to Grannie and Mum, now both gleeful. After lunch we walked to Harrods and Grannie bought me the Rod Stewart album, 'Do Ya Think I'm Sexy' and I was truly chuffed that I had met the man on the cover, dressed in tight leopard print trousers, in real life.

Needless to say, Grannie no longer lunched at San Lorenzo's or shopped at Harrods or Fortnum and Mason's, another favourite. That she would end up in council housing was clearly beyond her frame of reference, but there was no money left- except for a small but regular pension from the US- and there was no way Mummy was going to allow her to move in with us. She had fallen and broken her wrist and was still in the hospital, yet to take possession of her new council flat that she had no alternative but to move into. By this time her personal belongings consisted of a couple of framed posters- *The Ballerina* and *Les Folies Bergere* by Degas, a wooden Russian Madonna and child icon, a blue and yellow Wedgwood fruit bowl (crudely stuck back together across one side), some paste jewellery, a few oddments of clothing and a Burberry raincoat. My mother had kept her mink coat and various pieces of Cartier jewellery the last time she had recovered them from the pawnbrokers, her plan being to get the best price and hand over the money gradually to her mother, as and when she needed it, rather than when she wanted it.

Mum had arranged for us to stay at a friend's getaway cottage in a village, near Lewes. Maybe because we had stayed there before it helped her, knowing there was a familiar place to return to, after we cleared out and settled Grannie in her new accommodation which, judging by the state the flat was in, would take a few days to make clean and respectable, as well as organising a rental TV, buying supplies and settling Grannie in.

I had not seen Grannie for five years and she was a ghost of herself, frail and quiet, waiting to be picked up outside the hospital entrance. She barely greeted us, barking: "Where's your bloody car? Get me out of this bloody place now!"

She then demanded a trip to her bank. My mother offered to help her in but was told: "I'm not a bloody cripple." We waited and Mummy took on a pained expression. She seemed to take a long time and Mummy told me to run in and check that everything was okay, which I did, only to find that she was not in there.

"What on earth do you mean she's not in there? Of course she is! Where the hell else could she be?" Clearly Mummy is not in the mood for argument.

"I swear she's not- I don't know," I add, perplexed.

We catch sight of Grannie's slight, bedraggled figure at exactly the same time- I hear my mother's quick in-take of breath- emerging from an off-licence about 200 yards down the high street, carrying a jangling plastic bag. Impatiently, she waves us towards her.

"Oh that is just so . . . typical," Mum fumes.

That afternoon we return a couple of hours later to the one-storey row of council flats perched on a yellowed and littered hillside, loaded down with shopping. Mummy had left Grannie with a jaycloth and a bucket of soapy water to clean the dusty windowsills, but there's no evidence of any progress. The bedroom door is shut. Mummy knocks.

"Fuck off you fat fucking ugly cow!" Grannie squawks.

Mum pushes the door open and billows of smoke flood forth like something in a bad pantomime. Grannie is naked, lying on the unmade single bed, fag burning in the ashtray, glugging from an almost empty brandy bottle in her hand. She eyes my mother with what could only be described as pure and utter hatred:

"What? What are you doing here? I never invited you here- what are you doing here in my house. My house! Get out!!"

"Mummy, I'm sorting some food and essentials out for you. Radio Rentals are delivering a TV tomorrow afternoon. That'll be nice won't it?" My mother proffers.

Grannie slugs the remains of the bottle, seemingly oblivious to our presence. Her neck nods limply and she leans back against the white plastic headboard. She mutters names and places that are clearly from her distant past.

"His cock is gorgeous, simply gorgeous you know," Grannie tells an imaginary friend she believes she is having a tete a tete with. At this point, my mother suggests we leave. I put a packet of Rich Tea biscuits on the coffee table in the living room in the hope that Grannie might see them and be tempted, because she is so thin she looks like she could snap into pieces.

I walk into the kitchen where my mother is manically crushing something with a stainless steel spoon, on the tea stained counter top. She is crying.

"What are you doing, Mum?"

"Nothing!" She ignores me and continues her task. I see that her handbag is open and a blister of pills is now empty, next to another bottle of cheap brandy.

"What are you doing with those pills?" I am scared; this all feels somehow wrong and dangerous.

"It's for the best. She'll never know- it'll all be over very quickly."

She grabs a knife and starts to lift the white powder from the small mound, tipping it into the now open Brandy that she has tipped a little out of into a glass. I cannot believe my eyes. I instinctively grab the bottle, and some slops onto the worn linoleum.

"I know you're upset, but this isn't the answer!"

"What is then?" she demands, dark mascara tears running down her cheeks.

"Not this. It's not your right; she's made her choices. We need to go home now. Please just get your things and get in the car. I'll join you in a minute." Even to my own surprise, my voice is stern and complete; I will not take no for an answer and for whatever reason my mother follows my instructions. I wipe up the tiny white particles and flush them down the drain. Whatever is in the bottle will give Grannie a good sleep if she can make it out into the kitchen to get hold of it, but I somehow doubt she will before we come back tomorrow.

My mother and I do not discuss the incident further, but it gives me an insight into how difficult and painful it must have been for my mother growing up on her own, with her alcoholic

115

mother in New York City, with no decent male role model. She had often told me: 'You have no idea how lucky you are' and even though I did not feel particularly lucky, I thought she must be right and I just did not properly appreciate my own circumstances. My sense of guilt exacerbated when she would recount her experience of nights spent in Grand Central Station when there was nowhere else to go when Grannie became out of control. Mummy would lie sleeplessly on a bench in this public thoroughfare and splash her face with water from a fountain, on her way into school. Compared to the security, routine and care provided by Heathfield this was a horrific situation for any teenager to be in. It also made clearer her desire and need to get away from her mother which she did at the age of 20, by marrying my father, 14 years her senior.

I feel seriously let down by my parents and this sense of angry victim starts to pervade my daily thoughts, soon after my rapturous 'pink cloud' period that hits my third week at Promises. Basically I am really pissed off with both of them, but they aren't here to hear my thoughts and defend themselves. I argue to and fro with myself that if I had known more about the addictive cycle- been warned and had the severity of the situation explained to me- I might have seen sense before it was too late and not have ended up in Promises. My complex family matrix has turned me into a victim with no visible or tangible line of defence. My mind floods with memories of when I have behaved in an out-of-control fashion, and neither of my parents batted an eyelid, or did they even notice?

I consider what came first- the depression, or the desire to escape from reality? I have been warned umpteen times that my over-thinking will only land me back in trouble- aka addiction hell- but my brain will not stop. It is rattling away full-throttle. Dr Rubinstein, my psychiatrist and I discuss depression and where it comes from- whether it is genetic, circumstantial, a result of social conditioning, self-expectation and so forth. He draws my attention to my predisposition through genetic links on both sides of the family and the blame starts to spread.

"So it's not my fault I'm the way I am?"

"It's not about finding fault, but looking for the solution- that's why you're here isn't it?"

"No- I just want to be your keenest pill-popping human guinea-pig."

"Do you want to go off your anti-depressants?" he asks.

"No way! I was joking- ha, ha, ha!"

"I know that some people in The Program disapprove of taking any form of medication. I thought someone might have said something to you," he suggests, helpfully.

"Look, I don't sit there in meetings and tell them every detail of my scintillating life- It's none of their goddamned business."

I blush at my angry outburst, adding:

"Better to get it out than keep it in, right?"

"There's hope for you yet," he says.

CHAPTER 13

Digging

We are made wise not by the recollection of
our past, but by the responsibility for our future.
George Bernard Shaw

"I am falling down through the jagged scorched centre of
the earth with electrodes pinned to my eyeballs, slowly sucking
them from their sockets with a cloud of starved locusts
following at my heels, hungry for my flesh, snapping at my
painted toenails and humming for my soul. I'm shitting out my
own brain and watching the sand on the beach envelope it like
a sea of maggots, while my hands evaporate into the salty
night air. I'm locked out, but there is nowhere to be locked out
from because I do not exist- there is no ground to hold me up,
no trees, no wind, no world. Nothing." I describe my first and
last acid trip on Anjuna beach at a full-moon rave party in Goa,
India where I travelled on my gap year.

"Sounds like a terrifying experience." Dr. Rubinstein
remarks.

"Yes. . . my subconscious is not a place I want to re-visit
any time soon!"

I hold back that by the end of my travels through India,
last stop the magical Himalayan outpost Ladakh, I was
continually pinching myself to make sure I was still there- in my
body that is. I began to secrete away my food and drink as a
wolf protects her cubs, terrified that another traveller might try
to spike them with some unknown substance, or worse, the
dreaded LSD. My growing paranoia was consuming and I

backed off from other travellers whom I had before been keen to befriend. I naively hoped these feelings would dissolve once I hit the tarmac at Heathrow. The mind-bending acid trip was to become proof of the start of something that confirmed I was not exactly normal: 99% of the self that I presented to the outside world was a charade and I was a total fraud who'd been messing up my life since I was 17.

Undeniably, LSD had unravelled my senses and transformed my negative feelings into total dread and fear. When the hollow chasm invaded I found the warmth of the sun an irritation, a light breeze an imposition, the excited tones of a friend's voice hateful, food thick and gluey, drink tasteless, my own reflection huge, disgusting and to be avoided. I learned to hermit away during these times- ignore the phone, cancel commitments, lie if I had to- because the idea of covering up was too great a challenge, whereas sharing what I felt was unthinkable. It was unacceptable to those close to me because there was an accepted silent agreement between my parents and me: I was always 'fine', unless I had something physically tangible like a broken, bloody nose, or an arm in a sling. They had their own problems to deal with. How could the problems of a teenager compare with their adult grievances? I accepted the status quo, but as a result felt isolated: an alien who had ended up on the wrong planet.

Alongside the alcoholic gene running through the female line on my mother's side, I also have depression and schizophrenia on my father's side, again through the female line. A relative- actually the mother of my cousin Mia- had recounted with glee a story about my paternal grandmother whom I had never met and is now dead. She was Russian and had met my Grandfather in China where her father was stationed as a Judge. They married and lived in Shanghai and Tientsin where my Grandfather was the last British Commissioner of Customs for the Chinese government. He was a broken man following imprisonment by the Japanese during WW2 and following his death my grandmother, Olga, moved with her Chinese Amah- who had been with the family forever- to Hong Kong, where she rented an apartment on

Kadoorie Avenue and where chickens scurried about in the kitchen.

The story involved my Grandmother in her dotage. At this time in the 1970s various family members of the Vronsky family and cousins were living in Hong Kong. They would be telephoned in the middle of the night with her Amah screeching down the phone in Pidgin English:

"Come now, come now! Missy dying! Come now!"

They would drive over to enter a candlelit drawing room where they were greeted by her purple velvet back, ceremoniously perching at her grand piano, her prized possession. She would turn around to greet them, rows of pearls strategically strung around the rolled, turkey flesh of her neck.

"But we thought you were sick? That you were dying?" Someone would say, indignant to be called from his bed in the middle of the night. To which she would respond:

"Come, come- it's the only way any of you will visit me." She would elegantly smile at her captive audience and commence her recital- Tchaikovsky, Brahms and Schumann- while Amah dispensed cocktails to the guests.

In my youth, my mother would bang on about how 'weird and creepy' the family she married into were, because she had never met her mother-in-law and every year without fail a pair of flat gold and net flip flop sandals would arrive for her at Christmas, with no note, just the shiny plastic shoes. Why my father never took her out to Hong Kong I have no idea. From the age of 7, my father was sent back to England to prep school and parental contact was minimal during and after this due to the war, its aftermath, familial expectations and the state of world travel which was mainly by sea.

My paternal grandmother's sister had married another Russian called Vronsky who my Grandfather had introduced to some American entrepreneurs. Together they formed an insurance company that was to become one of the largest insurance companies in the world. And in turn, it is the Vronsky family who have played a significant role in my life. They were the family I wanted to become part of, and in a sense they had offered me this by bringing me to Brown. The thing is, however much you want to belong you can never really become truly part of another family while you still have your own. The reality is I am not an abandoned orphan, or even unwanted. But why do I feel that way?

According to Panda, abandonment is my 'big issue'. Dr Rubinstein is less keen on these kinds of labels, preferring to unravel various aspects of my life that might be of importance, as an indication of why I feel and behave as I do. To be frank, it all seems like mental masturbation a lot of the time- I mean who really cares? - but apparently that is part of my problem: I do not believe my problems are worth taking the time over because I do not want to cause any more trouble and expense. I hear echoes of my mother's high-pitched rant: "Oh for God's sake, just get on it with it!"- The business of life and living, she means.

I lament that I had never met my paternal grandmother because I am convinced we are very similar: misunderstood artists. The question of mental illness comes primarily through her eldest daughter, my father's sister. She was given a lobotomy in the late 1950's when this was the perceived wisdom and I often thank my lucky stars for the time I was born because I doubt my behaviour is really different to that of a schizophrenic. Dr Rubinstein insists it is and that it is fundamentally connected to my drug intake, whereas schizophrenia results from a chemical imbalance within the brain. But the truth is no one really knows how and why these mental illnesses come about and in a sense this is a terrifying prospect.

I soon realise- what with all these meetings, psychotherapy and psychobabble sessions- that the person I am the angriest and most disappointed with is myself. I am not yet at a place where I am able to accept this. I certainly do not believe Dr Rubinstein when he tells me I have everything I need within myself- the tools and intelligence as well as my survival instincts- to lead a happy, fulfilling life. Friends and acquaintance in The Program tell me that as long as I stay clean everything will fall into place, in time. But it is the slow passage of time that bothers me- waiting for it to all click together like lego. I want quick results.

Part of my problem is I have always wanted everything yesterday. My head is manic- an hour feels like a day, a day feels like a month and I am in a self-perpetuating angst-ridden state of self-pity, repressed anger and bundles of electric energy even on my antidepressant of 225 mg of Effexor (Venlafaxine) a day. I have no interest in TV because I am incapable of sitting still and the best release seems to be driving on the freeway, all the windows rolled down with the stereo on full blast.

The initial experience of Promises offers a pledge- a happier, healthier life based on sobriety, self-love and respect for others. The structure of daily life there, along with a group of us all living and sharing our problems together, boosts my energy and self-motivation. I am part of something that resembles a family, albeit a rather unusual one. But when I leave the structured rigours of Promises I start to flail.

I'd experienced a few counselling sessions at Brown but that is the closest I have ever come to discussing how I feel about anything, in a personal context. And now I am having intense therapy that's opening up a side of my self that I have kept buttoned down for years. When I heard that Ryan had passed away I had been unable to shed a liquid tear, as if to do so would release an unstoppable torrent, but now I am encouraged to 'feel and express these feelings' and the overwhelming sensation of doing so- they are incredibly painful and give a sick feeling in the pit of my stomach- culminates in a form of emotional paralysis where I am numb. It feels like an overload of my senses to go from pushing down my true emotion and turning the other cheek to digging these buried feelings out, processing, accepting them and letting go. I have been dishonest- tricking myself really- for many years now, and to give up this survival technique I have meticulously developed seems like a dangerous concept.

I am seriously depressed and the hole feels larger than before. A consistent low mood is not unusual for me- I have been experiencing this periodically since I was about ten years old- but whereas before I carried it on the inside and covered up on the outside, I now seem unable to play that charade. It's like this whole crystal meth addiction and the on-going repercussions have ripped off my mask and I am very naked and cold. There is a blanket on offer, of sorts, but it is not warming me up enough.

I had never been diagnosed before because it had never crossed my mind to approach a doctor about why I felt the way I did. I could sense that most of my friends did not feel the same as me- they had a lightness of spirit that eluded me- but I could never discuss this heaviness-within with anyone because I had no idea what it was. I suppose I believed there was something inherently wrong with me, but I was too ashamed to name it, because clearly it was 'bad'. In fact the inner work I am doing now is regressive because it revolves around digging up buried memories and recognising patterns of behaviour- most of it self-destructive- and I could not stop myself from thinking: what exactly is the point of all this? Dr Rubinstein assures me it is a necessary step to take but I am not convinced because I end up feeling worse, rather than relieved.

What I had before secretly labelled 'the hole' inside me had come at me from outside myself, as well as eating me from the inside out. I had accepted the existence of 'the hole' within me as part of me I hated, but had to somehow live with; I never spoke about it to anyone because somehow it felt dirty and bad.

I never thought of it as an illness or a problem, but as something only I knew about. It would fluctuate indeterminably and I would have to keep it hidden from everyone and anyone regardless of how diminished I actually felt. And after a while of doing this- always being 'very well thank you'- I did start to negate 'the hole's' existence as if I was slowly filling it in with some glue and then a few feathers and then some spare putty, until it gurgled from time to time, but did not fully express itself like it once had when I had felt the need to first identify and label it thus. That first time was at the crucial moment when a girl supposedly becomes a woman through menstruation. Unprepared- no one had said anything in warning- I had been scared and then duly horrified that this disgusting bodily function would take place every month. A sense of shame and self-disgust was seeded within me and directed at the 'womanly' part of my body. At age six I had questioned my mother about sexual reproduction and she had self-consciously denied it. This brownish-red bleeding added to my confusion.

In sessions with Dr Rubinstein we uncover and process some of these incidents that I had relegated to the dustbin of my past. But all they seem to do is compound and back-up my feelings of failure and self-hatred, as well as obvious stupidity.

It comes as a significant relief when Dr Rubinstein diagnoses my clinical depression. All these years I'd been feeling so terrible and thinking there was something very wrong and weird about me, when it is actually 'depression', a treatable mental illness. As far as I can work out I have been depressed for quite a few years, but how can one really tell when you are a child growing up and going through so many new experiences whether it is part of that process, or actually a state of clinical depression? At a rough guess I recall feeling this familiar void from my second year at prep school. The school had a very cold, inhuman atmosphere with no attempts by the starchy Matron and teaching staff to engender warmth or anything verging on a friendly environment to nurture children. It had a strict regiment that filled out each day in a plodding, dull fashion. Sundays were the worst when we had to walk in a crocodile formation- two by two- to Sunday school at the local church in Gerrards Cross. This was where I would see children going home with their families, whereas we would trundle back to school where we had compulsory letter-writing before lunch. We had to show our letters to the staff member on duty who would check them for errors and complaints against the school. This was forbidden upon the grounds that it would upset our parents and of course we would never want to knowingly do that because God forbid they actually knew the truth. I spent most of my time lost in my imagination where I wished and dreamed that everything was different from how it was for both myself and my mother and father. To me they both seemed unhappy, but in entirely different ways.

My Dad is a good man but he has repressed his feelings for so long I wonder if he knows what they are. He was sent away from China to boarding school in England at the age of seven and he clearly suffered from this disconnection, not in a drastic way but in a total lack of development of warmth and self-expression.

I will never forget the night my mother walked out on him- with me in tow- for the atmosphere was thick with latent sadness and unexpressed longing and misunderstanding. My mother could not meet his lost but vaguely pleading eyes. In that moment on the doorstep my father's world was ripped apart. She never did give him a chance to change or grow, but I know he would have given it his best shot if only he could break down his self-protective shell of arrogance. And I never questioned my mother's wisdom in these matters because she had fire in her eyes and I was scared to cross her. All I wanted was for them to smile and laugh and leave behind the sack of sadness that seemed to follow me, as well as them.

As a child I had to accept the state of affairs as they were presented to me, but when I leave for the US for the first time I am able to get some perspective and clarity about my parents. It is while at Brown I realise I am not a happy and well-adjusted young woman, but there is so much shame and guilt attached to this revelation that there is not a chance in hell I would ever share it with anyone.

Thus far crystal meth has proved the most effective anti-depressant because it totally blanks memory; it's the repercussions that cause so much havoc. I start to ponder if there is a way around this. I suppose this is what is meant by 'controlled use'. Maybe I can succeed as a functional user?

CHAPTER 14

Lone Visitor

What I try to say is that as human beings we
are more alike than we are unalike.
Maya Angelou

I am dreading today because my Uncle Boris is due to
visit me here at Promises and I have not seen him for over a
year. Luckily for me his visit fits in with the set Family Visit
Time: Saturday and/or Sunday from 2-4 pm, otherwise I would
have had to get Panda involved and she had already intimated
that she feels my family somehow set themselves above and
beyond the standard regulations of Promises, although I am
unclear how. They speak in riddles here sometimes and I am
convinced it is to maintain the upper hand.

Uncle Boris will be my only visitor and his secretary had
faxed through his California itinerary to the office a few days
back.

"This arrived last night." Pat thrusts a tube of fax paper
at me while I sit outside on my customary bench after
breakfast, smoking Marlboro Lights. I grapple with the curled
edges, scouring the purplish print in the smoky morning sun.

"It's my Uncle- well he's not my uncle really, he's a
cousin, a second cousin removed, or something like that- but
he's coming to visit me. Shit! - On Saturday."

"Good! It's about time someone in this vast extended
family of yours with all the big bucks made it here to see you."

"Oh come on Pat- that's not fair; they are on the East

127

Coast and my parents are six thousand miles away you know." Pat blows me her air-kiss that I usually find endearing, but right now find superior. Just because I messed up does not mean my family need to get on the next plane over from Heathrow, or Charles de Gaulle in my mother's case, but at least Uncle Boris can make it. The reality, however, fills me with terror- What is he going to say to me? I must be the only person to ever have been arrested in our family in the whole of its known history, except in times of war and that hardly counts.

Uncle Boris is here in LA for a couple of days on business. That he had squeezed me into his hectic schedule somewhat alarms me, while it also pleases me. Contradictory, but true.

And on a more basic level he's the one footing the bill for me to be here so he probably wants to check out what exactly his thousands of dollars are bankrolling- not a room of one's own, that's for sure. The first time we met was outside the Ritz Hotel in London, where the Vronskys always stayed when they are in London.

"Why don't they stay at your house?" I had asked my father.

"Well- I don't know really," he had quietly replied; years later when I paid a visit to them on ritzy Park Avenue in New York I found out.

Dad had come to pick me up for a day out from my prep school. They always made us wear our Sunday uniform on rare days out- purple acrylic A-line smock over a white polyester turtleneck- and today was no exception except that I was bursting with so much excitement I managed to forget how much it itched me, especially under the arms.

I chattered non-stop on the drive into London; I even forgot to put on my Abba cassettes that I always brought to play in the car. We pulled up in a side street near Green Park tube station; I avidly scoured the area between the row of columns in front of the elegant Ritz. The only person there was a stout, big-bellied man with a kindly rounded face looking out expectantly.

"Hello Boris."

"Bill!" The stout man turned about and then suddenly

leaned over to kiss my father's ruddy cheeks. To my amazement he did this three times. I had never seen a man kiss another man before, let alone three times.

"Are you really a Prince?" I blurt out. Silence. Both Dad and Boris catch each other's eye and chuckle together like they share some secret.

"Well let's see now- I guess I am. . .Yeah, I am."

That evening back at school I could not wait to tell my friends how I had met a real Prince- a real live Russian Prince who was related to me. I'll never forget that day.

Here at Promises, Uncle Boris arrives in a yellow cab. He looks surprised that Promises is a regular suburban kind of house, not a tucked away hospital with a gated entrance and security guards.

He double takes as I emerge from the front portico. I forget how thin I have become, although I am quite 'healthy' again compared to what I was when I arrived here, but then he knew me at Brown when I was forty pounds heavier. He kisses me three times the Russian way and gives me a big hug. I can see how hard it is for him to be here and I decide the most important thing is to put his mind at rest.

I bring him a cup of tea and we sit at the picnic table; I light up a cigarette. He is clearly at a loss for words beyond the polite observations of what a pleasant sort of place it seems, and such like.

"Uncle Boris, I'm really sorry. I don't really understand how this all happened but I guess that's why I'm here."

"I never imagined that something this terrible could happen to someone like you. I mean I really just don't understand it. You had so much going for you-"

"It can happen to anybody- addiction's a disease, almost like any other illness- that's what they teach you anyway."

"What about this psychiatrist? Is he any good? Is he helping you?"

"He's really good- my depression is improving and we're working through things." I do not mention that one of my most problematic relationships is the one with him and his family and my feelings of indebtedness, mixed in with an angry ingratitude.

"Good. That's really great." He smiles wanly and gives

my knee a pat.

"I'm sorry Dr Rubinstein is so expensive- I feel really bad about that. Maybe we can arrange some sort of payment plan for when I'm back at work and-"

"Please," his round, plump face harbours a pained expression, "the most important thing is that you get better Clea . . . You're such a pretty girl and it's all such a waste."

His reference to my prettiness knocks me off balance and I have to resist shouting back at him: 'What the hell does that have to do with anything?'

In essence his overall sentiment is kind, if somewhat clueless, but then he surprises me.

"Actually, I was thinking back to around the time when you first visited us in New York and it was Sonia's wedding. You were so excited and you'd come all that way and you looked so pretty in that bridesmaid's cream silk dress." Again the pained expression as he continues in almost a whisper:

"But then I remember seeing you later at the reception at The Metropolitan Club- that glorious setting with that huge Christmas tree in the hallway with the curved staircase- and I looked up and saw you clambering down those stairs- you had clearly been drinking and you were tripping and falling down the steps into the throng of guests milling about and they were moving out of your way and you'd dropped something down the front of your dress and my cousin Lola from Hong Kong was looking very concerned and came to find me to suggest someone call you a cab. Do you remember that happening at Sonia's wedding?"

"Yes- of course I do- well vaguely. I also remember you talking to me about it afterwards- I was surprised because no one ever had ever brought up my drunken behaviour before- so I was surprised and touched I think. You mentioned my Grannie and her alcoholism and that I should think about that quite seriously, that it was a grave matter. When I got home I told my mother and I remember how indignant she was about the whole thing. You bringing up her mother to me and everything."

He shifts his position like he has cramp and reaches for a Kent. I light it for him.

"I spoke to your mother; she's very worried about you."

"Sure, I know. But at least here I'm getting a grip on this whole alcoholism and addiction problem. We never talked about it at home- it was there, but never talked about. Actually we never talked about anything much; the most important thing was to keep the peace."

"That's what you have to do in a family sometimes- learn to keep the peace and tow the line."

"I'm sorry Uncle Boris but I need to go to my meeting now and I guess you need to get back to the Beverly Wilshire- I'll call you a cab."

I know he means well but I do not think he will ever understand my position and vice versa. I will feel eternally indebted to him for funding my time at Brown and now again here at Promises- what extremes I have travelled from Ivy League college to drug rehab- but at this juncture in our conversation I feel even more dislocated and alienated from my family than I ever believed possible. I have become the identified patient, the one with problems, and I can see my uncle's wife nodding her head, telling him: 'I told you so, I knew she was a bad bet'. The last thing I want is his mute form of pity, not exactly sympathy but a kind of resigned 'I guess it's in the genes' mentality. The thing is he is probably right- it is in the goddamned genes, and for that reason alone he has sympathy.

That is, however, never what I intended. Or is it?

CHAPTER 15

Crystal, Crystal, Wherefore Art Thou. . .

Don't mind if I do
It's Hollywood
Hot damn- hands in a jam
Never say can't
'cause you know you can
in Hollywood.
Hollywood Steve Tyler

While packing my things after a three month stay at a Sober-Living Accommodation located near Promises, I find Henry's pager number on the back of an old brown envelope stuffed inside my filofax. I'd scrawled Henry, (Elsie's bud) and the fives look like eights, or the other way round.

Before entering Promises I ripped numbers up, ritualistically crumpling and throwing them all away. It was par for the course that you changed all your beeper, cell and telephone numbers and throw out any telephonic links to your druggy past. While in Promises no one is allowed a cell phone for this very reason. Somehow I had overlooked this singular set of digits. Before I even think or calculate any possible consequences, I call the variations of numbers and punch in my new cell phone number. I kid myself that I want to check if my new cell phone works properly.

Within five minutes the phone rings. Stunned, adrenaline flows while I watch it vibrate on top of the communal chest of drawers in the cramped bedroom that three of us have been sharing. I attempt to busy myself with household chores- all of us in Sober Living have a list of them

to complete every day which are rotated on a weekly basis-
but a force seemingly greater than my self leads me back to
the cell phone. Whoever I paged has not left a message. In a
rush of excitement and subterfuge, I punch in the numbers
again and run outside with my phone so as not to be heard.
The cell rings immediately.

"Who's this? I just called and no one picked up- Who the
hell is this? Do I know ya?"

Gruff tones bark at me and I know it is Henry, a
Hispanic friend of Elsie's that I had met at her house. I place
an order for a gram of crystal meth; automatically the words
tumble out of my mouth, just like I had done it yesterday. I
arrange to meet him in the car park outside Ralph's at Santa
Monica and Fairfax.

Why am I about to throw away the progress I have
made, on what feels like a whim?- Quite simply because I
crave that unique high that only crystal meth gives me. I
obsess about the soon-to-be-realised burn in my nostril and
the familiar surge of euphoria. For the first time in months I feel
some sense of purpose- severely misplaced but purpose
nonetheless- and I am beyond caring because the obsession
has won over my newer desire to be the better and improved
version of myself. Confronting my past has unleashed palpable
demons and in this moment I choose the devil I know.

Henry is late and I contemplate saving myself, from
myself, one last time, but now I am literally salivating and
desperate for the crystal to be back in my blood stream. If I had
control over my desires and emotions I would head to a
meeting, or call my Sponsor, but instead I am going to risk
everything. I want to be high and it is as simple as that. I crave
release and soon it shall be mine. I know how sweet and
charmed it will surely be, because now with no tolerance I will
be riding a rocket through the stars.

Henry arrives in a beat-up two door black BMW with a
pretty Pamela Anderson look-alike sitting shot gun; she stares
vacantly straight ahead, raising a limp wrist in sulky
acknowledgement. I recognise Lissa from Elsie's, where she
had struck me as the definition of slutty. Henry is wiry, short
and muscular with a long, curly dark mane. His fine features
remind me of Jesus in a Ghirlandaio painting- he is almost

feminine looking, as well as very sexy, if you overlook his height. Right now to me he is as good as Jesus.

I slip the $50 into his manicured hand and revel in the feel of the plastic baggy full of potential, in my fist. We shoot the breeze and part as new best friends. Why are drug dealers so goddamned charismatic?

That first gram from Henry sets it all off again. I had been forewarned of this numerous times in Promises and at meetings. On average I place an order for a gram every 3-4 days and so far I am managing to control it. In fact I have arranged three interviews with modelling agencies, joined a gym and contacted a couple of acquaintances to meet up for dinner. Why didn't I try this before, I ponder? This way I have the best of both worlds- new friendships and support in The Program with the added bonus of an occasional buzz. It means I need to organise my tweak sessions to fit in with my new schedule which isn't hard because it is fairly flexible. I am ostensibly 'getting my life back,' so I have ample excuses: finding an apartment, looking for a job, attending interviews and taking acting classes (improvisation, sensory and scene classes three times a week) as well as NA meetings and weekly sessions with Promises aftercare and Dr Rubinstein. Do I feel guilty about betraying the trust of those who have helped and supported me in my drug rehabilitation efforts?- Yes, of course I do, but not enough to stop me from using and using gets rid of those uncomfortable feelings.

Will a fool never learn through her folly?

Dee is my new best-friend whom I'd met at Promises. She's a divorced Jewish mother with two sons from Beverly Hills who has impeccable family connections; she has a rather glamorous past life having worked with Michael Jackson and Motley Crue. Her family tree reads like a Who's Who of Hollywood Royalty- both her maternal and paternal grandfathers ran movie studios- and her father is talent agent to heavyweight actors and actresses. Like me, Dee has a 'challenging' relationship with her mother- hers exacerbated by her mother's published memoirs in which she recounts her involvement with one of the most famous unions of this century in which she was a bridesmaid. She also describes Dee's addiction to Queludes (Mandrax- a heavy duty tranquiliser) and cocaine in detail without ever having asked her daughter's permission to reveal her private life to the reading public.

With Dee you get what you see. I adore her dry sense of humour. She is on the level- unlike some others in Promises- and I suspect her relapse after seven years sobriety is due to the horrific way her ex-fiancé has treated her. Dee is the only person who knows first hand that I am using again. And that is because she reads me like an open book. Most of the addicts I have ever encountered have built-in radar as to who is or isn't 'using' because they recognise the subtle nuances of changes in behaviour. Dee drinks a little- the occasional Vodka mixer you can buy ready-mixed in a can- and the only reason I know this is because she hides the empties in her closet and I had found them when I was raiding her wardrobe. I now sneak them out of her house for her to throw away because her controlling freak of a mother has paid her maid Maria to spy and report back anything suspicious found in Dee's trash.

On my way out of her place, with a bottle run stuffed into my hold all, she suddenly reappears out of her bedroom and bounds down the stairs two at a time. I assume she has forgotten some bottles and is taking advantage of the fact that Maria and the boys are out for the next hour or so when she whispers: 'Can I try some crystal?' Her request catches me off-guard.

Amidst my self-proclaimed horror, guilt and my 'No way! Are you mad?' exclamations at the idea of being the friend 'to take her out' (another NA-ism) she reminds me that she is already 'out', indicating the small batch of clanking bottles in the garbage bag. I really do not want to give her any because I know first hand how lethally addictive it is. But like me she can be mighty persuasive when she sets her sights on something she wants.

"Owww-owwwww-owww- shit this stuff really burns!!" her hushed yelps punctuate the sacred silence created by our drug-taking bonding ritual. We addicts adore our rituals. I feel uneasy while I chop crystal up, locked in her en-suite bathroom on top of the rectangular glass of a framed photograph of her son Tim, grinning as a toddler. I suggest using some other surface but she is unsentimental, telling me to stop stressing and get on with it. I give her a tiny line because she has not snorted powder for years – and back then it was coke- and I do not want her having an adverse reaction. On the plus side at least I know this gear is relatively clean and not cut with Drano. On the other hand I am quite pleased- in a sick kind of way- that she is now part of my secret tweaking double life because she is my (new) best friend and sharing drugs dries the cement between friendships, especially if you are both addicts who have spent months in Group Therapy together.

Moving onto her King size bed, Nathalie Merchant on the stereo, we talk and share, revealing confessional things about ourselves that would make my mother blush. I believe our alliance is strong and am happy that now we will be even better friends.

She is the big sister I have always wanted. I know that we will stand by each other, whatever happens.

"Wow! What's this? It's amazing." I inspect a gold antique ring that has a circular glass pendant with what looks like a ring of auburn hair inside. I have never seen anything like it before and it is truly beautiful. It exudes the weight of history that only a family heirloom seems to hold.

"Isn't it? I love that. It's a Victorian hair ring. It belonged to my great, great grandmother. It's the only thing I care about that my mother has given me. Back then when your loved one died they took a lock of hair to keep because it symbolises their continuing life force and strength. I guess it's a symbol of the eternity of life and a way of being loyal to their memory. The eldest child would take it and pass it on to theirs and so on-"

"But you're not the eldest are you?"

"No but we're not the most sentimental of people and my eldest sister thought it was spooky. She's the spooky one. It's probably my favourite piece."

"I can see why."

Dee and I sit on her bedroom floor where we rummage

137

through her collection of jewellery that she keeps stored away in the attic. She had called me up at my new apartment and invited me over, telling me she was having a big clear out and she thought I might like to have some of her things. I have a garbage bag full of some great clothes and chotskes. Now I am amassing some cool junk jewellery. Only a couple of days ago I had come over and Chris, a junkie surfer-boy from Promises, was showing off a gold ring that spelled 'FUCK' which Dee had given him. I was jealous on two counts: Firstly that Dee had given Chris a solid gold ring and secondly that it served to seal their developing friendship. I think of Dee as my best friend and I do not want him usurping my position. I carefully put the hair ring back in the sky blue velvet box with a couple of other modern rings and gold chains.

"I'm not giving that one away." Dee states.

"It was rather nice of you to give Chris that gold ring," I comment.

"Yeah well, like a mother of two, just out of rehab is gonna walk around with FUCK in chunky, gold letters emblazoned across her knuckles. Great impression huh? In case you hadn't noticed I'm trying to clean up my act not increase the case against me darlin', as well as not alienate the neighbourhood! Anyway I've had it forever- some rocker guy gave it to me years ago. I know Chris'll probably sell it but otherwise it's just sitting in the attic gathering dust."

She gets up and stretches, heading into her en-suite bathroom. When she comes out she looks at her watch and whispers:

"Okay, listen up sister- one more line before I hit the hay. I've got a PTA meeting tomorrow afternoon and I don't wanna look like I've been up half the night doing drugs."

"Yeah sure- I'll cut it out in the bathroom."

"No shit Shylock?! I can just see Tim or Joey having a bad dream and bursting in: 'Oh hi Mom- happy to see rehab was such a success; hey Mom as I'm up can I have a line too. Or even better can I take some into school tomorrow, then I'd be the coolest kid in the class-"

"And the thinnest." Both her kids are overweight.

"Well they get that from their paunchy Italian Dad." Not from her that's for sure because Dee epitomises gamine and is petite and slim in all the right places, except her boobs- a 32D- which her ex-fiancé paid for. They look fantastic and sexy on her petite, slight but muscular frame. She gets a kick out of showing friends how lopsided they are- telling them as soon as her relationship started to crash her boobs followed suit- because the saline sack on her right side had slid under her armpit.

"I'm gonna go downstairs and get some tea- d'ya want one?"

"Ok yes please- I'll have a green tea, Mummy dearest."

I go into the bathroom and cut out the lines from her gram, leaving the compact mirror on top of the loo seat; I come back out and start putting my little bits and pieces together into a plastic bag when I take another quick look at the hair ring inside the velvet box which is now placed on top of a pile of assorted cases and boxes waiting to go back in a cardboard box headed for the attic. I grab the ring; I quickly slip it into my jeans pocket. I know she will not miss it because, as she herself said, it will only be gathering dust up there.

CHAPTER 16

Ajax

Well, there's a wide world of noble causes
And lovely landscapes to discover
But all I really want to do right now
Is find another lover!
Joni Mitchell

The man's happiness: I will.
The woman's happiness: he will.
Nietzsche

Right at the start of Promises I was warned of the insidious 13 steppers, constantly on the make with us newcomers in meetings. You can smell their unsubtle sexual desperation a mile off, like potent incense in a Hindu Temple. They cluster like starved piranhas at the close of a meeting. Following the obligatory Serenity Prayer, they stalk over with extended hand to mix with their prey: 'Welcome to Recovery-well done!' They solicit ever-so-understanding, sympathetic enquiries rounded off by the ubiquitous: 'Let's go get a coffee.'

But Ajax was different. I never heard him share at a meeting and his face was immobile, except for the third time I saw him and he waited outside for me.

"Come here often?" I ask.

"Not any more!" A grin spreads from ear to ear, creasing up his strong features. He is seriously handsome in a rough Mafiosi way. One look and you know he's bad. He waves a folded piece of paper:

"I got what I needed."

"And what exactly is that?" He opens out the crumpled

sheet: it is an attendance record of NA meetings, with various signatures scrawled down the page.

"My stay-out-of-jail-pass. . .

"Well congratulations are in order. . . I guess-"

"Hey you wanna take a walk on the beach with me and my dog?"

Ajax's dog is a gorgeous pit bull called Spanky. By some strange coincidence he'd got him as a puppy from Elsie's pit bull, Mumba - small tweaker world that it is.

On Venice beach Spanky frolics in the sea while we sit and watch; we are on the spot that I'd used numerous times when I'd visited alone to ponder the sea when I'd been blue, before I'd embraced toxic alternatives.

"By the way I know you're tweaking-"

"Huh? . . . what? Why'd you think that?"

"Oh sweet little English gal- so naïve and charming- like butter wouldn't melt in your cute, little mouth."

An embarrassed cough takes me over and I light a cigarette, inhaling dramatically.

"This your first date then?" He teases.

"Why do you think I'm tweaking?"

"I know you are."

"Actually, I'm really sorting my life out-"

"Did I say otherwise?"

"No. Sorry, I'm a bit touchy."

"Babe, I'm a tweaker. Takes one to know one and you're good. I'd say you had that crew at the meeting damn well fooled, but then most of them have fried half their brains anyway. . ."

He leans into me, planting a solid kiss on my lips.

"Do you want some then?" I whisper.

"I've got my own, babe."

Ajax and I spend the next ten days together at the house of a friend of his in Venice who's away. We talk and share like long-lost soul-mates only can and although we are both high I truly believe he is 'the one' I have been waiting for.

We connect on every level- sexually, emotionally, spiritually, intellectually and obviously drugs-wise. I am so desperate for the perceived intimacy of a romantic relationship I am capable of making myself believe anything and Ajax is undoubtedly an extremely handsome and sensual man.

We laugh together- a distinct novelty- and I think Ajax finds my youthful playfulness refreshing- different to the jaded women he is used to dating. It is another positive effect of crystal meth that any adult inhibitions are forgotten and fun is contagious from moment to moment: at the Bar owned by his friend I go round from person to person with my Polaroid camera, posing and snapping people- 'supplying their 5 seconds of fame'- and charging $10 per shot. The idea had occurred to me while I was chatting with someone and then my enthusiasm carried me off on this mini-adventure and because it was honest- not tricksy or trying to be clever- everyone warmed to me as this quirky, artistic English gal.

We talk a fair amount and there is no doubt that we connect on a deep level, but our time together is focused more on 'doing' than on intense self-revelation. And what a relief that is.

A major drawback, though, is Ajax's musings upon a number of crazy scams. He has not communicated with his parents for 'a while'. His father is Sicilian but he has not seen him for years and has no idea where he is. He hates his stepfather. They are wealthy and live in San Pedro- an affluent suburb of LA- and his mother has her own business. He has a brother who lives in Beverly Hills. He spent three years in juvenile jail for aggravated manslaughter, at age 17, when he stabbed to death an intruder who broke into his family's home. He mentions something about it being his fault because he knew the intruders. On top of this, his other brother was shot down outside a nightclub in Hollywood, and this is also something to do with Ajax, but he will not expand on it.

What I know of Ajax's life story so far- and this is only a relatively small part- would make most women run a mile, but not me. The anti-hero is my hero. I am convinced we are soul-mate, that have finally come together, and part of me hopes that we can kick drugs together and stay together forever. But in the meantime we'll enjoy staying high.

"I hope you used a condom?" Elsie says all matter-of-fact; she sees my face fall. Catastrophe.

"Are you insane? Do you want fucking AIDS? I mean what is your problem?" I stall for time, at a loss for words; I had stopped by to see Elsie to find out more about Ajax and this was certainly not the girly chat I was hoping for. I had mentioned condoms to Ajax but neither he nor I had any and our passion overtook a quick trip out to 7-11. HIV, pregnancy and venereal disease did not enter my tweaked mind.

"What the hell are you saying?! That Ajax has AIDS?"

"Yeah- probably."

"Probably??! Either he does, or he doesn't."

"He's the type of person to have AIDS. I can't believe you didn't use a condom. That guy's seriously bad news."

"In what way- why? What do you know about him?"

"He's a liar, a thief and into things ya better off not knowing-"

"Like what?"

Elsie polishes a turquoise stone with gusto, continuing her handiwork and ignoring me.

"Okay. . . How do you know him?"

"He worked for Gabe and he lived here for a while, but I had to kick him out. He had loser friends who kept coming over and he was holed up in that bedroom doing fuck knows what. I was pretty sure he was mainlining."

"I never saw him do anything like that-"

"Like you'd know with all those tattoos. Who's he leeching off now?"

"He's not. He's at this guy Tony's house in Venice. Ajax can stay there for a few weeks until the lease is up. I left a few things there that I got out of storage- my super cool 50s bar stools, my drafting desk, my computer-"

"You're not serious?!" Her tone is so patronizing I have to stop myself from smacking the cow.

"Yeah I am."

"They'll all be gone by now, duhhhhhh!"

"What d'you mean?"

"He'll have sold it all- the whole lot. I'm serious- he's a

total asshole. Mark my words!"

What with Elsie's tone and the thought of my computer being sold I blast round there, almost smash the front door down and demand my things back.

"What the hell is going on? What are you so fucking hysterical about?"

"I was round at Elsie's and she told me you used to live there and that I was mad to number 1) have had sex with you without a condom, and 2) that you will have nicked all my stuff by now and sold it."

Looking around I see that everything is as I had left it- almost: the bar stools are missing.

"Where are my bar stools- the 50s ones that needed re-covering?" I query, attempting to remain calm.

"I sold them-"

"What??!"

"Look Clea, you said I could- here." He pulls out a $20 from his back jeans pocket. He has to be kidding.

"Do you have any idea how much I paid for those?" I demand.

"Knowing you too much-"

"$180; not to mention the fact that I fucking loved them and I never said anything about selling them!" I whine.

"You were totally ripped off- I got $40 and I gave you $20 so what's the problem?"

"The fucking problem is that I never gave you permission to sell my goddamned property. So what's next- my computer?!" I am yelling now. He storms over and puts his hand over my mouth; I edge away, indignant and furious now.

"Look I'd never sell your computer."

"And why is that?"

"Coz I know how important it is to you and it has all your work on it."

"Aren't we a saint in fucking disguise?!"

"Babe you have serious memory loss when you tweak coz you totally said I could sell them."

Is he telling the truth? I have no idea; I am pretty sure I never suffered from memory loss before, but I suppose it is

145

possible.

I notice Spanky cowering under the kitchen table. I walk through and he whimpers when I crouch down, extending my hand to stroke him. Ajax comes up behind me.

"He hates women- even beautiful English ones- who shout and yell for no good reason."

"Yeah well- I was upset."

"Babe, I let you stay here for almost two weeks so I think it's fair I keep half the cash for the bar stools. They were fucking ugly anyway. You're better off without them."

"I liked them!" I manage a smile.

"No accounting for taste then."

I look at him long and hard; he looks away and goes into the bathroom, locking the door behind him. I gather up the remains of my stuff and load it into my car. I still can't shake the intensity of Elsie's proclamations; she had really scared me and I desperately want reassurance from Ajax but he locks himself away in the bathroom, refusing to come out when I knock gently and ask him to.

"Take your shit and get out." He yells through the bathroom door.

What with modelling shots, acting classes and wanting Ajax, I have painted myself into a box where appearance is paramount. The avenues I choose to go down are the ones where taking crystal meth can only help my cause, or at least I can justify it that way because it clears up my skin and keeps me skinny. Whereas before, I had many hang ups about my appearance, I generally accepted it. But now I am obsessed with it and unlike some addicts who let their selves go, I spend hours in face masks and creams, trying on clothes and mixing outfits, teasing my hair. It is almost like I am telling myself: Hey girl, let's forget about what's going on inside and entirely focus on the outside, because that is totally fixable.

And if I look fantastic Ajax can only like me more- fall head over heels in love- surely?

The problem with Ajax is that I have no idea where I stand. All I know is that the longer I am not with him, my whole body seems to ache with emotional need and physical desire.

146

In the past, when I was high I experienced some vague feelings of attraction for guys, but nothing close to this. It worries me because when I am high I usually have total control over my sexuality; I love to flaunt myself- in my walk, in the rhythm of my dancing, meaningful looks with suggestive eye contact while exuding real interest in whoever I'm talking to- but it is all part of my pathetic little game of self-esteem. I get to feel powerful without giving it away which is the total turnaround on what was happening before I discovered meth. I had been sleeping with guys I had not even particularly liked because I was desperate for love, but all I ended up with was serial rejection. That was one of my major motivations to take crystal- it bestowed upon me an untouchable, superior sexual self.

Because of the ferocity of my unexpected feelings for Ajax things have tipped and become topsy-turvy. I fear I am becoming obsessive over him but I cannot budge him from the forefront of my thoughts. In my mind's eye he is very determined to take centre stage. From what I have gleaned Ajax is a long-term drugs user and I'd noticed he had a habit of foraging under his skin, mainly on his scabby arms looking for bugs he believes are living inside him.

Over one of our lengthy interludes, I had told him about working at Propaganda and the screenplay for which I had had such high hopes. He had looked at me hard:

"Maybe you really don't wanna leave all that behind."

I knew what he meant: I can still turn back before it is too late, because crystal meth is not worth giving up my life for. But I convince myself I can have both- my life and my meth- although after three weeks of use I start missing my acting classes because I am tweaked. Waylaid by the familiar alleys, I had pulled over and dumpster dived instead. And where would Ajax fit in?

We all know old habits die hard. Maybe Marnie was on the money when she suggested setting up a Dumpster Divers Anonymous. The truth is I want Ajax, meth and a career. But you don't always get what you want, you get what you need.

The living room in the front is dark but I can see a light

147

on in the kitchen. I knock gently. Nothing. I wait and then knock again. No response. Where is Ajax? I bang. The door bounces open:

"What 'dya want- you're waking up the fuckin' neighbours and I've already told you about that how-many-times-shit!"

I smile winningly; his eyes zip up and down me appreciatively- tight faux-oriental sheath dress and heels- but he shuffles back slightly like he is going to close the door on me.

"Hey I'm really sorry. How are you?" I ask gently, opening my eyes wide for full effect.

"Fine- where've ya been? You told me you'd be back and then you disappear for days on friggin' end."

I rewind; I am fairly sure- as sure as one can be when tweaking- that I'd said I was going to see Dee to pick up some of my things.

A female voice from inside calls:

'Who is it?' I look at him while I feel my jaw drop. My heart crumples like a burned up ball of paper, dispersing in a draft. I am silent.

"I didn't know where you'd gone. I called my friend Tammy." He shrugs.

"Can I come in?" I venture unsteadily.

"I don't think that's a good idea." We look at each other for a long beat and then he backs up and closes the door gently. I have no idea how long I stand there. I am numb, paralysed. I notice tiny indents on the beige painted door that I am unable to tear my eyes away from. I will it to melt away and reveal Ajax on the other side with outstretched arms. When this does not happen I contemplate knocking and getting him here in front of me again, but I do not want to cause a scene, or freak out the neighbours that I know Ajax is already paranoid about.

I reason with myself: 'Okay so he was lonely and he needed someone with a car so he called up this kid Tammy' (I know instinctively that this girl- the girl behind the door where I should have been- is young, below-the-age-of-consent young). We all have our various means of survival. It dawns on me that he is in a vulnerable position and I am actually in a much better

148

one. After all, I'm about to rent my own one-bedroom apartment, I have a car and my family are still speaking to me, just. Ajax was in a bad position and he made that perfectly clear to me. All I can assume is that Ajax feels betrayed by me.

Floored by the scene that has unravelled not exactly before my eyes, but within my ears, and certainly within the realms of all my heightened and heady senses, I contemplate the unthinkable- have I been given the push? Self-talk, my old favourite, takes over: this is a minor blip and I shall find a way to distract myself and come back later. I disappear for a few days without word (I had crashed out at Dee's) and Ajax has to consider his own survival. Tammy is useful, that is all she is and useful people, well . . . have their uses. I congratulate myself on my powers of insight and rationality. Maybe I did learn something in rehab, or maybe it's the supersonic speed at which my brain is racing.

An angry car horn shatters my mercurial meditations and I slip lizard-like back into my car and purr away, desperate to draw no more attention to myself.

I am at a loose end and on my own, tweaked to hell. The CD in the car is set to *Let's Get it On* by Marvin Gaye which is due to wear out from my constant playing. The LA tarmac grinds beneath my thick tyres. If nothing else my raring '68 Chevy Malibu (half paid for by my mother and the rest due in monthly payments) makes me feel invincible and mission-bound.

At times nothing can make me happier than driving the endless streets of Los Angeles, but tonight I have ants in my veins. The only place I really want to be is off-limits, so I need a destination.

CHAPTER 17

Henry and Lissa

So this is hell. I'd never have believed it. . .
There's no need for red-hot pokers. Hell is. . .
other people!

Huis Clos Jean-Paul Sartre

I visit Henry, my new dealer, at his girl-fiend Lissa's house. All long limbs and peroxide hair, Lissa is the cheerleader type who has become a stripper. It's hard to know when she's serious and I suspect she is smarter than she looks. She looks ten years older than she is and she loves to tell you with pride and no trace of irony:

"Did ya know I'm an interpretive dancer-"

"Oh really! Where do you perform?" I ask.

"Jumbo's Clown Room. Have you been there?" Then she says with a beaming smile:

"You must come; it's totally awesome!"

Because I am now in Lissa's house I have to be polite and friendly and leave my Ivy League prejudices at the door. Henry and her use the same supplier so it is in my direct interest to befriend her. On top of that Henry drops in that she is friends with Ajax- 'they go way back'. Yes! God is on my side; I sit down with her on the hideous boat-sized cream leather sofa.

She asks me when my birthday is and when I tell her she looks excited and starts nodding her head up and down slowly, the way people do when finally the penny has dropped about something important to them. Her stare unnerves me, and her eyes are welling up:

"Why are you looking at me like that?"

"Coz you're born the same day and year as Ricky- it's like totally crazy! Brigitte promised me Ricky would send a messenger! It's you! It's you!!" She grabs my hand and starts dropping little kisses on it like I am St. Teresa of Avila. I am more and more spooked as each second passes- Lissa has gone from cheerleader to stripper to 'devotee at the feet of Clea' and I have only been on her sofa five minutes. Did someone say tweakers were weird? Attempting to cover up my discomfort I push out a laugh that even to my ears sounds fake:

"Who's Ricky and who the hell is Brigitte?" I ask.

"Shhhhhh! Keep it down- Henry'll flip."

"What? Why?"

She comes up close to my left ear and whispers:

"Brigitte's psychic. She was a starlet and then she married the son of a very famous crooner- they're divorced now. Ricky was my soul-mate and Henry hates- totally hates- me talking about him."

She then takes my hand and leads me through the house, out the back door and into the double garage that has been converted in a cute kind of tweaker way- with a miscellaneous set-up of junked furniture- into a den. Boxes on shelves line the room and streams of gauzy fabric staple-gunned to the rafters on the ceiling attempt a Moroccan harem theme. She tips out some crystal from a little baggy tucked into her bra onto a small picture of a fairy with a wand standing on an oversized green leaf. She picks up a clear Perspex tube broken off from a Bic biro and inspects it.

"Don't want someone else's bogeys going up my nose!" Lissa giggles. As if bogies are more dangerous than the supercharged manmade chemical concoction we are about to snort. She hands the tube to me and I insert it up my right nostril (I try to alternate between the two but for no clear reason I prefer the right one).

"Oh my God that is strong shit!" My nose membrane is on fire. I would not be surprised if bits of skin and cartilage start to disintegrate and fall into my lap.

"You bet girlfriend- it's the best. I just love that pain. That way you know it's really good stuff."

"Yeah, I know." The funny thing is that this is actually

true for me; the more it burns my nose the better high I believe I'm going to get. Lissa gets up to secure the garage door with a short plank of wood that she wedges between the metal inner handle and hoist. She looks triumphant.

"There we go! Now we can talk."

"Great- so tell me about Ricky"

Lissa hugs her knees to her chest and has the look of transient joy that only a major lottery win could produce.

"Okay! Well I met him in Sacramento- that's where I'm from. He stopped by my school and they hired him to mow the lawn. He was kind of bad coz he sold the mower- ya know those sit on ones- they're worth like over a thousand dollars and he took me with him to LA."

"What about your parents?" Now I think she is a lot younger than she looks.

"Oh they were really pissed but I called them a few times and they knew that Ricky was looking after me- He told them so, on the phone ya know and that shut them up. They got their own problems anyway so I think it was kinda a blessing in disguise for them if ya know what I mean?"

I nod in agreement. This girl needs to talk badly and talk she does. But it is a good enough story and I pick up a lampshade that suggests beading to me and I tweak up a new design. Lissa stops mid flow:

"Hey man, that's cool. Real psychedelic."

She continues to tell how Ricky came here to LA with really good intentions. His dream was to work at NASA, but he hadn't been to college so he was at a distinct disadvantage. He was willing to try to attend one here- at the very least a community college- but they could not save enough money for his education. All he dreamed of doing was getting an apprenticeship and designing rockets. She assured me that even though he had not graduated high school he was super, super smart; he studied molecular physics and electrical engineering in his spare time, buying second-hand text books from bookstores around UCLA and USC.

Lissa wanted to be an actress and she had some photos taken and got some representation by a seedy man who only put her forward for nude modelling. She got a job in a shoe store on Melrose. Ricky kept getting fired or quitting

153

from a string of jobs and then he met Gabe Doverman, the man I'd met last xmas at Elsie's house.

Ricky starts to work for Gabe. I can see Lissa's almond eyes well up again. She takes a deep breath and I can sense an ugly climax approaching; I am all ears:

Gabe really helped them out. He gave them a free place to live in one of his buildings off Sunset in West Hollywood. It was a bit of a slum but they did it up; it has since been pulled down because unbeknownst to them it had been condemned for years. So now they had an apartment that Lissa did her best to make as homey as possible, while Ricky did odd jobs for Gabe.

To start with these were above-board errands and handyman sort of things. After a few months the nature of the jobs started to change because Gabe began to trust Ricky. It started off with bully-boy jobs like strong-arming difficult tenants when they would not vacate their apartment or pay the rent in one of the many buildings Gabe owned and let out all over West Hollywood and Hollywood. Gabe drummed to the beat of his own drum and would burn up rental agreements in front of his tenants to make a point that his word was final. Ricky started to courier drugs around the US for Gabe, taking about four planes a week. The pay was good and the bonus of as much gear as he and Lissa wanted just made them more addicted and at the mercy of Gabe's whims. One time though Ricky refused a job that Gabe gave him- it was different to couriering drugs (a transaction that Ricky explained away as a simple matter of 'supply/demand') and Ricky refused to take the job on moral grounds. Few tweakers have any morals so Gabe was floored and Ricky never told Lissa what the job was. Some weeks passed and Ricky went on with the more usual work.

One night, following a run, a hooded man broke into Ricky and Lissa's apartment with a gun. Standing in the doorway he shot Ricky, who was on the sofa next to Lissa watching TV. A couple of minutes later Ricky died in Lissa's arms.

"I'm so sorry! That's terrible, I don't know what to say. Not much of a messenger am I?" I feebly jest.

"That's cool. We can still be best friends!"

"Do you know who was responsible for the shooting?"

"I have an idea, but what can I do?"

Lissa looks away with an impenetrable hardness in her bright blue eyes, before she turns back to me:

"So you really like Ajax, huh?"

Lissa and Henry bang on my new apartment door on Saturn Avenue in Beverly Hills Adjacent. When I open it with a welcoming smile they both look thoroughly perplexed and Henry steps forward and gives me a hug.

"What's that in aid of?" I ask.

"Shit man- we thought you'd gone and killed yourself."

"We were totally worried about you- where've ya been?" Lissa frowns suspiciously.

"Errrr. . . well. . . I was in the hospital a few days- it's okay. Why did you think I'd done myself in? I'm soooo not like that?"

I cannot bear the thought that even my tweaker friends doubt my resilience and substance. Lissa rustles through her maroon suede Jansport backpack that looks distinctly like one I'd owned. Pulling out a folded piece of A4 paper I recognise my handwriting. She reads it out:

"Did you ever think that one time, a long time ago, when you were a little child, you were visited by extraterrestrials? They say that when you are visited by an extraterrestrial, it puts this spell on you so you cannot remember the encounter at all, and you wake up only with this sad kind of longing for something, but you don't know what. And you carry that sad longing with you all the rest of your life. And they say that if, by chance, you get hypnotized, then you reveal the encounter under hypnosis, and when you wake up, you remember it, and then, it is no longer a sad longing, but a real thing, which you know about and even if people think you're crazy, talking all the time about your extraterrestrial encounter, that's ok, because in your heart you know what it was that had been locked up for so long and you are greatly relieved. I have often wondered what it would feel like to be greatly relieved. I am not a very healthy person-"

Impatient, Henry breaks in:

"We found that out in your yard and we thought it was a

155

suicide note-"

"No way!"

I cannot believe my ears: it is a monologue I had learned from the play *Brilliant Traces* by Cindy Lou Johnson, for my acting class. I had written it out on paper to help me memorise it. I explain this to them and we all fall over each other laughing at the absurdity of the whole thing. It sure feels good to have a belly laugh.

"Well thank fuck for that because we thought you were weird but that's pushing it!"

In truth, a few days back I had admitted myself to the psych ward in a West LA hospital. I had arranged ten days of work as an extra on the film *Nixon* and I had failed to show up the first day. I had recently joined Cenex, an extras casting agency and they had booked me for this job. I had dealt with Mitch who had made me promise I was reliable and not going to let him down. So when I failed to show the first day he called a couple of times and left relatively polite messages, but when I'd failed to call or show by the end of the day he was absolutely fuming and gave me a big piece of his mind; obviously I am at the end of a long line of extras who has let him down.

Dee had come by to check on me because I had not been answering my phone and when I saw her I burst into sobs and tears. She took me back to her house. For some reason I had no breath to speak, or listen and could not even vegetate watching videos. I was spent- figuratively, literally and spiritually.

All I could do was go to bed. I slept for two days and Dee was worried. She called Dr Rubinstein who suggested I go to the hospital. I know now what the problem was- I had come down and part of me wanted to quit the drugs, but I was not ready or willing to admit it, so I went along with the idea that I was suffering from some kind of suicidal depression. Yes, I was clearly depressed but not in need of hospitalisation. I was embracing this notion of myself as a 'poor damaged victim.' Also to be merely an addict who had a choice whether to use or not to use, is too simple; I want to be unique in all my psychological complexities, whether it be depression, attention deficit disorder, borderline personality disorder, anorexia or some other as yet undiscovered problem.

I spend only three and a half days in the hospital and experience a severe wake-up call. I know categorically that I never, ever want to return. At first rehab was weird but the psych ward in a hospital is a huge step beyond where I want to go. I quickly understand that this is seriously not a game, and not a place anyone would choose for a 'rest'. No nut wards for me thank you very much.

Henry now calls me the Unabomber. It irks me, but because it makes him chuckle, I put up with it because none of us laugh much these days. He has become my close buddy as well as my main dealer. It seems to go with the territory that you end up pretty close to your dealer and he is cool because he has yet to let me down- his Unique Selling Point. The fact that he is as much an addict as me is no doubt the reason that he is so reliable. He also has a very endearing quality about him, and does a brilliant Homer Simpson impression.

"Where the fuck does this Unabomber thing come from Henry- I don't get it?" I ask him in all seriousness.

"Have you actually looked at yourself in the mirror recently?"

When I had first met him at Elsie's I thought he was an idiot: he'd turned up with some GHB and Elsie and him were the only ones who wanted to take it, amongst the late night posse. Elsie snorted some and fell about like a laughing but drunk hyena, whereas Henry whooped up a pile and guffawed for a few seconds and then collapsed into a heap on Elsie's favourite zebra rug.

"Hey don't mess up my rug!" Elsie squawked.

"Oh my God, shit!! What should we do?" I exclaimed in horror, while every one else just sat there, totally nonchalant in the customary twilight zone that is Elsie's sitting room, surrounded by the candles and crucifixes that adorn all available wall and shelf space.

"He'll be alright man"- words of wisdom emit from Gary, a friend of Henry's who'd arrived with him.

"What the hell do you mean? He's overdosed on that

shit!! We need to call an ambulance!" I panic, scared that he is going to die on us.

"Chill the fuck out will ya!" Elsie, more normal now, tells me in stern terms as if I am somehow breaking up the party mood.

I am down on the floor feeling for a pulse and Elsie and Gary erupt into giggles. I find a slow pulse while looking at them both aghast.

"What the fuck is wrong with you guys? This is serious!" More laughs. Am I not seeing the joke?

"She obviously doesn't know Henry!" Gary adds.

"He'll be fine." Elsie rolls her heavy eyes- 'just relax dude'- and continues with:

"Honey, Henry is totally- and I mean totally- immune to all this shit- Let's just call it a momentary lapse of reason, okay babe?"

"Of fucking consciousness more like!"

"Whatever!"

I had been genuinely fearful for Henry's life, but I guess I am rather naïve.

CHAPTER 18
Mummy Dearest

If you look back, you risk turning into a statue of salt- that is,
a statue of tears. . .   Cocteau

I am in shock. My head buzzes with horrific outcomes and consequences. I had called my mother in France and my stepfather had answered the phone.

"She's on the plane right now as we speak."

"What?!"

I am completely dumbfounded. For starters neither of my parents had come for 'Family Week' at Promises where parents, siblings and spouses are encouraged to understand and help the addict recover, as well as air their grievances, resentments and concerns. This was all included in the overall fee, so why has my mother suddenly made the decision to get on a plane to LA? Her timing is appalling. I am using again but keeping up the pantomime of not using by maintaining a low profile, and making the occasional call to my outpatient counsellor Richard to check in. I long ago stopped calling my Narcotics Anonymous Sponsor who I really liked but could not bring myself to deceive. In fact, we'd had a blast together reading and then burning my 4th step (From the 12 Step Program: Writing a fearless moral inventory and sharing it with someone else) in her open fireplace in her living room up a windy lane in Brentwood. But I had relapsed and coming clean did not seem like an option. I was handling it this time- I knew the customary pitfalls- so I would manage my using with newfound knowledge learned about drug taking from rehab and meetings.

I had already passed my drug test at Promises the week

before by refrigerating my urine and then inserting it inside me in a narrow plastic canister I had bought at CVS. Granted, getting the pee out required some quick, accurate finger work but with my terror of the consequences I managed it even with Pat in the bathroom with me; fortunately she was not eyeballing me. Anyhow they probably assume that if you are using you are hardly going to turn up for the test, but I had no choice in the matter because I had my court hearing the following week and I needed Promises to vouch for my committed recovery.

So what on earth is my mother showing up for?

I find out much later that guilt has gotten the better of her when my aunt, my father's sister, had called her on the pretext of lending her the money to come visit me in LA. I do not understand my parents' attitude or response to my drug problem. I think they just want it to go away and they hoped that Promises would make that happen, without their involvement. Sadly it was not going to work like that for me, but that is hardly their fault. Because the financial side was being taken care of by the Vronsky family, part of me felt they could at least get it together to come out for a couple of weeks for family week so maybe I could feel some kind of resolution. I knew what had happened was my fault, but I also knew from my sessions in group and with Dr Rubinstein that my upbringing had some bearing on my current state of mind.

"Where is she going to stay?" I ask my stepfather.

"At the Los Angeles Athletic Club- it's in downtown LA." I had never heard of it but it has a reciprocal arrangement with the RAC that my stepfather was a member of in England. I am devastated; I do not want my mother here because it feels completely wrong. The only solution I see is to take more crystal and clean myself up. My mother has always been vain and I know that a good outward appearance will partly persuade her I am okay.

My mother waits for me in the bar at the rather smart members club, mainly used by businessmen. She is clearly rattled, on top of the jetlag and fatigue. I give her a hug- not something she is prone to initiate herself- and I sit down with

160

her. I am carrying a bottle of Snapple and she observes it with a look of abject horror.

"What's that in the bottle?"

"Iced tea- what do you think it is?" Her relief shows; I think she thought it was whiskey.

"My god you're certainly thin!"

"You can never be too rich or too thin, right Mum?"

"Actually you do look rather too thin compared to what I'm used to seeing but I suppose it suits you. So what about this court appearance?"

"It's on Thursday at 11am at the Courthouse downtown. It's really only a formality so the judge can know I've been adhering to the Diversion program and that I'm staying clean and out of trouble."

"So who's going to be there with you?"

"Someone from Edward French's office- this guy Steve Gold took me before when I was at Promises but now I'm out I'm not sure."

"I'm going to see this Edward French tomorrow."

"Great- I'll take you."

"No. I want to go by myself."

I'd hoped that my mother's trip would have healed old sores, or at least resulted in a band aid or two, but that was not to be. To be fair I think she was bamboozled into coming in the first place and was furious that my stepfather was not to be included in the trip. I had developed a steady hostility towards him since he had played emotional ping pong with my mother back when I was teenager- one minute they are separated, planning divorce and the day before the decree absolute they meet up and decide to give it another go. That in itself is understandable- people split and get back together again- but it was his behaving as if he had never left that really got to me. I felt I deserved a little more respect in the matter, or even an acknowledgement that I had been part of the mess that ensued.

I felt she had given up before she arrived- maybe something to do with mothers' instinct. I was using again, but I was not out of control and it was manageable, at least in my mind. I guess she did not know what to do and of course, I denied it flat out. She never saw me or caught me, but I was clearly different from the daughter she remembered.

Halfway through my mother's six day visit I arrive to meet her at the Los Angeles Athletic Club. I arrive on time and am waiting in the lobby when the Receptionist approaches me with the news that my mother had just called to say she was running a little late and she'll be here in about an hour.

I go for a walkabout and end up on her floor. I see that the maid's cleaning trolley is parked a few doors down from my mother's room. I wait. The plump short lady appears and I give her a friendly wave:

"Hi! My mother's in 408- She's down in the lobby and I came up to pick up something I left in her room but I left the key down at reception. I am so stupid."

The woman looks at me, expectant. I have no idea if she understands a word so I smile sweetly and mime unlocking the door. She looks me over- I am well dressed and presentable by anyone's standards- and she nods, telling me:

"Si, Si."

She lets me in and I head straight into the bathroom where I know my mother keeps her jewellery in a Chinoise silk bag. I am sweating profusely; all hell will break lose if my mother walks in and finds me in her room. I rifle through and there is very little- a couple of pieces of costume jewellery, an emerald ring with seed pearls all around and a small felt bag with two gold coins, from Africa. I have never seen them before and I figure that she will miss them the least because she can't wear them. Also they appear to be the only thing of any value besides the emerald. I tuck them into my pants- right down, as if by doing this I am somehow denying what I have done- and make sure there is no evidence of my visit.

I zip back to the lobby and calmly take a seat. My mother arrives fifteen minutes later.

We visit Dr Rubinstein together and it is an unmitigated disaster. He suggests she might be an alcoholic, or have 'alcoholic' behaviour (he had heard a fair amount about my family by now in our twice weekly sessions and was referring

162

to her upbringing with my Grannie) and she takes umbrage at this. She feels he is taking liberties due to the fact that they had literally just met and he calmly defends himself, saying that he is only making 'suggestions'. As far as mum is concerned she is here to support me, not look at her problems, because she did not have any and, 'besides that is not what this is about.'

By this time I could not care less, which is probably one of the distinct reasons crystal meth works so well for me- it totally erases painful experience: no memory, conscience or concern- and so confident was I now that I left the happy couple alone- my mother perched on the black leather sofa- in his plush office with the nice view across Sawtelle Avenue and Westwood, while I excuse myself and visit the bathroom for a toot.

To be frank it always did amaze me that Dr Rubinstein never realized I was high, or maybe he did and figured I would come a cropper soon enough. The other explanation is that I was still supposedly on the anti-depressants he was prescribing me so that could account for the pinned eyes and nervousness.

I make sure to reapply my lipstick and I walk back in to meet an awkward silence.

"We were discussing your depressive illness, Clea." Dr Rubinstein intones. My mother looks at me sharply.

"Yes. I wasn't aware of this- why didn't you say anything? One minute things are fine, then you're on drugs and in a clinic and now I hear you have a depression problem. To be honest I can't keep up."

"Sorry- it does sound a bit much I agree but things had been going wrong for a while. I just didn't know what to do about it."

"What Clea is saying is that she was depressed for a long time and her drug use was a form of self-medicating, but now she's on a new type of anti-depressant that has none of the side effects of the more traditional ones and we've been getting results, haven't we Clea?"

I nod in agreement and reach for my mother's hand which she awkwardly gives, but lets go of as soon as reasonably possible. She does not want to be seen as an ogre, but we all know she has not presented a sympathetic figure. In my calculating mind this all adds up to the newfound patient status that I am indulging in, in a sickening way. I like being the centre of attention and maybe Mum knows this. She certainly has no time for Dr Rubinstein, whom she denigrates as 'smug, rude and only interested in making money in those Gucci shoes'. I find her description quite apt, but also unfair because he has helped me- or at least tried to.

She feels insulted by my lawyer who gave her about five minutes of his time; clearly my case is small fry. I should mention that my mother is one of that breed of person who can say incredibly hurtful things to others but takes the slightest offhandedness towards herself as a hanging offence. Also, like my father, she has complicated feelings about America- at this point I think there is nothing she actually likes about it- and she somehow feels inadequate and/or ill-equipped to deal with my situation. I believe she blames me for having to ever come back to America again: first for my graduation- supposedly a celebration- and now for 'moral support' in my time of need. While at my graduation my mother seemed to feel things should centre upon her -and this had irritated me considerably- now I am used to it and not so willing to accept it. When she had annihilated my father with her aggressive comment: 'You're fucking useless', in front of me and my friends at dinner, I truly wished she had not bothered to come.

Similarly, here in LA when we face a small difficulty regarding the finalization and closure of my court case, she has another hysterical fit- her specialty- and loses it big time. In fact it is the inefficiency of Promises- or rather my aftercare counsellor Richard, who has held up the proceedings and not me at all. It is a technical error- some specific paperwork has not arrived on time- but my mother screams at me as if I want this to happen, which clearly I do not.

Mrs. Wade, whose stolen cheque I'd tried to forge and cash, has been subpoenaed to appear and the hatred in her eyes towards me is unquestionable. Along with her husband, she is dowdy, middle aged and furious with the aggravation, expense and inconvenience I have caused her for the sake of one measly cheque, nicked out of a black garbage sack. I apologise to them and they say nothing, although her look of disgust says it all. I absorb the shame- of my own negative creation- while having my wailing harpy mother scream me down.

On top of that I now know that in reality I would not have needed a lawyer as a first time offender. A Diversion Program (proof that you are dealing with your drugs problem by seeking treatment, attending ongoing NA meetings) is usually enough to bail out first time offenders- people like me who commit petty fraud under the influence of drugs and who have a strong likelihood of not re-offending. Basically it is standard procedure and I feel quite irritated with the top-drawer lawyer my family had hired at great expense when quite frankly I could have represented myself. Of course a respectable family is unused to being on this side of the law.

I feel overwhelmed by guilt about the amount of money that has been spent to get me 'better', when I actually spent a fifth of the portion- if even that- getting high. Oh the insanity. . .which reminds me of a definition of insanity: To keep doing the same thing and expect different results.

When my mother leaves the look of relief on her face is priceless and states: I am so happy to be leaving this dire situation with my drug addict, only child- who claims to be a misunderstood adult- who is a complete liar and thief and who has been on drugs my whole trip.

My mother confronts me about the coins but I freak out at her, telling her it must have been the maid and that her 'accusation was a typical example of how she always thinks the worst of me'. And on top of that how could I have stolen the gold coins when I had no access to her hotel room? After all I'm not a lock picker so the hotel staff must be dishonest.

"That's just the way LA is, Mum!' I inform her smugly.

But she knows only too well from her experiences with Grannie that where there is a will, there is always a way. And even though I do not seem desperate for money- I have not run out of it yet- a top up is always essential if you are seemingly incapable of getting and/or keeping a job. She had had a real go at me about that:

"Now you're out of rehab and had all this marvellous therapy with Dr Gucci-shoes why can't you do a relatively simple thing like get a job- waitressing or office reception or

165

whatever- to pay for the apartment you can't actually afford, the rest of your car payments- I still don't know why you bought this mammoth American jalopy rather than a Honda or some other economical Japanese car- and attend your acting classes in the evening? I'm sure that's what the majority of the wannabe actors do here. They can't all be from rich families who are happy to fund their dilettantism . . . Oh sorry your 'true purpose' as you call it, that I have never supported you in! By the way is it still acting you are now pursuing or is it something new this week that you've forgotten to tell me about, or have you gone back to the original plan to be a screenwriter?" She had paused for a long in-take of breath and a glug of her drink:

"Sorry Clea but I'm finding it hard keeping up with you. And you are very different to how I remember you. I know you think I've been unsympathetic about my divorce from Daddy and this other stuff with Phil and whatever, but you are an adult and you can't blame every thing on me."

"I'm not! Why do you think that?" I retort.

"Because of the way that doctor went on, like I was the cause of all your problems. The truth is I have hardly seen you more than a few weeks a year- if even that- in the last five or six years. In fact, since you have been in the USA. Yes!- That is really when everything started to go wrong in my opinion; ever since you went to Pine Manor and were so desperate to go to Brown and then you actually got in and went and then you ended up in LA of all places . . . Okay, do you want to know what I think?"

"Of course I do! You're my mother for Christ's sake-"

"I think you should pack your things up and leave LA. America does not suit everyone. It didn't suit me, it certainly didn't suit Daddy and it doesn't seem to suit you. . . There! I've said it now, for what it's worth."

So now, as if to prove her wrong that I am doing the right thing staying in LA, I do find a part time job- about 24 hours a week- working for an Iranian eye doctor who is partially blind. I call her immediately to let her know and she sounds pleased but again repeats her belief that I am not suited to LA and I should come back to her in France for a few months. I cannot think of anything I would hate more.

The eye surgeon is involved in the advent of corrective

laser eye surgery and he wants help with general administration, correspondence and the like. I manage to keep the job for almost 3 weeks and then I flake out and forget to go and because he is so nice- I had even eaten mezze lunch (correction: picked at) with him and his Persian family in their ornate dining room- I feel too embarrassed to return his call and make up some huge lie of an excuse. The basic fact is that tweaking and regular life don't mix.

CHAPTER 19

Full-Time Tweaker

I had nothing to offer anybody except my own confusion.
On the Road Jack Kerouac

I am back into my familiar 'tweaking' routine- four days awake followed by about 30 hours sleep. This lifestyle resembles an ongoing security operation because I am constantly guarding my belongings from other tweakers. Tweakers are like magpies. Anything bright and glistening ends up in their pockets.

After sustained use my appetite for food returns. Sometimes I crash with a spoon in my mouth and a spilled bowl of Campbell's Cream of Mushroom soup down my front. Experience has taught me to let it cool down.

I have been up for almost three days when the phone rings. I take a deep breath, reminding myself that I need to sound like a normal person going about my regular daily routine when it dawns on me I have no idea what time it is, or what day it is, let alone the month or year. This throws me into turmoil as I seek out my Breitling Divers watch- given me by Amory in what seems another lifetime- and manically rifle through a batch of clothes on my sofa and then I notice it swinging round my neck on a piece of brown leather thread, knotted round my neck with my apartment and car keys. Then I recall how I had rifled round for a chain in order to tie my essentials onto my person, because I keep losing them in the chaos that is my domicile. How had I not realised, when they clank and knock the pointed collarbones of my scraggy neck continuously? The watch proved its own problem because it was floating up and down my arm. I had tried switching it over to my right wrist- the marginally thicker one because I am right handed- but it still ended up around my bony elbow.

On my 'own' time, with no job to go to and no one to let down (again), real time is of no consequence. Time now exists in two clear categories: tweaking time and crash time. I have to be careful and make sure I am home near the end of a four day run because I often fall asleep while in the midst of driving. Once I was caught out in a traffic jam and I prayed hard that I would get home, my erratic foot jerking on the brake, jolting me awake.

Dislodging the watch face glued to my chest by dry sweat- I had been dismantling and re-stuffing an armchair- I see it is almost 11:00am. The phone continues to ring. Or maybe it stopped and started again? I grab the receiver.

"Is that a Miss Clea Myers?" a female voice enquires. A couple of beats pass while I decide whether I want to be me, or someone else.

"May I ask who's calling?" I politely say in my best American drawl.

"Well, the thing is, we have her suitcase."

Suitcase? What suitcase?

"I'll just see if she's home, okay." I tiptoe into my bedroom, slip on a pair of heels and clipetty clop back across the tiled floor.

"Halloo- this is Clea."

"Oh hi. Yes- we've found your suitcase- the Louis Vuitton one- someone chucked it over our hedgerow into our garden."

"That's great!"

"I guess you weren't counting on seeing it again? Luckily there was your credit card statement inside with your phone number on- you didn't fill in the tags so we had to look inside."

"Right. . ." The plot thickens; I have never owned any LV luggage in my life.

"So when 'dya wanna come and pick it up?"

"As soon as I can."

She gives me an address on Laurel Canyon Drive and tells me she will leave the suitcase inside their porch door because they will be out for the rest of the day. That suits me because it crosses my mind that they may expect a reward, or something.

I am buzzing with excitement when I lug the very heavy case into the trunk of my car, which I do as speedily as I can because I feel like a thief- in fact, I am a thief. I race home and spring the case open on top of my bed.

Inside are a stack of CD's- what could only be described as 'easy listening' (The Carpenters, Kenny Loggins, Jennifer Rush)- clothes including some cute designer tops and a Gucci bikini and matching wrap and some credit card details of two men I have never heard of, alongside mine. I empty the case and am about to push it under my bed when I notice a slight cut in the lining that has been glued down. I can feel something flat against the structure- some computer discs perhaps? - and then the phone rings and I forget about it for the time being.

"Clea I need to talk to you about something serious." Ajax says. I lean up against the breakfast bar, all ears, trying not to drown in his emerald eyes. Why is he so gorgeous? Even tweaked out of his mind he exudes that intangible charisma, aka 'star quality'.

"Yeah shoot."

"Babe, you're not getting it!"

"Getting what?" I ask impatiently; I am in no mood for riddles.

"You just don't get it, do you?"

"Get what?" I demand.

He goes on, concern clouding his handsome mask.

"You don't really understand what these people are totally about. The freaks that you let wander in and out of here in the middle of the day and night."

"Yeah like you can fucking talk!" About two weeks ago I had invited Ajax and his so-called girlfriend Tammy to stay. She looks like Sissy Spacek in *Carrie* and trails Ajax like a younger sister, wishing some of his cool would rub off on her. I am not quite sure what was rumbling around in my brain when I opened my door to them- I guess that I figured if I invited Ajax to stay he would ditch Tammy and we could take up where we had left off. What I had not considered was his reliance on her for a couple of things- namely cash and the most vital necessity in LA, a car.

Unlike me, she did what he wanted, when he wanted without question or just sits around with a forlorn look on her pale face. I have never seen her take drugs either, and that makes it even weirder because why else would you hang out with a bunch of tweakers like us?

The situation between us was certainly weird and at breaking point. The thing with Ajax and me is that we completely relate in that soul connection way that means you know what the other is thinking. He even admitted he felt the same way but that it 'was too damn weird and I was the last thing he needed'. We'd never had sex since our stay together in Venice, but having him near me was enough. I have never felt like that- before or since- about any man, but then I have never met anyone like Ajax either.

What scared me about Ajax was the way he accepted his 'junkie' status (as he called it) and he is always trying to scam some way to set up a meth lab. I am in love with him but I do not want to nail down my own coffin.

"So what is it that's so important Mr wise guy?" I prompt while he gives me his surly smile that makes me want to kiss him. Not that I would ever let on.

"Ya know you've got a lot of stuff sitting around in drawers and stuff here that I'm surprised is still sitting here."

"You shouldn't be in my drawers!" I point out. Only yesterday Lissa started rifling through my desk drawers as I stood there aghast while she flung a copy of *Surrealists in Love* on the floor.

"Huh! Nothing of any interest here". Lissa slouched off to the bathroom; later on I realise that half my earrings and all my bangles have vanished.

"I think I've hidden anything of value- gold and stuff, or I've taken it to the pawn shop already." I tell him, unconcerned. The junk jewellery Lissa took I do not really care about.

"But check out this beauty!" I lift my right hand to show off the ring I'd 'borrowed' from Dee.

"What is it? It looks like a piece of rabbit shit encased in glass!"

"Ha, ha, you ignoramus- it's a Victorian hair ring; it's a beautiful token of love!"

"Huh . . .I'd check your stuff if I were you. Gotta run babe- Tammy's waiting at Henry's for me to pick her up.

"Aren't you her knight in shining armour!" he looks sharply at me and for a split second something passes between us that could have spelt the beginning of something real.

Dee's cell phone rings and she passes it to me.

"Hi- is that Ajax?"

"Who the fuck is this?"

"Calm down will you! It's Clea- I'm borrowing a friend's cell."

"You're fucking lucky I called you back man coz I don't call back numbers I don't recognise."

"I feel truly privileged!"

"You should- So what do you want, trouble?"

I giggle like an awestruck schoolgirl and Dee gives me an odd look.

"Well my best-friend Dee and I want to see you about a dog- Can you help us out?"

"Probably- what are you thinking about?"

"Four old gramophone records, but we're kinda flexible. Have car, will travel."

More banter follows and we arrange to meet in Venice. We set off in Dee's Lexus because she cannot stand the way I ride the brake when I drive, claiming it makes her need to vomit. She calls her live-in Hispanic maid Maria to pick up the kids from school and make their supper. We are free to groove.

We join the freeway and cruise towards Santa Monica when Ajax calls back on the cell. This time Dee chats to him and they discover that he knows her younger sister Audrey, who Dee cannot stand. But at least they move in similar circles, kind of. She hands her cell over to me:

"Hiya- we're nearly there. What's up?" I ask casually, dreading an excuse that he suddenly cannot meet up with us.

"Now this is really serious Clea- I need to ask you something important. . ."

173

My heart beats even faster than it already is: He's dumped Tammy and wants to spend the rest of his life with me? I take a deep breath- cool, collected I prompt:

"Yeah babe, shoot! - I'm all ears."

"Are you being followed?"

"What?"

"You fucking heard me- are you being followed?"

"Who the fuck would be following us?!"

"Not you, but if my phone is tapped then they could be following you to get to me." Ajax slowly explains like I am retarded.

"Who the hell is 'they'?" Dee gives me a concerned look.

"Look- that is none of your fucking concern, or problem-

"Well it is actually coz we don't want to get arrested you know, by association with you."

"I'll repeat the question, once and for all- Are you being followed?"

I turn to Dee while leaning up to glance in the rear view mirror, pointedly asking her: "Do you think we're being followed? Ajax thinks we are."

She whisks her cell back:

"Hi there again. Of course we're being followed- we're on the freeway! Currently we have a few hundred cars behind us so in answer to your question yes we are definitely being followed, but I'm sure it's nothing personal. I'm about to turn off in half a mile so I'll be losing them okay!"

We laugh mighty hard until we get to the corner on Abbot Kinney and Venice where Ajax, in shades and baseball hat, sits on the wall by the 7-11. His beloved Spanky sits patiently at his feet on his thick leather lead. I instruct Dee to pipe down her giggles because Ajax cannot cope with being the butt of anyone's joke.

Dee honks the horn and he slopes over. I jump out the car and he lets Spanky off the lead. He bounds over and leaps on top of me, jumping up, trying to lick my face. At least his dog is on my side. I had spoiled Spanky rotten the morning Ajax had had his court date downtown, in the week we had first met.

"Homies, can you do me a favour?" Ajax asks, taking Spanky's collar, shoving him up onto the back seat.

"What?" I ask, clambering in next to an excited Spanky who will not settle; Ajax is the kind of man who expects to sit up front, shot gun.

"Can we stop by Erewhon coz I need to pick up some food for Spanky?"

"It's up to Dee, not me-"

"Yeah okay, where is it?" Dee asks, turning the ignition.

"Why don't you just buy some dog food at 7-11?" I ask.

"He won't eat Pal, or Bonio- he likes that organic stuff from Erewhon-."

"Clearly your dog's got better taste than you then." I recall Ajax's 'junkie' diet of Big Mac, fries and Coke, when he actually ate anything. Even though he is lean he is also surprisingly muscular.

"Well I'm not so sure babe- he's pretty keen on you!"

"Exactly!" Dee glances up in her rear view mirror and gives me a wink.

Ajax decides it is better if we go somewhere public rather than back to where he is staying. Part of me suspects he does not want me to know where that is. What he thinks I will actually do with that information is anyone's guess.

He is very paranoid and I have to keep nudging Dee to keep a straight face. He thinks the FBI is after him because he keeps pointing out ordinary cars with nondescript people inside them, claiming they are watching him. Dee, suppressing her sniggers, asks:

"What have you done that's so bad the FBI have a whole troop of people out looking for you?"

"Don't wanna talk about it- Hey, stop over there; we'll find a beachside bar."

"Must be pretty bad if all those cars are after you .. . " Ajax glares Dee down. Clea, suddenly the peacemaker, jumps in. The last thing I want is Ajax strutting off in a huff, something he is prone to do, especially when in a super paranoid state. He even thinks homeless people on the side of the road are undercover agents. From the way he goes on one would think he is America's Most Wanted and maybe he is for all I know, but somehow I doubt it. Like most tweakers he has an over-active imagination.

We walk along Venice Beach which is relatively empty

since it is a Thursday afternoon. We settle on a surf bar that has some tables out back.

"So who wants what or shall I get us a pitcher of Margaritas?" Dee enquires. When Dee walks off to the bar I lean in to Ajax and tap his arm:

"Are you okay?"

"Not really but. . ."

"What?"

"It's really complicated-"

"Oh for fuck's sake, isn't it always really goddamned, fucking complicated- I feel like we're all living in some really shit B movie, or something!"

"If only. . .Watch your back, Clea- I'm serious." And he does look serious but then a damp pitcher and glasses plonk down in my line of vision. The moment is gone.

"Hey d'ya guys mind if I take a couple of photos- I'm trying out a photography course and I've just got the hang of the light meter and today was supposed to be a 'photo day'."

"Yeah sure." I like having my photograph taken and even better is the idea of having a photo of Ajax, or Ajax and me. Dee poses me against the wall with a cigarette- very Garboesque- and clicks away with the light meter and adjusts the aperture to cover all her bases. She then poses Ajax leaning on the side of the armchair he is lounging in, in a very Humphrey Bogart way and I realise now why his intonation had always struck me as familiar; clearly he has modelled himself on Bogey. She looks down to get the accurate light meter reading.

"I don't believe it!" Dee exclaims while Ajax helps himself to my drink, having slugged down his ice tea.

"What? What don't you believe?" I ask.

"This reading- it's what you get with studio lighting!"

"So what's the big deal?" I do not get her point.

"Well the thing is only a few, certain people radiate this much light energy that they get such a high reading- basically they did an experiment with movie stars and they discovered that they radiate at a much higher frequency than other people."

"I guess that's why they're stars." Ajax drolly cuts in.

176

"That's right, and according to this you should be one!- My teacher was going on about it the other day in class and now I've proved it." Dee looks excited by her discovery. I am perplexed:

"What about my reading then?"

"Sorry Clea darling- yours was average."

"Let's drink to that." Ajax clinks his glass to hers.

The next day I'd received a phone call from Dee, asking:

"Clea- do ya remember if I took the roll of film out the camera while we were in that bar? My memory's kinda hazy and I really need to develop it for my project that's due next week-"

"I don't think so, but to be honest I really wasn't paying much attention by that time in the day, if you know what I mean? - Sorry!" I lie. In truth I had witnessed Ajax swiftly pocketing the film after Dee had re-wound it and taken it out of the camera. At the time I had asked Ajax what he was doing and all he said was:

"She doesn't need it." He was cryptic so much of the time I let it go; after all I knew Dee could take more photographs- of me anyway- if she liked. My energy lacked conviction too; it was easier to ignore people's irrational behaviour than question it. I was changing in my core- I could feel it slowly rotting- yet I had no impetus to check it, or forestall it; somehow it seemed inevitable and part of some bigger picture I was not able to pull into focus . . .yet.

A few days later after some sleep, I scoff down some Crunchy Nut cornflakes with cold milk- the most delicious meal after a speed run- and I am ready to tweak again: Into my bathroom I go, free from prying eyes because there are no windows, where I have some meth laid out, ready to roll. I always leave a line, or two, on a small dark ceramic tile, tucked away in a bathroom cabinet under the sink for when I first wake up. I have different stashes set up all over my apartment. Ceramic tiles provide the best surface, rather than mirrors, because the dry porcelain is unslippery and I don't get to see the gaping hole up my nose to my brain when I lean over.

Once it is flowing through my blood again I sit and

tweak in front of a gilt 1950s table mirror I have set up on a circular dressing table in my bedroom. I tweak over my face and adornment, because my physical beautification ritual is still a priority, especially as I never know when Ajax might turn up. I also enjoy admiring myself in the privacy of my bedroom.

Whereas the drug cutting, laying out and ingesting with paraphernalia ritual used to be part of the 'fun' experience of drug taking, it has now graduated into pure necessity and something of a bore. Hence, I try to prepare a run in advance. I also have my own cut-down straws that no one else uses which I replace from time to time, taking a handful from a fast food joint.

I am placing one of them up my worn nostril and counting down the split seconds to inhalation when out of the ether I remember my hidden collection of pearls kept in a red velvet Mikimoto jewellery case. I have not seen them for ages but I have kept them in the same place forever.

I had put the pearls in the desk purely because I rarely wear them- pearls conjure up the Sloane Ranger image of my teenage years too vividly for me. I figured they must be worth something and had hidden them in the case of a burglary because they were gifts of sentimental value: A three row set of Mikimoto pearls given me by my stepfather on my 21st birthday and an antique strand with an emerald and diamond clasp given to me by the Vronsky family for my 22nd birthday, when I had spent spring break with them in their villa on St. John in the USVI while I was at Brown. If I had not forgotten all about them I would have pawned them anyway because that's what tweakers do.

I rush over to the desk and drag out the second drawer down- stuffed with theatre and concert programs, photos, a couple of Propaganda screenplays from my days with Amory, and wrapping paper- and frantically feel for the silky velvet underneath. I yank out the box, relieved. I knew I could not be that stupid.

I ease it open and the click of the joins echoes my sharp intake of breath: Black satin glares back at me. Empty.

I hurl it across the room in fury, grab my keys and storm out to the car. I fail to notice I am still wearing my skimpy nightdress that barely covers my butt until I arrive at Dee's building on North Palm Drive and a passing car honks at me.

I can see the back of her auburn, cropped head of hair through her bathroom window upstairs but to my surprise she quickly pulls the blind down. I ring the doorbell and wait for at least ten minutes on her doorstep; she does not come to the door. Now I am furious: I lean on the doorbell. I yell:

"Dee! Dee! Are you home? Please I really need to talk to you about something! Please, let me in. I'm your best friend, I really need to talk."

Nothing! No response whatsoever and I am stumped as well as deeply disappointed because she is the only person here in LA that I really trust.

I wait for at least fifteen minutes and she does not appear, either at the door or out of one of the many street-facing windows. Perhaps she is sick, or worse: something terrible has happened to her or someone in her family. These thoughts take the edge off my confusion so I return home to change my clothes and make another plan, indignant and smarting at my own crazed stupidity to leave the pearls sitting in that desk drawer with all the tweakers around my belongings.

Back in the apartment the first thing I do is call my messages. There is one from Henry, 'Yo dude what's up?' and the other is from Dee, in unfamiliar terse tones:

"Look Clea you cannot come over here anymore. Things are too weird with you and quite honestly it frightens me. I can't have the kids seeing you the way you are not to mention my neighbours; I've already had two complaints and lots of the weird looks. I just need some distance from you. I really mean it, okay. And by the way I'm not u-know-what anymore, okay, so please leave me alone. You can send back the clothes and stuff I've lent you or drop them round the back in my garage, but if you do that then do it quietly please! And I am serious."

Then her tone softens and sounds maternal:

"Oh yeah, I don't know who these new friends of yours are but they are totally bad news . . .take care of yourself, okay." Click.

I had known things were becoming stretched between Dee and myself, but I never ever thought she would cut me out. Granted we had seen less of each other in the last month, but nonetheless, weren't we soul sisters?

She had always been there for me, since the day I had met her in Promises when she had just left the alcohol detox at Cedars Sinai. She had needed to talk- really spill her guts- and I had stayed up with her till 4am in the airy den at Promises, chain smoking, drinking tea, listening and sharing our woes.

On more than one occasion she had seriously helped me out. My mother had just come and gone from LA, and almost immediately afterwards I had been arrested for stealing a packet of Marlboro Lights from Ralph's Supermarket, on La Brea and Santa Monica.

I had paid at the checkout for one pack on the understanding I would pick it up at the exit. In LA they have this weird system where you pick them up by the exit so instead of taking just the one packet, I snuck another one, assuming no one would notice.

"Excuse me Mam- can I speak with you." A gruff low tone sneaks up on me.

Play it cool I tell myself- an easy mistake to make, after all.

"Yeah what sir? What can I do for-" A uniformed Ralph's Security Guard is at my side.

"I saw you take that extra pack of cigarettes- you only paid for one" he accuses. I look down dramatically at my hands:

"Did I? – Oh my God! I am so sorry- I'll go straight back in and pay for them."

"Can you come with me please, Mam." People stare at me as they wheel their groceries back to their cars.

"Errrrr- yeah okay, but I need to just-" I step back and suddenly he is very close, his body language letting me know I am trapped.

"It's better if you just come this way, Mam!" He firmly takes hold of my elbow- in a resolute no-nonsense grasp- steering me back into the store, past the leering teller and through the swinging staff doors at the back, up some narrow stairs and into the Manager's office. He undoes a fold-up chair and places it down in the furthest corner of the room away from the large desk, like he thinks I am going to raid the Manager's stationery supply.

The smell of shame reeks through my pores. The now-familiar sensation of fear and dread gathers momentum inside my palpitating chest. Oh god why?

I can see the Manager and Guard confer in the corridor, through the glass panel in the door. I sit there and hope: A pack of cigarettes is one thing- with any luck they will just give me a warning and ban me from Ralph's- but my real concern is my hidden stash. I had believed I had been doing so well. I had cleared the court case, alongside the Diversion Program assigned to first-time offenders- and was back in the legal clear. Complacency mixed with a tweaker mentality has put me back in the hot seat.

The Manager struts back in, ignores me, walks round the side of his desk and takes up his phone.

"Hello there . . . Hollywood Division . . . yeah . . . thief. . Yeah, pack o' cigarettes. Madam here thought she could add a free pack to the one she paid for. . . "He laughs heartily, then his tone becomes droll:

"No we're not running a 2-for-1 offer on cigarettes right now. . . He throws me a withering, tired once-over: "You guys know the type."

Gently replacing the phone he appraises me in an unnerving fashion.

"Hollywood are tied up but West Hollywood will be here within an hour. . . Have you got anything you shouldn't have in your pocketbook there?"

He raises his eyebrows for added effect. I estimate that this is probably the most exciting event in his sorry existence.

"Like what exactly? - Tampax, make up, keys-"

"I will repeat the question: Do you have anything that shouldn't be there?"

"I still don't understand what you mean?" I realise he is not going to let me walk so now I am obnoxious.

"Do you have any controlled substances on your person?" he demands, a flash of anger in his eyes.

"No!" I spit.

"Then you won't mind if I take a look then, will you?" He walks across his office with extended arm; I shove my bag in his fat, grubby paw eternally grateful that I did not slip Citri Lemon Conditioner inside as I had been tempted to do while I

181

walked the supermarket aisles earlier. Citri's bright yellow packaging and blazing Ralph's price ticker tag of $7.99 would have really made his day. Not that it would have made much difference, in terms of shoplifters' procedure, because it seems there is an issue of principle operating here, rather than a question of the material cost of stolen goods. A pack of cigarettes only cost $3.45, for fuck's sake.

Yet again LA's 'Zero tolerance' policing policy will prove to be my downfall. It had completely slipped my tweaker mind that in LA shoplifting is an imprisonable offence- maybe not for long, but time in jail nonetheless- even for a lousy pack of cigarettes.

His fat fingers are surprisingly nimble in their search of my things inside the black leather holdall. I am consciously praying in my head- 'please god, please god'- while offering serious penance for my sins. The hand lands on the Kodak film canister, with the roll inside and my stash inside that. He slowly pulls it out- 'What do have we here?' I look away casually and try to take in the Degas poster of *The Dancers* on the greying wall opposite, just like the one Grannie once had. Poor guy, having to call this shit-hole his office, but at least he has made an attempt to personalise it. Maybe he will become human and let me walk?

"I love that picture." I say quietly.

He moves onto my wallet, unclipping and unzipping, and flicks through the note section.

"You've got nearly 20 bucks and change in here! Why on earth did you steal the cigarettes?"

"I've already told you, sir, I made a mistake. We all make mistakes sometimes, don't we sir- No one's perfect and I've been working really hard and. . . ."

He nods his head in disbelief:

"I don't get you people, I really just don't get you. Why? Why on earth do you. . .?" His voice trails off, distracted by the sound of sirens approaching, announcing the arrival of the West Hollywood Police. I shrink into the hard chair with my head bowed in my hands. I push down the tears of humiliation that are welling up.

"Next time maybe you'll give things more thought and this'll be the last time you have to hear sirens on their way to pick you up?" He almost looks compassionate.

Following further discussion outside the door with two huge cops, one of them undoes his cuffs and signals for me to stand. He fixes them tightly on my wrists. They pinch and the coldness on my skin matches my rapid comedown.

"Sir is that really necessary?"

"It most certainly izzz." He hisses in an accentuated monosyllabic way.

Walking through the car park is even worse, with shoppers stopping in their tracks to gawp at me. In my leather and bead-adorned Versace jeans and silk wraparound blouse I clearly do not fit most people's stereotype of the common shoplifter.

In the back of the chilly panda car, all doors firmly locked with a grate separating me from the 'good guys', their chat is drowned out by the crackle of the radio. I slide down the vinyl seat wishing I was invisible.

Further discussion ensues back at the station- you would think LAPD had nothing better to do than worry about petty shoplifters- alongside extensive paperwork and a property search. I am eventually locked in a cell overnight. I take my one phone call and call Dee; I get the answering machine and leave a message, careful to speak in code in case the boys hear it. The cops do not find my stash.

They release me at 1:45pm the next day. I cross the road and use the payphone to call Dee.

"Please, please come and get me! I beg you, I'll do anything for you for ever after."

"What's going on now Clea?"

"I was arrested for one lousy pack of fucking cigarettes- I've just been released."

"You're unbelievable- you total idiot!! What were you thinking??!" She laughs with a mixture of hearty disgust and disbelief.

"Well that's the problem- I wasn't." I tell her drolly.

"Clea, you're heading for a fall and it's making me edgy."

"Okay, it was stupid, I know…but please. Just come and get me. . . okay?"

An hour later she pulls up in her Lexus. We drive back

to Ralph's and to my further horror my car has vanished from their car park. It had never crossed my mind that they would tow my car overnight.

Adding insult to injury I have to go in and find out which depot they have used. The bastards.

The tow yard is down La Brea at Crenshaw. Dee puts the $160 charge on her credit card for me because I am out of cash- I have about $95 in the bank- and credit cards are a luxury of the recent past. I promise, on my life, to pay her back within a week. I actually manage this because I finally get my state security sickness benefit allowance through for $980, four and a half months out of Promises. This windfall comes just in time because on top of my debt to Dee, my $650 rent is due.

There is also something wrong with the fuel pump on my car but because I have now missed my second payment I am unsure what to do about it. I am confident that I will soon get an acting or modelling job and pay off anyone I owe, including the Vronsky family, although it will obviously take quite a few jobs to clear that enormous debt. My plan to take control of my life seems to grow murkier with the passing of each accelerated day.

CHAPTER 20

Chrissie

Tell me why are we, so blind to see
That the ones we hurt, are you and me.
                    Gangsta's Paradise Coolio

Dirty: that's my first impression of Chrissie. She walks in with Henry and I find her vaguely repelling: She has slightly dirty, mousy brown hair, bad pale skin, too-tight clothes that need a wash, stubby nails and a stale smell- like a mild combination of rotten cheese and sweat- comes off her. She mumbles 'hi' and sits down on a bar stool, adrift in her own world.

I go into the bathroom with Henry (I never do deals in front of other people) and my face says what I think of his uninvited guest.

"Chrissie has been through a fuck of a lot ya know-"

"Like what?" I am genuinely interested, with a mix of compassion and curiosity.

"She had a baby-"

"Your baby?- You're kidding! No way!" I am shocked.

"Will you slow down and hear me out you fucking speed freak- not my baby, this other guy Sick, who's in jail at the moment."

"Oh how charming. What kind of a sick name is Sick? That's a joke right?"

"No- so she had her baby, a little girl called Taylor, but they wouldn't even let her hold her after she was born. They took her away straight off an' had her fostered- the foster parents were waiting at the hospital for Chrissie to give birth so they could take her immediately-"

185

"But that's horrific- how can that happen?"

"They declared her unfit-"

"Oh. . . right; that's sad, really sad- she looks messed up." Even my cold heart thaws a little. Henry continues:

"She needs a place to stay for a few months and I thought she could split the rent with you?"

"What? Where's she going to sleep?"

"I don't know- in the living room, or you could share your double bed, or something?"

I do need to pay my rent. I have fobbed them off three times already and it is becoming serious. I hate having to avoid the landlord and act like some scuzzy lowlife.

"Yeah, but she looks broke; does she actually have any money?"

"Her mother sent her a check to help fix her up after all this shit went down."

"I'll need $300 up front for the first month and we can see how it goes, okay?"

"Cool man, let's go talk to her about it." I snort up a fat one and follow Henry out into my living room where Chrissie appears to be reading one of my books. She looks up and gives me a sort of half smile and in that moment I figure I have a new friend. And let's face it: we all need friends, especially if they can split the rent.

~~~~~~~

I am relieved to unlock the apartment door and find it empty; thankfully Chrissie is out so I do not have to deal with her presence and her undesirable friends. She knows people that can only be classified as serious 'down and outs' and if I had known that was the world she was part of, I would never have let her move in. One time a guy showed up with a bleeding stab wound and refused to go to the hospital. He then tried to steal my car keys but fortunately for me I noticed just as he was creeping out the door; within a second I pounced on him and grabbed them back. Stealing from me and in front of me made me so furious that I kicked him out the door and slammed it hard, double locking it, despite his bleeding wound.

"Chrissie! I can't have these people in here!" I yelled at her.

"He found out I had a place- I didn't tell him." She shrugged, like that served as an excuse.

"Actually this is my place, not yours!" I tartly replied.

"And who covered more than half the rent last month?"

"Yeah, well, I let you borrow my car and I know you took it out when I crashed, coz you so kindly emptied the gas tank!"

Chrissie is the last person I would ever have chosen as a roommate; I barely even like her and I am sure the feeling is mutual. Another problem is her conversion to Islam that she has not entirely committed to, but boy does she rattle on about it and how we are all sinners, especially me. I agree with her and tell her I am perfectly happy to be a sinner and I'll take my chances in hell rather than walk about with a pale moon-face and a black shroud wrapped around my head like a deranged washerwoman that strikes me as insensitive to real Muslims. I suspect her supposed 'conversion' is her way of dealing with her feelings of loss and guilt over her baby girl, Taylor, although I am tempted to point out that thieving and drug-taking are hanging offences in Islam.

There are some material benefits, though, in terms of some new furniture- a huge navy corduroy sofa and decent stereo system- that she has taken out of Sick's storage facility, while he serves his time. When I ask about his jail sentence she gets a weird look and evades me so I have no idea what he is in jail for. But I do know that he had a fine line in humiliation: I heard one story about a guy who owed him money for drugs, came round to score and Sick had made him clean up, scrub down and vacuum his whole apartment while in the nude. And the guy had been so desperate he had actually done it.

I find a rough letter that she had written to him in jail, in one of my A4 notebooks:

Dear Vincent (Sick's real name)*,*

Thank you for the flyer and vocabulary sheet. I've already submitted to Islam through Shahad. I was debating for the past 3 months but it was time. I'm not living in the back of the store anymore. I needed an apartment for when I get Taylor back. I live about 2 blocks from Beverly Hills. I pretty much have a car now so I'll be able to get to work. I hear you're going to try and get Taylor. The social worker Lisa said I haven't shown enough stability yet but if I stay stable now I should have her for the 60 day visit and then permanently, after about 2 months. If it's any longer I'm just going to go to Arizona with her to my mom. I'd rather not have to do that but if that's what it takes to be with her all the time I will do it.

I'll always have some love for you, Sick. I do want to thank you for providing for me when we were together and you were out. Take care of yourself and peace unto you.

Love, Chrissie

PS: If you want Taylor you have to show up for court (which I know you can do), take parenting classes, drug and domestic violence counselling, drug testing.

Have you even started or tried to find out how she is?. . I guess it still bothers me how when I was sick just before I had her and you knew I was burning up, you never even brought us a Tylenol, or checked to see if we were even still alive. If Kath and Jerry didn't come we'd both be dead. Plus you weren't there when she was born. Or after. You never even came to see her at the hospital (how could you not even come see her?) Or ever try to do the things I told you they wanted you to do (the classes, and you said: "Counselling is for white folks")? . . . I'll never forbid you to see her. Except, if you go back to your old ways (tweaking, selling shit, guns) because your daughter deserves a father who is willing to do change and become the best he can.

She and I have a bond because when you hit us, hurt and upset us and left us (especially being that sick) it was just us together and we made it and it was just us in the delivery room and in the hospital. It still is just us. . . Never mind now, I'm getting too angry and I don't want to!

Anger is my initial response: anger at the horrific nature of her situation and fury that it is somehow destined to pollute mine, when the main reason I am on crystal meth is to banish pain from my memory.

Also, a sobering sense of messy confusion strikes me. How am I here sharing this apartment with a young woman so clearly in need of help? I cannot help her because I am seemingly incapable of helping myself. Also her lies about the apartment, work and having a car tip me into red alert.

~~~~~~~

I almost blow it, but somehow I get back just in time to get Chrissie to the Children's Court out in Monteray Park. She had made me swear on my life that I would drive her there for the hearing at 11:00am regarding Taylor and her foster parents. To me her situation seems unbelievable- verging on surreal- but I can hardly let her down over her baby girl even when I am collecting up a storm dumpster-diving. Picking through the contents of a dumpster was preferable to the all-too-real situation of Chrissie, the Muslim/tweaker/mother desperate to reunite with her baby. It touches a very raw nerve in me, but I still try to keep my promises.

Whenever she talks about Taylor I find myself leaving the room. It all seems so contradictory to have a baby when you are living as we do. Not in a hundred years would I bring a baby into this world I live in- it is plainly wrong. I guess I am not the only one who thinks like this considering that the nurse took her newborn away immediately, following her birth, on the orders of the hospital administrators. Chrissie has told me how they refused to let her hold her baby girl for even a second after the cord was cut, and the pain in her eyes and voice is intense and makes me feel incredibly uncomfortable. I have no idea how state law operates in this kind of case. From what I gather Chrissie was in a diabolical state when she was admitted to the free County Hospital. Sick, the father of the unborn baby, had gone awol and a few days later Chrissie was thrown out of their apartment in Hollywood.

Chrissie is furious that I am cutting it so fine, yelling and swearing at me.

"Just get in the fucking car okay!" I order because I can

189

see she is at breaking point. She wears a black sweater over a long grey skirt resembling attire more suitable for a funeral, but I assume she has given this some thought because I have never seen these clothes before.

Once in the car I ask for directions. She looks at me blankly.

"What do you mean you don't know how to get there?" I scream. I cannot stand her inability to take some control over the proceedings. She looks at me with doleful, tear-brimmed eyes, begging for my help; she is a lost soul for sure and she needs me right now. I pull over and rummage through my trunk for the Thomas Guide. I am a horrific map-reader but I need to get us there by 10.55 at the outside. Desperation and fear of the outcome- for all of us- focuses my tweaker mind and I manage to work out a route.

We get there on time. She runs in and I arrange to come back in an hour and a half. I drive away quickly as the circling patrol cars and uniformed personnel freak me out. I head into a gas station and spend about half an hour in the toilet, doing my make up and a fat line to give me the courage to not bail out of here.

Chrissie sits on the low wall outside the courthouse. She holds some paperwork close to her chest. Her eyes stare ahead, glazed and dulled.

I drive and smoke a couple of cigarettes. Clearly she is in no mood to talk. We are waiting at the lights when I hear a strange hissing sound. Alarmed I think it is coming from the engine but then realise the unusual sound emits from Chrissie. A seething, angry hiss from deep within her:

"I'm gonna get back my baby! How dare those fucking assholes tell me what is right for my baby! She's my baby! My baby! My baby! How dare they judge me- who the fuck are they? I'm gonna get back my baby and you're gonna help me, okay!" She does not yell exactly, but her voice penetrates the air with a newfound determination and vigour that I find frightening. I do not want to be part of her life in this way; I only needed a room-mate to help cover the rent. What have I got myself into? Her evident pain and frustration fills every molecule within the framework of the car and I find myself telling her:

"Yes of course we'll get Taylor back for you. . ." I say it with as much gusto and belief that I can muster, because I know that is what she needs to hear. And quite frankly her ferocity is scary and I do not want her turning on me in a state of misplaced anger and frustration.

Back in the apartment Chrissie is more focused than I have ever witnessed. Lissa stops over on her bicycle and joins forces with us, apparently determined to help Chrissie with her court battle; maybe she too has lost a child for all I know? They read through paperwork together and discuss a plan of action. Their sudden togetherness is irritating and Lissa tops it off by announcing:

"We all really need to get our shit together. You too Clea!"

"Yeah sure, you bet!" I acquiesce.

"That means quitting crystal meth, guys!" Lissa catchs my eye; I cannot tell whether she is sincere because she has been on crank for at least 4 years and I have never heard her mention getting clean before. Maybe this is her incentive. But it certainly is not mine. I say nothing, go into my bedroom and pull the door to.

I am too far along this dead-end road now. I have no idea where I am going, what I want or what I need. All I care about is maintaining this suspended state by knowing that my next line is taken care of. My escape from myself with these semi-derelict characters is pathetic but I do not have the energy left that would be required to reform it. That is where I am at and no girl and her lost baby is going to change that.

Chrissie and Lissa's head fuck must have sent me off to sleep because the next thing I know I am being prodded awake alongside Lissa's whiney yell.

"Clea, Clea- wake up! Ya gotta wake up!"

"What the hell's going on?" I muster, confused and in very bad humour. Why won't these witches get lost and leave me in my wholly dysfunctional peace?

"Get up, Clea, get up!" Even Chrissie is almost foaming at the mouth.

"You got the part in some commercial- Budweiser Beer I think. Girl, move your ass!" Lissa excitedly tells me, adding:

"You're gonna be a movie star."

"You gotta call them- your agency left, like, five messages!"

"Okay, okay- I'll call."

I had gone to a casting for a beer commercial- was it weeks or months ago? - and I had forgotten all about it because I had stopped calling the Model Agency due to the reality that even getting to that one casting had been a major trial. I had taken hours to get ready- the part was for a 'sexy barmaid'- and I had been in heaven tweaking over what to wear. Eventually I had gone with a pair of paisley Versace leggings that Dee had given me, a boob tube, heels with a denim jacket. That was the fun bit. Finding the venue had thrown me into total disarray and after three calls to the Agency, I eventually found the casting suite. They were ready to call it a day when I stormed in with total attitude demanding to be seen. To my amazement the advertising posse, the director and casting director sat back down. Then the director outlined the scene: 'You're serving drinks at the bar and this totally evil dude walks in and freaks ya out, but ya can't take your eyes off him, like he's mesmerised you'. All I had to do was visualise Ajax and I was in the right frame of mind. It was the best fun I'd had in months.

"Very real, powerful stuff- you're good." The Director says, while the casting director nods in agreement. I beam and privately thank crystal for giving me the chutzpah to waltz in there late and pull it off.

A buzz of excitement infiltrates my weary being- maybe all is not lost? - and I phone my agency who tell me what time to go and where. They also make me promise that I won't let them down. The fee is $3000 so I would be a total fool to mess this one up. And that money would enable me to kick Chrissie out and get my life back on some kind of reasonable track. Finally, I see a way out that does not involve breaking the law.

The shoot is in West LA- about 20 minutes drive away- and I make it on time, making sure I clean myself up. My personal hygiene has started to slip. With no job to go to and a life dedicated to tweaking this is not surprising, but I want to appear shiny and fresh- like a professional.

A runner takes me into wardrobe and I change into a diner waitress uniform and then have my make-up done and

192

my hair poofed up into a bouffant do. It feels great to be back on a set and a little part of me realises what I have been missing. We shoot the set up, which requires me to walk to and fro for a few times, without saying anything, and to carry a tray of beer. It only takes about 40 minutes and I am done.

People hover around the craft service table and a couple of the camera crew flirt with a pretty brunette who is a production assistant on the team. Their easy banter and flirting serves to make me feel like the total outsider and I try to strike up conversation, but I sense the young guy thinks I'm either a freak, or weird or both. I cannot read people anymore and I decide I need to leave as quickly as possible because I am becoming distinctly paranoid that people can tell I am tweaking and it is freaking them out. Or they are freaking me out because they are not tweaking and I am only used to being around tweakers these days.

The truth is I have lost my basic social skills; I have forgotten how to hold a regular, friendly conversation.

Thankfully the production manager approaches me and releases me, before I become more agitated by the fact that something I had previously taken for granted is now a serious challenge:

"Thanks for the good work. Take it easy."

Does he suspect I am eager to get away because I have a date with my dealer? Can he see straight through me? Anxiety rises in my chest and throat and I virtually rip off my costume, desperate to escape this everyday set-up that feels like a foreign landscape to me now.

In a state of panic I pull into a strip mall and enter a liquor store. I buy a couple of beers and miniature vodka. I rip off the vodka top as soon as I am out of the store and drink it down in one. I really need something to take the edge off and the vodka does the trick. I rarely drink alcohol now so its full effects on my empty stomach are noticeable. My anxiety disappears and I feel 'normal' again. I console myself with what I hope is a reality check; I mean how would the people working on the commercial know I was a tweaker? I was letting my paranoia get the better of me.

CHAPTER 21

Betrayal

Damaged people are dangerous. They know
they can survive.
Damage Josephine Hart

A sharp metallic twang awakes me; someone is
knocking on my window:
"Clea, Clea. . ." over and over.
Immediately I recognise Ajax's voice. I struggle to stand
because my toes are massively stiff. I realize I crashed
wearing my cowboy boots. Like a giddy child I am overcome
with joy and I race to unlock the front door. This will be the first
time we have been alone together in months and my
imagination is racing. I quickly check my face in the bathroom
mirror and I look okay, considering I have just woken up. I
quickly apply some lipstick and pinch my cheeks for colour. All
my fury, jealousy and suspicions vanish at the prospect of
being with him again.
"Well hello! Come on in." I smile warmly.
Ajax stands there, poker faced. He takes something
from his jacket pocket and flashes some kind of badge at me.
"I'm with the FBI and I've come to pick up Dee's things-
the ring in particular." Is he for real? His voice is deadly
serious. What ring? What is he talking about? And since when
is he an FBI agent?
"I don't have time to hang around- just get the ring."
"What ring...?"

"You know perfectly well. Just quit your 'I'm such a cute, little English girl act' coz it doesn't wash with me anymore. You showed me the goddamn ring yourself!"

Dee's hair ring! I had forgotten all about it. Why is he here asking for it? How does he even know about it? And then I recall how I had shown it off the night I had taken it- months ago now. But how is he connected to Dee and how does he know it belonged to her?

He struts around my apartment as if on important business; in fact who exactly does he think he is? I remember my pearls- the stolen pearls!

"Now hang on a moment Mr. Bigshot-I'm-an-FBI-Agent! What the fuck happened to my pearls? It's strange how one day you're warning me about thieves and the next day my pearls are gone and you're suddenly driving round in a 4x4?!"

Ajax does not even look at me but continues to rifle through my belongings on the counter like some nosey bureaucrat. I continue, gathering more steam:

"And then you have the audacity to waltz back in here accusing me of god-knows-what when I know you sold my stuff at that pawn shop on Santa Monica- I know you did and you can lie all you want but I know!"

Ajax comes up close now and in that split second I think- and hope- that he's going to kiss me and make all this badness vanish. Instead he quietly says:

"When I met you, I liked you. I thought you had a chance to do something with yourself, but look at you now; you're disgusting, pathetic- you make me sick! You play out your little 'sweet, English girl' routine but I'm telling you once and once only that you are going so far down you will never see the light again. Give me the ring."

I am in shock. How can he stand there and speak to me like this? It is beyond my comprehension. What have I ever done to him to deserve this vitriol and hatred?

"Give me the ring!!" Ajax yells.

"No!" I yell back.

He steps forward and his hands are round my throat. Is he testing me further?

"I told you I don't have it!"

"Give me the ring!"

"No!"

He starts to exert pressure; I am unable to breathe- he does not let up. I choke. I panic; I raise my arm in defeat. He eases off. I hate him. I do not understand him- one moment he is my friend, now he is clearly my enemy. Why? What have I ever done to him?

"I'll find it. . ." I splutter, spittle running down my chin. My appearance has taken a back seat now.

"Get it, bitch!"

I had forgotten about it- guilt perhaps- but I rummage through a shelf in my bedroom and find it sitting in a small beaded, green purse. Funny really because I have not worn it or taken it out of that little purse since the night I showed it to Ajax.

I give it to him; he throws the purse on the bed.

"And I had thought you were a nice English girl." He smirks.

"Get out, you bastard."

I am confused. Then it hits me. The only explanation is very simple and explains why Dee suddenly turned against me- Ajax is with her now, but how and when did this happen? Then it dawns on me that I had been the one who introduced them.

I jump in my car and I pull up outside her building. I am not clear as to what my purpose here is but I know I want to see Dee and know if my suspicions are right. She had known how I felt about Ajax and I find it hard to believe she would betray me like this or that she would let a fairly suspect character like Ajax into her life and her family's home.

I ring the doorbell. No answer. I ring again. I step back onto the lawn and I look up; Ajax is at the window, looking at me, a triumphant look spreads across his face. A flood of emotion hits me- confusion, pain, anger- and I ring the bell again. I hear muffled voices from inside, or am I imagining it?

Now I lose myself- I bang the door, I lean on the bell and I scream:

"Dee, you fucking bitch. You owe me an explanation. How could you betray me like this? I was supposed to be your friend. Doesn't that mean anything? I know I shouldn't have taken the ring- I was going to give it back. I promise I was. I just want to talk to you, hear it from you first hand."

I am kneeling on her front lawn, wailing and sobbing to myself: "I just want things to go back to how they were before." The content of my bag has tipped out and a man walking his Chihuahua has crossed over to the other side of the street. I look up and all the curtains and blinds have been closed. The message is clear. I have no choice but to gather up my belongings and get back in my car. I can barely see to drive through my tears. I am gutted like a flailing fish that won't die. It is as if my own mother has abandoned me all over again and everything bad that has ever happened is being relived in this precise moment.

My world has collapsed and where does the fault lie? The fault line is filled in with crystal meth- evil, clever, insidious and toxic- and I know I have only myself to blame. But Dee playing a part?- She was my good friend and no friend has ever betrayed me over a man, a thieving, deceptive man who seemingly had us both wrapped around his little finger.

Back at my apartment I pack up the car with anything that I deem valuable- namely my computer, some china that I wrap in clothes in a suitcase and cosmetics. Besides my art deco collection nothing here is worth much, not even the computer, but I still want it with me so that maybe I can get writing on one of those projects stashed in its memory. I cannot remember what they are, but maybe if I can find a safe place I will be able to re-connect with that lost part of my mind? Maybe. . .

I am in the car park at Ralph's on Fairfax and Santa Monica where I had first met Henry to score that first gram following Promises. I go in and buy a packet of cigarettes. Then I page Henry from the payphone outside and I have to wait for him to call me back, while holding the phone down but speaking to an imaginary person because two people are waiting to use it.

"What?" Henry growls.

"It's Clea- I'm in the car park at Ralph's."

"Okaaay- something up?"

"Yeah- an emergency. Can you meet me here?"

"Take me a couple of hours-"

"I'll be here waiting."

By the time Henry arrives I am enjoying the attention of the security guard who seems to find me amusing. Henry pulls up in the space next to mine, jumping out of his new, glaring white Golf convertible, that I had gone with him to buy last week with wads of cash.

"What's going on? Are you okay?"

"Yeah I'm good-"

"So why's your car packed up with all your stuff, Clea- Are you moving? What's going on?" I give the Security Guard a look that says 'I'll catch ya later' and he heads off back to guard Ralph's (pity he was not on duty when I got arrested for the unpaid-for pack of fags!).

"I'm not sure why I'm here. I guess to score-"I suddenly feel really stupid.

"Ya said there was an emergency- I was having Sunday lunch with my mom! It doesn't look so hot when I get ten pages just as we sit down to roast chicken ya know; she'll think I'm a drug dealer, or something. . ."

"You are a drug dealer Henry." I remind him.

"Yeah but she doesn't know that; so you called me out here for a deal and I only saw you yesterday! For fuck's sake- your nose'll melt soon!"

"What?! Keeping records now are we? . . . Okay look there was a situation with Ajax and"- Henry looks away, embarrassed:

"Right . . .I guess ya found out he's living with that friend of yours then?"

"You knew?!- Why the fuck didn't you tell me? I can't believe it?!"

"What difference would it make? Ya know what Clea- as I told ya already 500 times Ajax is seriously bad news; he'll fuck her up real bad, I know, girlfriend!"

"Well, that's real consolation, I must say."

"Forget it! Forget about him and forget about her- they're not worth the head space."

"Believe me I intend to. So where's the party?"

A couple of hours later I sit on the edge of Lissa's bath while Henry prepares his syringe. Lissa sits on the floor, head tipped back against the wall, eyes closed. She never says much when Henry's around, but somehow still manages to look pretty in a doll-face way; if you look close, though, you can see the ravages around her eyes and mouth, like little slits tearing through from the inside of her taut skin.

Henry rolls up his sleeve and Lissa hands her jeans belt to him that he uses as a tourniquet. He finds a vein easily- he's quite new to injecting- and eases the mixture into his wiry frame. Smack and crystal hit him and he sways, grinning from ear to ear like a happy tramp.

"My turn now!" Henry hands over the gear to Lissa who sterilises the needle with a lighter and sets about getting her hit.

"What about me?" I ask.

Henry explodes with guffaws of low, deep sounds that resemble a strange form of laughter:

"Are you fucking insane Clea! Man oh man- you fruitcake."

"What the fuck are you talking about? Why am I insane, exactly? I only want to get high."

"No! No needles for you! You couldn't cope- you'd be dead within a week." Henry's tone of voice is surprisingly adamant.

"You don't mean it?" I am unsure how to take this.

"Unabomber, I don't want your blood on my hands- we're friends right?"

"Yeah- I guess we are." In that moment I see beyond Henry the addict and his drug dealer persona to the truly good man he could be.

200

CHAPTER 22

Coming Around Again

We're visiting the Castle of Fear. She's
the mistress of the house.
Leonora Carrington *The House of Fear*

A knuckle bangs frantically against my car window-
'what the fuck?!' The middle-aged man with a crooked smile
knocks and waves intermittently. He must think I know him. I
take off my sunglasses and pull my car up alongside Kanter's
on Fairfax, where the man had approached me, while I was
stopped at the lights.

I do know him. Of course, it's Jeremiah, who I've not
seen for what feels like an age, but is in reality only six months.
I'd met him with Marnie a few times- they were occasional
lovers- and I had visited him alone, because I found him weird,
but great company.

Bizarrely he was also the father of an acquaintance from
Brown who had graduated in the same year as me. The fact
that he is a father gives me comfort, although he is as far away
from the suburban dad-image a man could possibly be and
certainly the polar opposite to my father, but there is an
unrecognisable similarity that may be to do with his pale skin
and the clean smell that comes off it. Maybe they just use the
same soap: Imperial Leather.

I roll down the window.

"Hey can I get in?"

Before I have time to respond he is opening the
passenger door.

"How are ya Clea? Well there are no coincidences coz I was just talking about you yesterday. I've got someone at my place who really wants to see you. . . Actually she really needs to see you."

I know he means Marnie. The question is, do I want to see her?

"To be honest I don't think I can deal with her recriminations right now- I've got enough on my plate."

Jeremiah looks vaguely confused; he shakes his head.

"Let's go back to my place? She'll be thrilled to see you, I promise."

"I don't know. . ." I mumble, seriously torn.

"She really needs a friend. Please."

I park in the familiar back alley, parallel to Fairfax and about 5 minutes walk from Kanter's.

Strangely, there is a sense of good about Jeremiah that makes me feel safer than I have in a long while. Entering his place, in the far corner, is a stepladder leading to a loft where I can see the edge of a mattress and bedclothes. He gestures that I should go up:

"Marnie's up there- she hasn't moved for four days. Maybe you can talk some sense into her?"

"I'm hardly the good Samaritan, now, am I?"

"Well she can't stay up there forever and it's beginning to get on my nerves- she's off about that Gabe Doverman again."

"I'll do my best."

I climb up the ladder and lift myself onto the edge of the bed across from where she is scrunched up in a ball, with a cream and blue floral quilt tucked around her. I had not expected to find Marnie like this. The feisty, headstrong redhead who had taken umbrage at my skittish behaviour and tried to mother me is reduced to a balled up, whimpering mess. Part of me wants to gloat but I can sense the tensed up anxious pain emanating from her. She always claimed we had been Native American Plains Indians together in another life and maybe she is right. I gently pull back the quilt from her tear stained, pale face- she looks terrible with dark circles round her eyes- while strands of her thinning hair stick to her bony temples.

"Marnie, what's happened?" She shudders and pulls the cover back over her head. Quiet, rhythmic sobs make the bed pulsate.

"Please Marnie, It's Clea, your friend. I'm here to help you."

"Go away! Just leave me alone; I wanna be left alone. Alone!" Marnie growls. Her message is clear, but this is not the woman I know; the woman who was straight up- harsh, yes- but honest, so I decide to give as good as I had been given by her, in better times:

I stand up, fling back the cover in one strong move and eyeball Marnie, who shrinks more in amazement, than anything else:

"I am not going to leave you alone, alright. Jeremiah ran into me on Fairfax and asked me back here for a reason. Now you are going to tell me what has been going on. What has happened to put you in such a state? I need you to be honest with me."

Marnie scrambles under the covers for a clump of tissues and blows her nose with vigour; this is more the Marnie I recognise.

"Have you got a cigarette?"

"Yeah, sure." I find them and we both light up, smoke circling around the small dim spotlights fitted into the ceiling.

"Jeremiah's is some crazy kind of place to live in," she comments

"Certainly, different to before.. . . when I lived with you."

"You won't believe me if I tell you; no one else does, so why should you?"

"Try me Marnie, for fuck's sake!"

"I found a kid's body in a dumpster- a little boy. He must have been eight, or so. . . he didn't have any fingers or toes." Tears start streaming down her face. I put my hand on hers.

"Go on."

"His body was in a real mess- cut, bruises- oh god . . . "

"So what did you do?"

"I went home and I called the police and arranged to meet them there but when they opened up the dumpster he was gone."

"What did the police say?"

203

"They asked if I'd been taking hallucinogenic drugs and they laughed- can you believe they laughed like it was some kind of funny joke when some poor little boy was dead and. . . "

"Actually I can believe it-"

"Then they gave me a citation for wasting police time; some kind of dumb ass warning-"

"So what happened to the body do you think?"

"They took it. . . somewhere else- to dispose of it properly."

"Who's 'they'?"

"Who 'dya think?- Gabe Doverman and his goons; I know it was them coz I found something else-"

"What?"

"A locked up garage- it belongs to Gabe." Marnie is alert and frenzied.

"Are you crazy?- You can't go breaking into his property- that's asking for serious trouble!"

"Clea, we're talking about innocent children here. What do you expect me to do?"

Somehow I wish that Jeremiah had not seen me driving along Fairfax because things were spiralling in a way that made me feel decidedly queasy. But at least Marnie now had the gleam of hope back in her blood-shot eyes:

"You got any crystal? Then I can take you and show you."

Marnie pulls up on North Citrus and Waring. She leads the way to the back of a boarded up house, pointing a flashlight. I am very nervous even though there is no one out on the streets. It must be 3:00 in the morning and any noise our feet make seems to amplify ten-fold. Marnie leads the way in a highly purposeful manner; any inkling as to her state of mind two hours ago has vanished. Now she is on a mission.

The front of the garage in the back is bolted down in the two lower corners. She creeps round the back where there is a patch of overgrown weeds and some discarded broken pieces of furniture piled up haphazardly.

She flings a chair to reveal the handle of a door that has been clearly broken into. She yanks it open and takes my hand. We enter and the first thing that hits me is the smell of strong disinfectant that makes my eyes sting and water.

Marnie leans in, whispering:

"Now you'll see what I mean!" Her tone is jubilant, if a little off-key. She shines the torch around the small rectangular space and it is empty, save a disgusting futon folded and stuffed in the far corner.

"I don't believe it!?- All the stuff's gone. . ." Her face shines likes the moon in the half-light; she is paler than before if that is possible.

"What's all gone?"

"The stuff- the torture stuff- it was all attached to the walls and there was sound-proofing material up on the walls. I promise you- I swear on my life!"

"I never said I didn't believe you, Marnie." I try to sound like the voice of reason.

She is now down on all fours, closely inspecting the wall:

"Look! Clea please look! There was this device here with wrist holds and these holes here-" She frantically moves around flashing the torch at holes in the plaster and at remnants of strips of polystyrene covered in some kind of silver material:

"This is the sound-proofing stuff- it's the cheapest you can get, but totally effective."

"Marnie, I'm not saying I don't believe you but maybe it was some kind of weird S&M club for consenting adults?"

"I have something back at my apartment I need to show you- they've already cleared this place out. All I can say is these guys are professionals."

Marnie has the knack of drawing me in, even when I try to make a conscious effort not to be drawn in. She has mentioned nothing about the weirdness that had resulted between us after she threw me out, or anything about my sojourn in rehab, but looking at her she is clearly using and drinking a lot. She always had a beer on the go and I would guess she probably drinks about 20 bottles a day now to hold herself down. She also pops pills but she will not let me see what they are, keeping them hidden away in her pocket.

Back at her apartment she goes to her fridge and gets something out of the freezer. She unwraps the plastic wrapping and opens a small black enamel-like box.

"This might really freak you out Clea- you might wanna sit down?"

"Oh come on! I'm not that much of a pussy-"

Marnie slowly opens the box and I am faced with a creamy white thing that at first I do not register but then it dawns on me that it is actually a frozen finger tip, with the nail intact, about an inch long. Judging by the size it must have belonged to a child. I run into the bathroom, retching.

Marnie yells after me:

"Sorry but I did warn you."

"I wasn't expecting that for fuck's sake! Where the hell did it come from?"

"That garage- I found it in the corner, hidden under some skirting."

"I can't believe it- that's so sick!"

"Now 'dya understand why I was so upset?"

"Yes of course. But what did Jeremiah say?"

"He said don't get involved in things I'll never understand. All he cares about are his goddamned conspiracy theories." She pulls a face.

"So where's the . . . thing?"

"My evidence you mean?"

"Yeah-"

"I put it back in the freezer. I'd like to reunite it with the body but I doubt that'll be possible."

"This is seriously frightening stuff Marnie- I mean what can we do?"

"I really don't know, I just don't know." Her eyes well up again and I go to hug her. We hold each other for a long time, crying together.

CHAPTER 23

Car Trouble

Thanks to our desperation for speed,
we live in an age of rage.

Carl Honore *In Praise of Slow*

"What the hell's going on?"

I run out the sliding doors and through the back gate to see my Chevy Malibu backing out of the driveway. I vaguely recognise the man in my driver's seat.

"Wait!! What are you doing? For fuck's sake, stop!"

He slowly brakes, rolling down the window, turning to face me with a smug grin across his unshaven, course features:

"Tough shit, baby- I found ya again an' she's mine!"

"But you can't do this- that's my car!"

"You owe me over a $2000 – did ya really think I was just gonna let that go?"

"Please- can't we talk about it? We can work something out? Payments, or something. Please!" I plead.

"Honey, you had payments but ya didn't keep 'em up, now did ya?"

He is right but I had wanted to contest the final ones because the gas pump needed a total overhaul and I felt they should have knocked that off the overall price because that would cost about $800 to fix. I had left some messages, no one had responded and then I had . . . forgotten. Like I had 'forgotten' to keep up my car insurance, my rent and my phone bill- the list goes on and on. But taking my car? No!

"How did you find me?"

"It's not that hard, ya know babe! See ya!" And he is gone. Is this the beginning of the end- again? Back again in exactly the same weak and desperate position like some perverse deja-vu. I cannot fathom how I'd had the stupidity and naivety to believe it would be different this time around. Same result, different circumstances: whereas before I had totalled my Volvo and then been arrested a few days later for trying to cash a stolen cheque, now my car had been repossessed because I had reneged on my car payments. I wish I could turn back time, knowing full well I cannot and the only person I have to blame is myself.

I lock myself in my bedroom and sit at my dressing table for minutes or hours- I cannot tell- snorting lines and pondering, the thoughts clustering my tired and worn brain, what to do. I am almost in a trance state- I have not slept for two days- and I need to make a decision. But decisions are based on a selection of choices and what choice do I have?

And then it comes to me- I'll steal the car back. All I need to do is find it. After all, I still have my keys and it could be parked on the street. I know the Auto Dealer lives near his business from past conversations when we had been on amiable terms. I know it will be in Venice somewhere.

A beat-up, black Cadillac curb-crawls while I walk along Venice Boulevard. It is at least the fifth car that has followed me in the last hour. Why won't they just leave me alone? I am looking for my car, not business in the sex trade.

I am a woman obsessed. I comb every street from Venice Boulevard to Main Street to Rose Avenue and all the streets and lots in between. On foot this takes me three days and by day three, the heavens have opened and I am drenched to the skin. I am ready to collapse when a maroon Chrysler pulls up to the curb and I find myself drawn to the car, my exhaustion overtaking any fear. The car window glides down:

"Hi- I saw you yesterday on Abbot Kinney. I'm on my way home from work. 'Dya need a ride somewhere?"

I look at him through my rain-soaked hair, pushing it back to see whether he looks regular enough. Is it possible that he is just a person taking pity on me? He is about twenty-four and he looks like he works in a bank.

"Which way are you heading?"

"Towards West LA, but I don't mind dropping you off somewhere-"

"I'm really wet-"

"I can see that- I thought you looked lost- no offence but. . . it's kinda dangerous round here when it's dark." No kidding! He leans across to the passenger door, easing it open for me.

"Get in- I'm not gonna hurt ya, or anything. I'm Phil by the way."

But I might hurt him if he tries anything because I have my knife tucked into my jeans. However I keep this to myself.

"So ya gotta place I can drop ya to?"

"I live near Beverly and La Cienaga- anywhere near there will do- Thanks."

The traffic is slow which comforts me because I know I could make a run for it if he tries anything.

"Wha'dya doin' out in Venice walkin' around all by yerself?"

"Someone stole my car- I'm trying to get it back."

"Why don't ya go to the cops?"

"Errrr- yeah, could do I suppose."

"Ya hungry? You look kinda like ya could do with some food-"

I am famished, but I have no money on me- beyond bus fair- because now the only way I can get any is to write cheques with my English chequebook- for a maximum of £50- and I have to go into the bank to do this and I have been too absorbed in my mission to retrieve my car.

"I am a little actually." A mile or so on he pulls into a drive-through Jack in the Box.

"Well. . . what 'dya want?" He looks over and smiles like he is talking to a four year old.

"Large curly fries, please."

We drive out and I tuck into the fries, oblivious to him now, as my desire for food takes over.

"You're pretty hungry, aren't ya? So ya got a place?"
He says with disbelief. His tone is starting to irritate me, like he
sees me as some kind of pet project, casting himself as the
good Samaritan. I continue to stuff my face.

"I guess ya don't have a job?"

"What's it to you?" I demand.

"Well a job is always a good place to start when things
are rough, ya know."

"Oh really!" Sarcasm spits out the side of my mouth.

"Where I work In Venice at the Post Office they have
some vacancies- I could put in a good word for ya. How'd ya
like that. It could get ya off the street and give ya some self-
respect back. Wha'dya think of that little idea?"

"Pull over here!"

He ignores me.

"Pull over here!" I scream. He indicates and slowly
moves across to the side of the road; his eyes flicker
nervously. Before he brings the car to a stop I have my knife
out- the one Henry had given me 'just in case'- and I lean up to
him, the knife glinting and darting from the street lights and
sheets of rain all over the pale skin of his neck.

I now tower above him and wallow in the fear in his
scared eyes. A low evil laugh erupts in me.

"Whoa- steady now miss. You can take whatever you
like- my wallet, my cash, the car, whatever-"

"I don't want anything from you, you judgemental
bastard! What gives you the right to judge me? I'll tell you
what- Nothing! Who the fuck are you with your cosy little job at
the post office and your neat and ordered little life- Well I say
fuck that!" I move the knife away and click it closed.

"You know what I am?- Huh? Do you know?" I shout.

The poor guy shakes his head slowly, like he is fearful
any quick motion might bring the knife out again.

"I am tired, very tired, and the last thing I need right now
from a goddamn fucking stranger is a pep talk, okay. . . thanks
for the fries." I shove open the car door and stand there until he
regains his composure and drives away.

The two mile walk home is fast because I am buzzing
with hate- hate for the good Samaritan, hate for LA, hate for life
and pure hatred of me.

I suspect that I have become one of those people that Amory had warned me about when I first started working for him. One of those people on the street that parents point out, as they drive by: 'Hey kids, stay away from drugs otherwise you'll end up like her'. I have become a warning to others of what no one in their right mind wants to become- an isolated, violent, self-destructive, self-hating person.

At the entrance gate to the car lot I follow closely behind two young Hispanic men. I wear a baseball hat low down in case the dealership owner is on the premises. I had remembered how once, when I had been considering buying the Chevy Malibu, one of the workers there had told me the owner was down the road at the other car depot. It had suddenly dawned on me that was where my car was, locked away in that huge lot. I had passed it on my travels throughout Venice but had passed it at night when it was locked up with at least three dogs on guard, who howled if I even touched the wire mesh fence. I deduce that the only way to possibly get my car back was to get in there in daylight hours when mechanics were there working on cars in the front.

I follow closely behind the men and they seem to know the lot; one turns and smiles at me while I tread lightly but purposefully towards the vast array of lined up cars. I see mine in the far right corner parked between a blue and a black car, her snotty green colour making her highly visible. My heart is racing. I had arrived early that morning to stake it out and see what the chances were of entering without drawing attention to myself. The place is so large and thus far I had seen only two mechanics at work. One was under a car and the other was speaking with a middle-aged salesman type when I had tagged along behind the two guys.

I yank out my keys; I halt my urge to run to the car as this could draw attention to me. I sidle along and they turn off to the row of cars before the last row where my Chevy is parked. I speed up now and get to the car quickly unlocking the door. I jump in, shove the key in the ignition, and turn. Nothing. I turn again, foot down hard on the gas. Nothing! The battery is

211

dead.

The guys are driving towards me on their way out when I jump out the car, waving and plastering on a friendly smile:

"Hey, you guys?" I incline my head suggestive of my dire need of a favour.

"Whazzup?" The driver responds.

"Could you please give me a jump? I've got some cables- it'll take a couple of minutes, that's all- I promise!"

"Errrrr, yeah okay." They pull in close so their car is nose to nose with mine while I fling up the bonnet, having retrieved the cables from the trunk. I have never moved this fast before in my life but I figure any second now one of the mechanics is going to guess that something is not quite adding up. I attach the prongs to their battery and to mine. The passenger gets out to help me, but I have already set it all up.

"Thanks!" I shout as I jump behind the wheel and turn on the ignition again. For a second my heart sinks with a dread of failure but I try again and the engine fires. Yes! I jump out and rip off the cables from my car battery, then smash down the bonnet. The guy standing by starts yelling:

"Whad th' fuck lady- we helping you out here! Fuck man. . ."

I ride the accelerator and zip round almost clipping their car. Now they look really pissed off but all I care about is getting out of the lot. Right now I could be done for stealing, but once I am back on neutral ground I am in the clear because possession is nine tenths of the law.

I go hell for leather through the gates; nothing will stop me now. A tied-up dog barks and I hear yells from behind: 'Hey stop, you there stop!' but I do not even check my mirror because all I want is to get as far away as quickly as possible.

I speed off along Venice and onto the 10 freeway. I am exploding with exhilaration and joy to be back with my baby. All is not lost- I have my car back. I drive for over two hours leaving Venice far behind. The car needs a long run to re-charge the battery and I am thrilled to be back behind the wheel. I am so damn pleased with myself I buzz with adrenaline. The only thing now is to find a place to store the car when I am at home because they know where I live.

Having my car re-possessed was a shot of reality, once

the initial paralysis had worn off. But stealing it back was a dangerous thing to do- if I had been caught on the way out they could have literally done with me what they wished because I was on their property. I was lucky! I am buoyed by my 'triumph', as I perceive it, but this is short lived because the rent is due and there is no way I can pay my share. I am now selling all my appliances- TV, video, microwave- at the pawn store to cover my necessary expenditure: crystal meth, gas, cigarettes, Snapple Iced Tea, Oreos and Reeses Peanut Butter Cups- in that order of priority.

Each day I feel weaker and my eyes and ears spin, depending on the light and weather; my muscles are wasting away. I admit- at least to myself- that I have failed miserably. I really had believed that I could beat crystal meth in my own way, having learned some new tricks. I had deluded myself into thinking I could control my usage enough to maintain a regular routine and lifestyle. But once crystal meth is in my system- surely now part of my DNA- it is entirely impossible for me to comprehend such an idea.

The trap of crystal is terrifying in its powerfulness. Even when Chrissie had voiced her intention to quit crystal meth once and for all, I had recoiled and literally hidden from the conversation.

Because I live in constant fear of Chrissie and her weird posse I have selected an assortment of my most precious and favourite things- mainly art deco china, chotskes- anything I like that I know magpie tweakers will grab and take if it is sitting around, even in my own apartment- and packed them away in the large LV suitcase. I then stored it in a locker out in the garages which I padlocked; the locker needs a ladder to get up into and my landlord had shown it to me when I first moved in. I am the only person who knows about it, as far as I know.

Henry cuts lines out on a plate; he passes it to me having snorted two fat ones. He is even more agitated than usual and he starts to rifle through a satchel bag he had come in with. He presents a frayed piece of newspaper from the LA Times and shoves it at me:

"Take a look at this!"

I read out the headline:

Decayed Body of West Hollywood Grandmother found in rolled up carpet in locked closet.

Uhhh! So what about it?"

"Read the rest!" His tone races with urgency.

I really have to concentrate in order to do this:

"The decayed body of a 79 year old woman was discovered yesterday inside a rolled up rug, inside a closet in a West Hollywood apartment on Crescent Heights. The body has now been identified as belonging to Mary Rubens. According to Forensic Scientists she had put up a strong fight and had survived inside the carpet for almost two months, finally dying from dehydration and starvation. Her apartment had been ransacked and according to her niece who had been in Europe throughout this period, about $25000 worth of jewellery had been stolen, along with many other possessions, some seemingly of little to no value. The police believe the thieves were inexperienced and panicked. They are still at large and the West Hollywood Police Department request information for the night of the 24th December. Please call this number. . ."

I look up at Henry; the look in his spooked eyes demand an 'Aha!' moment from me, but clearly I am slow to catch on.

"Can't you fucking guess, Unabomber?" Henry hisses.

"No- but I'm getting a vague idea here that you know something that I don't-"

"It's Lissa and Ajax- they did it!"

"What!? No way- that's crazy, really crazy."

"You ask Lissa where she was that night and where she got a serious amount of money at Christmas last year and why she had scratch marks all over her face, chest and back with cuts and scabs in her hair where it had been pulled out in what she told me was a catfight with a tweaker. And where she got the little diamond brooch with the initials MR from?"

"Henry, there are many ways she could have got money and found the brooch and-"

214

"How come she keeps changing her story then and the only person who will vouch for her is Ajax? She went all weird and took off for about 2 weeks; I never knew where she went and when she got back she'd totally changed her hair, clothes, everything, she even moved-"

"She's moved twice since I've known her and that's in the last three months!" I point out.

I'm really shocked that Ajax is in this equation because even the suspicion of his involvement in such a heinous crime makes me feel violently sick, even with meth flowing through me. For the first time in a very long time I feel serious compassion for this poor old lady who was caused such diabolical suffering by inhumane thieves. The sensation is far stronger than when I grew uncomfortable witnessing Chrissie's pain after I drove her to the children's court. Has crystal meth stopped working for me?

Not wanting to address this possibility I reason with Henry that, even if they had done it, surely some evidence or their DNA would have been found at the crime scene.

"Are ya kidding!? They're untraceable- d'ya know how many false ID's they have? The only way is to actually turn them in!"

I cannot believe my ears. Here is Henry the drug dealer telling me he wants to snitch on his girlfriend Lissa for murder, with the flimsiest of proof imaginable. In fact, he is going purely on what sounds like a hunch to me. However, I know to tread carefully because Henry has a temper and he is already mighty paranoid.

"Are you sure Henry that this isn't about something more personal between yourself and Lissa? Maybe because you've been fighting . . ." I speak gently, in what I hope are soothing tones.

"She's fucking begging me to stick with her, but I see into her soul and what I see is black and evil!" Henry rants, stalking round any available floor space, banging his fist on the wall to emphasise his conviction.

"Okay she's a bit dodgy, but murder? Come on!"

"Man, you really don't fuckin' get it do ya?"

"Get what? I know we take too many drugs and we steal bits and pieces but. . ."

215

Henry comes up close to my face and his eyes glisten with what can only be described as zeal and purpose. He speaks quietly:

"Get out of here now, before you become part of something you don't understand. Promise me Clea, please, go anywhere, but get out of here!"

It didn't take long to lose the car again. I'd been hiding it in a garage nearby, but on this occasion I had parked it briefly outside my apartment and typically ended up staying in longer than planned. As my luck would have it, the dealer showed up and towed it away.

I knew that this time it was gone forever.

CHAPTER 24

No Turkey This Thanksgiving

Those who go beneath the surface do so at their peril.
Oscar Wilde

The day starts promisingly enough with Lissa calling me up; she'd left a denim jacket at my apartment and wants me to bring it over to her at Brigitte's house where 'we can hang out'. Lissa is staying with Brigitte, a fat wrinkly ex-starlet friend in her 60s, who lives up Laurel Canyon, very near where I had picked up the Louis Vuitton suitcase a couple of months ago.

Lissa tells me what bus I need to take up La Cienaga and then I'll have to walk up the hill from Sunset. But I end up getting off the bus early at Beverly because a surly, dark haired man in some kind of security uniform keeps giving me the evil eye. My paranoia is fiercely evident, even to myself: Yesterday I ended up on the next door building's roof, pulling out all their aerials because I could hear people in an apartment- next door and above me on the first floor- discussing me. I was unclear on what exactly they were saying but I kept hearing my name. The voices sounded like Ajax and someone I could not pinpoint but they were definitely talking about me and I was not ready to tolerate it. I crept around the building (it was not locked) and listened at the various apartment doors in case they had moved apartments (for all I know they might have taken over the whole building). The doors were heavy so it was hard to hear anything at all so I decided the roof was the best way to 'disarm' them, at least electronically speaking. Up on the flat roof I disconnected all visible wiring. No one below seemed to notice or be bothered and this made me even more suspicious. But then a little later a couple of cars pulled out of their lot and I deduced they had lost radio contact and needed to reconvene.

Even though some part of me recognises that my mind is over-thinking everything and adding things together in an obtuse manner, I still know that all these people and things, noises, looks, brainwaves, electricity are part of a universal conspiracy to undo me. I do not actually know the man on the bus but I am caught up in the sickly excitement of feeling that I am a mouse being chased. The cat is invisible but I sense its slow approach- in different forms- that is all part of the 'cat and mouse' game where I am teased to beyond a second of sanity.

I arrive in West Hollywood on foot. I notice a beige car following me. It turns off and drives east but I know it will do a u-turn and be back. I sit on the low wall of a bungalow on Fountain and Olive to wait. I want them to know I know.

Now two beige cars appear- clearly they are raising the stakes. I gather myself and stalk along Fountain but there are so many cars- many of them in that inauspicious beige- that I am having trouble identifying the original. Maybe Gordon had been right when he had said the cars with the Enterprise sticker attached to the back bumper were undercover agents. I had laughed at the time but now I scrutinise the back bumpers for the 'E' sticker. A blue car has one but none of the beige. They are trying to trip me up with a cheap trick.

I am becoming hot with rivulets of sweat soaking my shirt and my neck is damp and clammy. It strikes me that I could change my clothes around- lose some even – and throw them off my trail. I climb over the low wall of a well-kept bungalow on Alta Loma Road and quietly creep down the narrow, fenced side into the small patch of overgrown back garden. I take off my jacket and hide it under a small bush. I have my pager on me too and realise that this is what must be working as a tracking device. How could I have not realised this sooner? What insanity! I crouch and pull up tufts of yellowed grass and weeds. The earth beneath is hard so I dig a small hole with my straining fingers and lay the pager down, covering it with some dry earth and the tufts of grass in the form of a hasty burial. I am back on top again.

My exuberance is short-lived when I notice a blonde, floppy haired man looking out the window at me, dialling a number into his phone while eyeing me suspiciously. What does he have to be suspicious of?

I run out anyway, just to be on the safe side. But where am I running to? Where had I been going before the game commenced? I am now on Sunset. I walk and the sun burns my eyes. I am breathing heavily due to the sprint up the hill far away from the bungalow with the blonde man inside, who had threatened to harass me for no reason.

I sit on the corner of Sunset and North Kings Road where there is a large billboard with an ad for Budweiser. Cars pull up and park along the side road. People get out of cars. Some of them carry flowers and dishes of food. I look at them and they look at me, but no one dares to maintain eye contact with me. After a while, when the stream of people-traffic entering the apartment building eases, I cross over so I can better hear the muted mumblings from inside. A grey-haired lady with her hair in an elegant pleat comes out; she pretends to be looking up and down the street for something. She addresses me:

"Excuse me but have you seen a white Persian cat at all?"

Is this a trick to bring me inside? I cannot tell. I do not say anything, but just shake my head. She glares at me now. I jump up and rather than stay on the roads I agilely climb the railing at the side of the Billboard. I reach the top horizontal frame that reaches across the back, supporting the vertical hoists that hold it down into the ground 30 feet below. I climb right on top so I am virtually part of the billboard and I chuckle to myself as I momentarily recall my mother's hopes and dreams as articulated in the autograph book I had as a child. She had written: 'I know I'll see your name up in lights one day'. Well I am up on a Billboard so I figure that is kind of close in a perverse way.

But how do I get down? Like a fireman seems to be the only answer so I wrap my bony legs around the rusted metal tube and ease myself down. When I reach the ground below- my hands are chapped and slightly bleeding- I am trapped inside the back of a row of buildings that have emergency doors leading outside. The opposite end is a sheer drop leading onto the sloping hillside which would be impossible to climb up without a ladder. My only hope is a small building that looks more residential than the others.

I bang on the far door. I wait. I bang again. I sit down against the door. I feel it move and I leap up.

"What the hell is going on back here?" A man of about 25 opens the door. He has a shirt with an undone maroon tie around his neck.

"Can I come in, please?" I eye him pathetically, desperate for his help and pity because I need to replenish my stash and Lissa is the best bet for that right now. How did I become so diverted?

"Wha'dya doin' back here- how 'dya even get back here?!" He pokes his sleek, dark head out and looks around the desolate concrete space.

"Not too sure really-" I attempt a friendly smile.

"Are ya in trouble, or something?"

"Kind of. . . but not what you might think; not with the police, or anything!"

"Where ya heading?"

"Some friends nearby- my car broke down and I got kind of lost. I haven't lived here very long and-" I use my plummiest English accent.

"Hey you sound just like that English chick, that-actress-wassername? Errrrr, whatever, come in."

He opens the emergency exit so I can ease myself through. He gives me the once-over, I guess just to make sure that I am not armed and dangerous, and then glances at himself in a small mirror, rapidly doing up his tie, telling me:

"I'm off to my folks in the valley for lunch. Okay, I'm ready to hit the road. I'll let you out the front entrance of the building, okay?"

I grab his arm and he looks startled:

"I'm sorry but before I go out there can you check on something for me?"

"What?" I sense annoyance.

"Can you check to see if there's a beige car parked outside on the street with someone sitting in it?"

He looks totally perplexed, and regards me intensely:

"You must have been quite pretty once. . . before ya got so. . .ya know what I mean-" He makes a weird kind of gesture at me and moves his hand in circles like I will understand what he is unable to spit out.

"What are you talking about? Please can you check for me, otherwise I'm not moving from here." I dig my heels in the dense carpet to make my point, like a stubborn child.

He emits a slow whistle and I regard his features more closely and realise I would have found him incredibly attractive before I became permanently tweaked.

"I'll drive ya over to your friends okay? That's the best I can do"

"It's really near. Just off Sunset a little ways." I cannot believe my luck because quite frankly my legs and back are seriously sore, as are my blood-crusted hands that I have kept out of sight thus far, not wanting to freak out this nice guy.

"I'll go get my car and pull up- I'll honk 3 times so you'll know it's me, okay?"

"You're my saviour! Thank you." And I mean it.

When he pulls up outside Brigitte's house he turns to me; I recognise the look that says loud and clear: 'You really need help.'

"Good luck- "

"Oh piss off; you've done your good deed for the day." I had not meant to be rude but that look makes me want to hard-boil his eyes.

"Hey look, I was worried about ya doin' something stupid out on the busy road." He gives me an almost apologetic smile. Why is he being so nice?

"Thanks- you're a really decent person." I tell him.

He shrugs and waves, driving off back down the hill. For a second I ponder whether coming here was the right move, but I am here now so choose to ignore my misgiving.

There are three cars I do not recognise outside Brigitte's house- a classic Mercedes, a new BMW convertible and some non-descript jalopy, alongside Brigitte's jeep.

Lissa takes ages to let me in; she is half undressed with her black bra barely covering her small breasts and a flared, short brown suede skirt with no shoes.

221

"Ya took ya fuckin' time! Where ya been?"

"Is Henry here?" I change the subject, remembering I have forgotten her denim jacket as well as having taken hours to get here.

"Haven't ya heard? He's in jail!"

"No way? How? What happened?"

"Wha'dya think happened? Someone snitched on him. Anyway ya get arrested when ya need a rest. He was acting real crazy, making shit up about me n' stuff so. . . whatever."

Lissa seems to be taking his arrest very much in her stride which is very odd considering he was her lifeline. She has something up her sleeve for sure.

"Look ya can't hang out here now coz there's some people over n'-"

"That's cool. I just need some shit-"

"Lissa- I need yer help down here!" A male voice yells.

A trap door opens up into the kitchen and someone climbs the stairs, carefully shutting the door behind. For a second a stench pervades the atmosphere; a smell that has some familiarity but mixed in with something heightened, possibly sexual but tinged with an unidentifiable aroma.

The man skulks into the dark living room- the drapes are closed with only a dim table lamp on- where Lissa and I are sitting on the purple velvet sofa. I recognise this man, but cannot place him.

"I'll be back down in a minute, Gabe." Lissa tells him.

I feel uneasy, queasy even. It hits me with a thump in the chest that it's Gabe, the one I had met at Elsie's briefly who had prompted me to drive around all night seeking out a Jesus statue, and the same Gabe that Marnie believes is the devil incarnate. I am thrown.

"Hey shit I'll have a toot while I'm up here." Gabe has less hair than I remember, but still the pasty face and black eyes that bore into me.

Lissa has laid out some lines; she rolls up a bill.

"Having a party down there?" I ask.

Gabe and Lissa look struck by some unknown force:

"No- what makes you say that?" Lissa's tone is panicked.

"Nothing- I just thought I heard laughing and music and

222

stuff."

"No party. Just helping Brigitte clear out her basement." Lissa is resolute.

"Do I know you? We've met before haven't we?" Gabe looks at me pointedly. I raise my head directly to meet him on the level:

"I've never seen you before in my life, but nice to meet you."

He ignores this and takes the bill. While he leans over to snort up some meth, I notice little scratches- small but deep- on the side of his neck that had been hidden by his shirt collar.

"Back to work then." When Gabe lifts the trap door to go down, the smell hits me again and I recognise it as the potent, viscous smell of fear: a combination of urine, sweat and other secretions that I wholly recall from when I escaped a gang of Indian men on the beach in Goa during my 'year out' when I was 18. I had fought myself free from clutches and grabbing fingers and hands. I had run and run for miles, urine flowing and sweat drenching my cotton dress. The smell would never wash out and I burnt it a week later to kill the putrid smell that served as a blatant reminder of violent and brutal men.

"Okay, well you can take this- it's about 2 grams." Lissa hands me the bag.

"So come on, tell me what's happening?" I coax.

"I told ya- clearing stuff out." Lissa is casual.

"What are you doing down there?" I sense things are wrong, very wrong indeed.

"Nothing- you're really paranoid. Please don't end up like Henry for fuck's sake!" Lissa's laugh is tinny.

"Paranoid or not, something weird is going on down there. . ." I attempt reason, rather than an accusatory tack.

I stand and slowly walk towards the kitchen where the trap door is; Lissa darts up and gets there before me, leaning her back against it and grasping the round brass door handle with both hands. Her 'Off Limits' message comes over loud and clear.

"I need a glass of water; I'm a little parched." Her eyes follow me suspiciously as I rinse a smudged glass, wipe it on a rag by the sink and pour the water.

"You need to leave- Now!"

223

"I'm going." She is not moving away from that door.

I am almost at the front door when Lissa bolts towards me:

"Actually gimme that baggy a second." I take it out my pocket and hand it over.

"Now go!"

"You bitch, that's mine. You owe me, you said so yourself!"

"Look at you panic now- can't survive without this, can you!" She waves it at me and I clutch at it. She is a complete witch with her long, scraggy hair and pointy nose. But it's her black eyes that give her away: in that moment I see she is truly evil and readily capable of murder.

I jump at her and snatch the bag; she goes to hit me but I am prepared, hitting her hard instead, directly on the right brow. Her eyes are on fire now:

"I'll get ya for this you tweaker bitch!" Lissa yells at me as I slam the front door in her cold ugly face.

I am terrified that they will come after me now and I have no idea what to do- I am convinced someone was down in that basement against their will. I know it but I cannot do anything by myself. Overcoming Lissa was a fluke and I know Brigitte and Gabe were in the cellar so already I am outnumbered.

I run down the hill, fuelled by fear, anxiety, adrenaline and crystal meth. I am drawn over to a dirt track- really a footpath- that is a steep shortcut down the hill leading to a makeshift car park that has only a worn white van parked in it. I walk by and see that the keys are inside the van. I cannot believe it! Surely this is a sign- a sign of what I am unclear- but if nothing else it can get me out of here and I can fetch help.

I look about and see no one; I yank open the door and climb in. I turn on the engine and back it out and round so as to be able to drive down the sloped driveway to Sunset facing forward.

"Ehhhh!! Stop! Thief! Stop!" I am half way down when a short, angry Hispanic man appears and chases behind me. I freeze at the wheel; my foot has hit the brake. Caught in the act, I grab the hand brake and jerk it up. I fling open the door, just missing the man's outstretched arm and I run back up the hill. I end up in Brigitte's garden when I hear the sirens approaching. I dart up the side of the house where there is a ladder. I start to climb and make it half way up when two strong arms grab my legs and pull me down.

"Got her!" The cop shouts over his shoulder, while cuffing me.

The other cop- a woman with fair hair in a ponytail-bangs on Brigitte's door. No one comes. She tries the doorbell, then bangs again. We stand there and wait.

Lissa opens the door slightly:

"Yes?"

"We're arresting this woman for attempted car theft; she was on your property and we want to know if you know her." I detect Lissa's smirk beneath her nonchalant act.

"Never seen her before in my life." Lissa eyes me with utter hatred.

"Lissa, don't lie. She knows me officer, I promise."

Lissa recoils and shakes her head like 'clearly she's crazy'.

"Sorry to disturb ya Mam."

"That's quite alright officer." Lissa smiles with a nauseating graciousness that I didn't think she had in her.

"They've got someone locked up in the basement inside that house, officer. I promise- please just go take a look." My plea falls on cynical ears.

The cops shove me in the back of the panda car. I am so alone in this moment; even a fellow tweaker refuses to vouch for me and here I am again- powerless in handcuffs- on my way to jail. I want to break through and help whoever is down in that basement, but I know I have seriously blown it. The police do not even acknowledge me as a fellow human being- rather as something sub-human and a pesky nuisance. I ponder why I stalled so long before legging it out of the frame, or maybe they received the radio message when they were only a street away because they must have arrived within a minute or two. It makes no difference now.

To my hope and surprise our first stop is Cedars Sinai Hospital because the woman cop has noticed I am barely able to walk. I am not even aware that it is Thanksgiving until I am on the gurney. I recognise an English accent through the dividing screen, addressing a nurse:

"I beg your pardon Miss, but may I please telephone the people I'm staying with to let them know they can pick me up soon?" he asks courteously.

I close my eyes and imagine I am somewhere back in England- my bedroom at Gravesend Farm, lying on the softest feather mattress ever, with rain pattering on the panes of the creaky windows.

"I need to wait and hear what the doctor has to say. It shouldn't be much longer now." The nurse tears away my memory with her authoritative tone.

"Well I must say this is a grand way to spend my first Thanksgiving- in bloody hospital!" The young man laughs.

"Yeah, it's pretty funny. Ya gotta be careful with those turkey bones!" The nurse cajoles.

"You're not joking! Somehow I feel it rather verges on the absurd."

"Excuse me nurse, but may I please have some painkillers for my back? The other nurse was getting me some but that was hours ago." I raise my voice to reach across the screen.

"Hardly hours, minutes more like- hold on." Her tone is wholly dismissive of me.

"Excuse me, but you there across the divide- are you English?" The Englishman asks.

"Yeah, I am."

"Cool. So how long have you been out here in LA?"

"Too long."

"Seriously, how long? How do you like it here?"

I cannot calculate time for him: years, months, days, hours, minutes, seconds, milliseconds melt into a mass of unknown matter while I reduce to something that vaguely resembles a human being, a skeletal creature with thinning hair and bug eyes. I hazard a guess:

"A few years, but I think I'll be leaving soon."

"Can you believe I choked on a turkey bone! How embarrassing is that? I'm such an idiot."

"Well as they say- shit happens." The cops that brought

me in reappear waving some paperwork at me:

"The Doc here said there's nothing serious wrong with your back. Now we're gonna book ya at Sybil Brand."

My heart sinks into my boots; the stop at the hospital had offered a brief glimpse of relief on the inevitable path to jail. The cops push the gurney with my right arm handcuffed to the rail, past the English guy who watches in amazement. I meet his shocked eyes for a split second and quickly turn away; the shame and self-hatred is too much to be witnessed by myself, let alone others. His confident, British tones recall a life that I had once been part of- only a few years ago- and this adds to my remorse and catatonic reluctance to leave with these angry, frustrated men and women of the law who resent working on Thanksgiving and hate petty criminals like myself.

Oh what have I done? Where am I? Who am I?

~~~~~~~~

The previous events wholly represent the nadir of where my crystal meth addiction has led me. To this day, I grapple with the eternal question of what was, or wasn't true. I have many questions and no concrete answers.

What I've written is what I believe to be the truth, but my mind was addled with paranoid delusion. However, there is no doubt that I was in the presence of evil. I have no tangible evidence, only my instinctive and intuitive memory to back this up. I also know that crystal meth creates such perverse character changes- a hungry, animalistic and angry life-state within the user- that violence, torture and murder become palpable realities.

Crystal meth is synthesised with toxic chemicals, with zero beneficial medicinal content. It is a drug of pure excess, at the farthest end of Dionysian extremism. All of us have the potential to create good or evil with our own lives, relationships and actions: crystal meth can only result in evil because it only ever unleashes the brutal and destructive parts of ourselves- our anger, resentment, hatred, fear, frustration, impotency- that we keep under wraps through conscience and an ethical code. Crystal meth rips away our civilised blanket to reveal an ugly

227

face: human baseness in its purest form.

In my stupidity and ignorance I did not understand this, but allowed myself to exist within these terrifying parameters where I also became very sick. At this point in my story I am a pitiful wreck of a young woman, governed by fear and out of control. I'd allowed crystal meth to take me over, but my true nature- my better self- quietly fights in the corner, willing me to wake up and see the self-perpetuating 'living hell' in which I choose to live.

In that situation at Brigitte's house I made the wrong choices. Unfortunately, the universal law of cause and effect does not take into account personal flaws or drug psychosis. Part of the reason I wanted to tell my story is because I want other young people to understand that crystal meth is unequivocally dangerous and vile. Put simply, it destroys life, the most precious aspect of the universe.

I have cried many tears but that does not change anything. Positive action and awareness are what count, not regrets, self-pity and excuses.

CHAPTER 25

Sybil Brand

The road of excess leads to the palace of wisdom.
William Blake

I am booked for GTA (Grand Theft Auto) at Sybil Brand penitentiary, on the outskirts of Los Angeles County and will remain there until my court hearing, because I have no one left who will stand me bail.

I deserve top marks for turning the dream inside out. There is nothing to do but wait, adding ironic credence to the tongue-in-cheek remark that LA is one huge waiting room: we're all here waiting for our big moment, our fifteen minutes and now I'm waiting for freedom. The four payphones are switched on for two hours a day- an hour after lunch and an hour before dinner. While my car was my lifeline outside, the telephone is my oxygen vent in the gas chamber that is jail.

Eventually I garner the courage to call my Uncle Boris in Providence, Rhode Island. I had no choice but to throw myself on his mercy. Aunty Tess had answered and her complete disgust burned through the line before she passed the phone to him; she had nothing to say to me.

Uncle Boris takes my call and he is going to discuss things with my parents. He spoke to me like a retarded child, but here I am- supposedly an adult- in a very grown-up place. I have been issued with a state attorney, paid for by the state, whom I will meet when I am due in court.

I have had the phone snatched away from me twice in mid-flow by a skinny white girl with very long, lanky brown hair that's always backed up by her waddling partner- a huge buxom black woman with enormous thighs who enjoys yelling at me:

"Hey bitch- ya takin' too long. How many times I gotta tell ya 'fore I break ya fuckin' neck bitch!?"

I get her point as they slit-eye and jostle me; they certainly do not like me, but why I have yet to find out. In a brave moment I ask Nicky, a toothless junkie prostitute who I share a bunk bed with, why I rattle their cages. Apparently I do not understand the 'code' in here and also that all my bruises look like I let some guy beat on me all the time and that is a sign of cowardice. I heatedly deny this is the case and try to explain that I bruise very easily but she is not buying it. Also Nicky says they can tell 'I'm egicated' so how come I've ended up in jail when I have had choices in my life, unlike them.

There is a real push and shove mentality here that can result in violent fights which the guards take their time to break up; personally I think they take bets to amuse themselves. I keep to myself as much as is humanly possible considering the close quarters. My ability to sleep anywhere proves a godsend.

The food is abysmal. Powdered eggs and milk, everything else is straight from large tins- watery pale pink baked beans, grey peas and toxic orange carrots. I have never felt so hungry in my life.

The drone of the drill bell each morning at 6am permeates my senses, jolting me back to the reality of my inch-thick prison mattress. Just for the millionth of a split second I float in neutral, unaware of where I am and who I am- then bang I wake up and it all floods back: that aching sensation of dread floods through me to the pit of my famished stomach.

The greyness is inescapable: grey-washed walls and floors, grey cylindrical bars that bleep, whenever they open and close, like depressed daleks assaulting my sensitive eardrums. The grey floors are painted with different coloured lines, as are the walls; the red one leads to the eating area, the green to the visitors' area, the blue to the laundry where you change your obligatory hospital blue shirt and elasticised waist trousers once a week. At least you only have to spread your butt cheeks once when you arrive and hand over your own clothes. Everyone wears rubber-soled slippers- one of mine fell apart on the way back from dinner on my first day. I am pleased as the need for a replacement means twenty minutes less in the lock-up dormitory cell. I ask the round-faced, jovial guard with crooked teeth how many women have already worn them and she replies, "Hundreds".

A trolley of worn paperbacks was wheeled into the block today. I had signed up for the Drug Prevention Group, but it was cancelled for the rest of the week, of course with no explanation. It had only been two hours a day but it had relieved an iota of the monotony. I flicked the pages of a book- a Harlequin romance and a postcard fell out. It was worn and faded like it had been bleached in the sun but I recognised it immediately- it is a postcard of a Leonora Carrington painting *The Cabbage*. I thought I was beyond squeezing any more tears out, but this image here with me now feels heaven-sent. On the back in a very tight neat hand is the message:

> *Hi Sandy,*
> *You can see this 2 ways- either it is the beginning of your life, or the end.*
> *It is your choice.*
> *Love Dadxxx*

It is as if my father sent this to me. Even though I know I am not Sandy, I know I was meant to find this worn postcard. Who am I? A car thief, a drug addict, a fuck-up who was given many chances and blew them all big time. My mind floods with memories like it is trying to get me back for the months I have deprived it of life. And things snap in and out of mind like Polaroids, trying to build a collage to explain what actually did happen to land me here because this is not a mistake, a coincidence or an accident- it is real life and it is my life.

Events start to come together in my mind. Finding the postcard has given me hope. Hope and faith- in something, though I do not know what- keeps me from crumpling and giving in to the ever-present chasm of doom and utter despair. As long as hope exists in me I know I will survive this. Rather than see myself as a sinner I perceive the events of the past three years as possibly instructive, if I can find the true message within. I plot my path in reverse and recall my arrival in LA. I was full of hope and dreams, but I wore a mask that said I must be this great success, I must prove my family that they were right about me- I deserved to go to Brown, to graduate, to follow the American dream and I must see my father- my dear, kind, struggling father- as the counter role model who had come to America and been given great opportunities but failed to make gold. My mother, given little guidance by her own drunkard mother, had done her best with me but how good could that possibly be? I had shamed the family further with drugs- even more heinous than booze.

Obviously I wanted to escape everyone and that is why I chose Los Angeles. Now I see it is my self I had wanted to lose and I have succeeded. But why did I have to take it to this extreme, trading respectability and decency for the strange and unusual, the downright weird and dysfunctional? Because I am an addict and addicts destroy themselves no matter what.

At the courthouse in downtown LA we all sit and wait in another holding cell, having been unshackled.
Ms. King, my court appointed Attorney, comes to speak with me. She is an attractive brunette with kind eyes and by some miracle she is on my side. Really on my side.

I tell her what I believe to be the truth:

"It's the drugs- not me, not the real me- that made me try to steal that van! I've never stolen a car before. I wouldn't even know how to. I wasn't thinking straight and I had a sort of panic attack. . ."

I decide not to bring up the suspicious incident with Lissa and Gabe at Brigitte's house, because I know it will sound like I'm mad.

Ms. King slowly nods and I can see she is adding up what the best way forward is.

"I can see you're not a career criminal; what you need is drug rehabilitation. Because you're English I might be able to sort this out quite simply but it will mean you have to leave

Los Angeles as soon as you're released- well, they'll give you a few days to pack. But do you agree to that?"

"Yes! I'll agree to anything to stay out of jail." I know that if her bargain fails then I will be looking at a year stretch. The possibility of this sends cold shivers through my whole being. Now I know how valuable freedom is. If I can recall the sensation- abject fear and dread- whenever I am tempted to use drugs again I will be free of my addiction. . . if only.

I know how lucky I am. I do not feel elevated by my apparent good fortune but just greatly relieved to be walking through that loud, electric gate for the last time. And it is definitely the last time because I am under oath to board a plane out of Los Angeles and California, out of the US, back to my homeland. That was the deal my attorney made to keep me out of jail. My two week stint showed me how tough jail would be on me. While free and tweaking on crystal meth, walking around the streets acting all tough and mouthy is one thing, but in jail with no drugs to provide the armour, it was a terrifying charade I cannot possibly maintain.

Freedom! What an intoxicating sensation. I understand now why people have risked or given their lives for it. Free to leave but to do what the court has instructed, not as I please. I am back in the realm of a freewill that was so out of control it had landed me in jail in the first place! On my last night in the slammer I vow to Nicky and her crew that I am never going to use crystal meth again.

I insist that I have come to my senses and I am finally getting out of this mess. Nicky revels in throwing me spiteful challenges: "You'll never do it! I bet ya'll be back on that shit the same day you get out of this shit hole." I bitterly protest and she starts to snigger:

"Not my problem girl, but I don't think ya got in ya to quit- you're just like the rest of us poor fuckers in here- weak."

I hate her in that moment because she is absolutely right.

233

Many hours later- at least five- I am back at my apartment. I take a bus part of the way and then walk the rest, enjoying the sights and smells of the city of angels like I never have before; even petrol fumes smell beautiful today.

I let myself in. The apartment is not as I had left it. There is the scent and evidence of the presence of others in my domain and they have tried to rub away my identity like you rub a steamed up mirror.

I can tell my bed has been used- the sheets are not mine- so I do not want to lie down on it although my body is begging me to. I am in a semi-trancelike state, physically and mentally. I feel like I have been robbed- and I have- but of something more substantial than material possessions- CD's, clothes, furniture. Nothing is mine, nothing at all, and I am completely and utterly alone. I have lost my soul. Or maybe I have destroyed my soul.

Papers are all over the bar top. I notice opened envelopes addressed to me. What? I hastily pick through the strewn papers- it is all my mail, opened and read and left on the counter by someone not expecting me back. I find a letter from Natasha dated September (we are now in December), a court summons, bills and a cheque from the advertising agency for the Budweiser commercial, although this has also been tampered with and has worn edges. It arrived the day after Thanksgiving!

I pick up the phone, amazed to hear a dial tone because I have not paid the bill for months. I call my cousin Mia and ask if I can stay with her for the night, possibly a couple. She needs to ask her house-mate and tells me to call back in a few minutes.

When I call back she is apologetic:

"I'm really sorry but she won't have it, with you being an addict and everything-"

"But I haven't used since jail. I would be so grateful-"

"Look I'm really sorry, but she's adamant."

"Yeah, okay I understand." What a total bitch.

A bang on the window makes me start.

"Hey Clea- I wanted to come by the jail and get ya, but they only just released your name. I gotta gift for ya-" Henry's gruff tones sound hollow, but comforting.

I know the gift is drugs. Part of me is yelling out for the familiar release from myself, but my conscience is saying: No! No! No! Prove Nicky wrong! Prove you can pack your things (what's left of them) and get on that plane to a new and better life.

I look around the apartment and that hollow thump inside my stomach beats faster and in time to Henry's thumps on the window: "Come on dude, lemme in!"

"Hang on- I'm just finishing a telephone call-" I lie, picking up the phone and placing it by my ear. I wish God was on the other end telling me what to do.

I am torn. But then, I reason, I am so weak and unfocused; surely it will help me get packed and organised. I unlock the door and let him in.

I take shower after shower to scrub the jail of my skin and out of my hair but it sticks like gum on the sole of my shoe. The crystal makes me edgy and paranoid so I pick up a six-pack of beer and some sticks of beef jerky at my local 7-11. I need something to slow me down. My limping heart is demanding my attention but I refuse to listen.

At the counter, I rifle through my purse gathering and counting coins.

"How ya doin'? Haven't seen ya in a while-" A chubby, pale man asks me in friendly fashion which totally takes me by surprise because I have never made acquaintance with an LA shopkeeper. People come and go too quickly here for rapport to develop at your local shops.

"I'm fine, thank you." I give him a quick half smile because all I can think of is opening up a can of beer and slugging it down.

"Hey, can I come over when I finish up here?" He hands me my change.

"Excuse me? What?" He leans over and whispers:

"Ya know, can I come over and see ya. Like what I done with your room-mate Chrissie?"

"I don't know what you're talking about!" And I don't, but a picture is coming to mind.

"I'll pay you more coz you're better lookin'." My shock is

235

switching into fear combined with rage.

"Don't come near my apartment, you hear me!" I yell at him.

I grab my things and storm out. Now I need to change the locks on the apartment because that has really done it- there is no way I am letting Chrissie back in after she has turned tricks in my bed and stolen my mail. But where is she and what if she gets back before me? My heart is racing so fast that soon it will break out of my chest if I do not calm down.

Marnie comes to stay. Desperate like me, she has been ousted from her apartment and even Jeremiah has had enough of her. What a circle Marnie and I have travelled, sometimes apart and now back together. I know this is the end; the end of this life I've been leading that has almost destroyed me, yet I still cannot quite let go.

On my second-to-last day in LA, we go dumpster diving.

'For old time's sake' I'd begged of Marnie: one last drive down those familiar back alleys where we have spent weeks combing other people's trash in search of the Holy Grail.

But it's falling flat because I can barely drag myself out of her car and she makes excuses that it's a 'thin pickings day' anyway, while she swigs surreptitiously from her vodka bottle.

In a day and a half I will be on a plane back to London.

I know if I don't I will end up in jail because my nerves are fried. I see familiar faces whenever I go out, but I cannot place them. I decide they are Gabe's goons. They carry haunted expressions that tell of sustained electrical torture techniques. I think they are really controlled by a grand master puppeteer. This idea would be backed up by Jeremiah's theories- especially the chip-in-the-brain theories- but these goons are even more deranged that that. They also whistle all the time, especially during the night, and the whistle is a secret code that whines constantly in my head.

Chrissie appears, demanding to be let in. She yells from outside through the window and starts begging my forgiveness.

236

Apparently she does not know why she stole my mail. I stand my ground and arrange for her to return with a ride to move out her belongings.

"By the way, Ajax came over to see you on Thanksgiving." Chrissie drops in casually, as she lifts a box of CDs.

"Well I wasn't here was I-" I state the obvious.

"Just telling ya-"

"What did he want?"

"Dunno. But he's bad news. He's still on the run for pushing that cop down the elevator shaft anyways so better not to be associated with him, that's for sure."

"What are you talking about?"

"Serious shit. Sick told me about it- he was there with him at the fire in the Magic Hotel in Hollywood."

"And Sick would know-"

"At least he's not dumb enough to kill a cop!" Chrissie states smugly.

"I'm leaving. I don't care. Get out!"

I go out to the hardware store to get some tape and sticky labels for my boxes that will be shipped over to England. On foot the store is about fifteen minutes each way and when I come back I notice a stooped male figure leaving the emergency exit at the far side of my building. He is about to get in a parked car when he turns to look for something and I recognise him. Then I see a pit-bull and know right away the man is Ajax.

"Hey Spanky, Spanky! Come here boy," I call.

Ajax whistles and the dog stops in its tracks unsure which way to go; Ajax whistles sharply again and the dog trots to the car and jumps in. I run towards the car but they drive off before I get there. Ajax does not look around once. But what the hell was he doing in my apartment building if he had not come to see me? I have no idea what to make of this but then I remember the LV case that I had hidden away in the locker, outside of my apartment. I had almost forgotten about it and I had always suspected he had something to do with it.

The padlock has been broken off, but the suitcase is

there with everything inside, just as I had left it a few months ago. This distinctly surprises me but I find another padlock to fasten the cupboard and make a mental note to fetch it when I am ready to leave for the airport.

If it was up to me I never would have boarded the plane. Already I'd changed the flight numerous times, much to my mother's anguish and fury, but my cousin Mia keeps guard at the exit points, once I am actually through customs and at the gate.

I have enough stash on me for the next three days, or so. Otherwise I have no plan. I am at a point where I am incapable of making any decisions and questions of legality completely slip my mind.

I do not really believe I am leaving LA. I am living in a hazy, warped underworld where people trail me and send me signals. I live in perpetual fear and anxiety, yet I am unable to drag myself away. I telephone Marnie one last time from the airport. She is taking my departure very badly, even though she's inheriting my apartment (at least until the landlord kicks her out). Despite the fact that I do not feel very much these days her response to my last phone call while on American soil shakes me up.

"Just go, go! Get the fuck out of here! Get on that fucking plane."

I am abandoning her. Now the tables have turned.

When I board the full plane I am in the aisle seat and the man on my left tries to be friendly to me, but he freaks me out by asking me questions that are not the sort of thing to ask a complete stranger:

"Been having a good time in LA then? Lots of great drugs aren't there?"

"I don't know." I shrug and pretend he is not there. Other faces in the nearby seats look familiar and I am convinced that one of Gabe's goons was near the check-in desk. He was not waiting to check in, but staring at me, and then he seemed to vanish. I have gone through customs assuming all this will stay behind in LA.

My mind and body are in constant overdrive, but I can

feel a sense of exhaustion overriding the anxiety because I know I am stuck in this plane seat for the next eleven hours. I drift off and when I open my eyes we have landed at Heathrow. Passengers are already out of their seats gathering their things from the overhead lockers. My neighbour has gone.

I am disoriented. I exit the plane and decide I need to have a quick wash and wake up. I have about two grams on me hidden inside a dental floss container under the wheel of floss. I find the bathrooms before customs and when I come out refreshed and with my face on, all the other passengers have gone through. Suddenly I have renewed confidence after my sleep on the plane and my toot in the bathroom; I decide things will be better now and I almost feel normal, like I am back to visit my father for Christmas. I stroll through customs breezily and locate the baggage carousel. There are only a few suitcases and bags still going round; I haul my three off and look for a trolley. I sense eyes on me, really boring into me. Across the carousel, a grey-haired man of about 55 and a young blonde woman- presumably his daughter- give me the serious evil eye. They have a trolley stacked high with Louis Vuitton luggage. I look away telling myself I am imagining it, but when I look back they are still staring at me.

And then they are gone.

CHAPTER 26

Gordon Revisited

But it's the truth, even if it didn't happen.
One Flew Over the Cuckoo's Nest Ken Kesey

Patient as ever, Dad waits in Arrivals at Heathrow looking just the same- calm, well dressed and conservative.

I sense he is surprised by my appearance (I think he expects me to look like the guy in the heroin posters from the 80s) and happy that I am alive and surprisingly cheerful, ebullient even. His relief is evident in his blustery, up-beat manner which is as excited as I have ever seen him.

We are to visit Dad's elder sister in Devon, the next day, for Christmas and we are booked to take the coach to Exeter from Victoria Station at 8.00am on Christmas Eve. The trains are overbooked and this is the last available form of transport; he no longer keeps a car.

The evening before we had walked to The Hurlingham Club- a posh traditional British 'country club' in Fulham- to have a drink and a snack; I chattered away, sipping Merlot with crystal buoying me up, along with the newness of this situation- father and daughter together. I am incapable of thinking past each moment and have given no thought to saving my supplies. I continue to tweak after my father has retired to bed but feel strangely immobile and spend hours reclining on my bed in a sort of trance, periodically jumping up to adjust the curtain. Familiar whistles- similar to the ones that had haunted me from inside my apartment on Saturn Avenue in LA- emanate from the back of the house. I can also hear agile feet fleeing across the aluminium roof of the Jane Shilton factory that backs onto my father's garden. From my front-facing bedroom I can see directly across to the window of the house opposite, over the road, where I am convinced someone is spying on me. Whenever I bolt up to throw back the heavy drape they turn off the light as if we were playing some childish game. What do they want from me?

With all this activity sleep is impossible, although my jetlagged body cries out for rest and I experience periodic twinges of pain in my lower back. I need to keep guard; I have no choice but to remain vigilant and alert. I have lost track of how many lines of crystal I have snorted and I know my paranoia is strong but believe it to be wholly justified.

The next morning, after no sleep, I board the National Express coach at Victoria Coach Station.

And I see him! There he is- sitting there waiting- the man from the plane. He is biding his time waiting for me to arrive. It is the same man that was sitting next to me on the plane. I am terrible with names but I have never, ever forgotten a face. My father has already boarded the coach and taken his seat while people are jostling each other trying to find theirs. I retrace my steps and grab my overnight bag that has been loaded in the undercarriage.

"We're leaving in five minutes," the driver points out.

"I'm getting off!"

I have no idea where I am going, but I know that I cannot stay on the coach with that man. What does he want with me? Who is he?

I lug my bag and walk for a while; I am unsure where to go. I stop at a café on a side street in Victoria. I sit with my coffee and look at a tabloid paper that someone has left behind. Inside the front page is a story about a homosexual MP, and a photograph of him with his wife and daughter. I cannot believe my eyes! In the black and white photograph are the man and daughter that had been staring me down at the airport. But why have they taken umbrage with me? I deduce that they are connected to Gabe and his ring of crime.

I walk and run. I hail a taxi; it stops and then his radio stops working and he drives away. I continue to walk. The streets are almost empty around Eaton Square. I am now scared to return to my father's house because I will be alone there. It seems safer out on the open road so I head past Peter

Jones. I walk along and a familiar face waves at me from a VW beetle- It distinctly looks like Lissa's friend Brigitte and she's laughing at me. What is she doing in London?

I keep going until I end up on Finborough Road, near Earl's Court. I sense that whoever they are, they are getting nearer and the traffic seems to be increasing. I see a YMCA Hostel on Earl's Court Road and I enter. An Indian woman comes to the reception desk.

"Can I help you?" She asks in a slightly arch tone.

"I'm looking for a place to stay. I think my life is in danger. . ." I start to dry heave because tears cannot form.

The woman looks at me hard:

"Wait here. I need to speak to someone, okay?"

She goes back from whence she came and I realise she must be in on it too. My gear! I take it out from inside the secret cave in my wallet and shove the whole bag in my mouth. The bitter taste of the crystal powder makes me gag, but I swallow it down and shove the baggy in the dried earth of the office plant on the desk. I pick up my bag with renewed strength and flee out the door before she returns. I am not falling victim to her caper.

I head back to Chelsea. I will find a payphone and get someone- an old friend- to come collect me. An old friend I can trust to not be working with these goons who operate on both sides of the Atlantic with their underhand, corrupt methods. I move into the middle of the road because I am nervous of being cornered on the pavement. If they do get to me I can throw myself in front of a car and end up in hospital, rather than in one of their torture dens. I know they have it all planned out and it will give them immense pleasure to finally catch this mouse and give her what she deserves.

One or two cars honk their horns but I walk fairly straight along the centre divide. Once back on the Kings Road I feel safer; at Wellington Square I stop for breath a few feet away from the flower seller. And then they swoop.

Four officers are present which strikes me as rather unnecessary- I only weigh about ninety pounds. Two of them back me up against a tree.

"Where are you going?" One of them asks.

"Back home to Fulham." I answer sensibly.

243

"Is that right?" He continues, smirking.

"Yes it is."

"No you're not!" He tartly informs me bringing out the cuff. They crowd in on me and I am cornered, but I still fight them with all my might, clawing and kicking, desperate for flight. I am not going to make it easy for them this time!

I dart across the road. Men crowd me- spiteful uniformed foot soldiers- and hem me up against the window display of Gap. Shoppers start to gather round the commotion suspiciously. They also suspect foul play; they too fear for me in the face of this firing squad.

The growing crowd fills me with newfound courage and confidence- I stoop down suddenly and push through the wall of menace until a sharp pain stops me dead in my tracks. At first I cannot identify the sensation. My struggle is cut violently short by temporary paralysis to my arm and caved chest. This strange and sharp sensation invades as if from nowhere- a dangerous current of intense electrical energy.

I freeze with abject fear.

"You're not going anywhere now- you stupid girl!" A pasty, narrow-faced officer growls this at me.

"What are you doing to that young woman? She's not doing anything wrong." An elegantly dressed, well-spoken woman enquires.

"This is police business, madam."

The electric shock has the desired effect: Temporary surrender. Similar to the LAPD, the British Police have no patience with people like me; clearly we really bring out the worst in them. My memory habitually recoils as I try to piece the sequence of events together and even now it does not serve me clearly. One thing I am positive of is that their method of arrest, holding, and subsequent sectioning was unnecessarily cruel and very heavy-handed. To this day I am trying to get a copy of the police report.

I am carried and violently hurled face-down onto the rusty, filthy floor of a police van- the windowless type with two oafs sitting on rudimentary benches either side and above me, their heavy-booted feet holding me down flat as if I might rise up and bite.

I hear mention of needles and realise they think I have some hidden on me. From the obstructed front I can hear a nasally voice issue instruction:

"Gordon! Only place for the likes of 'er!"

Gordon!? These words were equivalent to the heavens opening, Jesus appearing before me, Buddha beckoning, a phoenix rising up out from the ashes.

I understand. I have to experience suffering to reap my reward.

My feelings of shame, desertion and isolation strike me now as worthwhile penance. Of course! Everything falls into place. Back to Gordon I will go. Where else could I go but to Gordon- the first man I had fallen for in LA and the one who introduced me to my nemesis, crystal meth. He was my mentor, my teacher, my lover, my friend, the one who set it all off, set me off like a boisterous child smashing a stink bomb, running off and leaving his playmates to inhale the rancid eggy fumes while giggling outside the window.

Gordon is my self-proclaimed genius and finally he has returned to rescue me. I will pay homage to my genius Gordon!

I am deposited in a cell at Chelsea police station. The desk clerk asks me a few basic questions, but I refuse to answer. Once in the cell I try to decipher the carved messages left for me on the wooden berth and scribbled on the walls. But the names- Darren, Monica, Joe- are unfamiliar... unless they are in code. My mind is too restless right now to decipher a code.

I stand at the cell door straining to hear. I see wires all around me. I am terrified they will turn them on and fry me alive. Oh what have I done? Am I to die without the knowledge of what my crime is? I collapse onto the dusty floor and close my eyes. My father! What of him? I assume he is still on the coach. And then I realise that because I left the coach, the man from the plane will escort him off the coach, somewhere along the way, and lead him away to kill him. My father will protest and attempt reason, but the man will ignore him. I start to scream:

"No! Not him! Take me! I am the bad one! Not him!"

"Keep it down in there, will you." A gruff voice scolds me from outside the cell.

I sob my heart out. How can they take my sweet, kind father when I am the one they want. No! I will give them whatever they want. Anything and everything to spare him. But maybe it is already too late? I strip off my underwear- a lycra body with under-wiring- and stuff it into the toilet and keep flushing until it goes down. I figure that someone somewhere will find it and trace it back to me. When I show up dead it will serve as evidence.

I hear a loud drill of some kind in the near distance: A brief moment of hope enters my soul- Ajax will come and rescue me! He is going to bulldoze his way through this thick, brick wall and rescue me from our oppressors. After all this he will reveal himself as an undercover operative who has been forced to watch me play out this sting to uncover international paedophile circulation methods. I will have aided in the exposure of a sick ring of paedophiles.

The perfect explanation falls into place: A weak woman (myself) is targeted and used unwittingly as a courier of illegal material from LA to London; all they need now is to retrieve their disk, chip or whatever form of the latest technology they have used to store their illegal material. Their plan went slightly awry when I spent so long in the bathroom at the airport and the man from the plane lost me so now the police (someone has been bought) have my property, with my house keys inside, and they can go to my house and enter easily and retrieve their smuggled goods from my luggage.

I wait. But the drill has almost dimmed to nothing. Where is he? I cannot stand the wait. The cell door opens:

"The doctor's here now to see you. Follow me."

Doctor! What do I need with a doctor? But anything to leave the disguised torture cell.

Inside an Interview room a middle-aged doctor sits across from me.

246

"Do you have any medication or drugs on you?"

"A couple of Vicodin." I tell him.

"What's Vicodin?" He asks.

Huh! Please- how can a doctor not know what Vicodin is? He is trying to trick me. I decide to keep my mouth firmly closed. He leaves the room briefly, only to return with the officers who had arrested me.

My bony shoulders and feet are grabbed and lifted roughly. I am taken out to the same van and pushed down on the floor of it again. I shiver all over, my bones stiff and cold. I close my eyes and accept that death is coming. They drag me out of the van and up onto my feet. A hospital doorway evilly beckons with fluorescent overhead like the entrance to hell. It darts open on an electrical spring.

I panic. I pull away, arms flailing. Struggle follows and people in white coats and navy uniforms blend together like one big monster trying to squash me into nothing, dragging, poking and pulling at me. I am a mauled animal, considered dangerous, a threat to myself and others. Then a quick sharp jab from nowhere enters through the layers of wool I wear into my tight, scared skin.

I am a lump of pliable putty, calm- Oblivion.

I am floating, the air is fresh and I am whole once again as the universe always intended me to be.

No one rescues me. Gordon turns out to be The Gordon Hospital- a small mental hospital in Victoria, central London and not Gordon, my long-lost ex-boyfriend from LA. What a mistake. I had wanted to close the circle and in a way I have, just not as I had envisioned.

How on earth do I end up here? For this was surely hell. Days later- how many I have no idea- I lie encased in starched linen in a sterile room. My surroundings consist of one wooden chair against the far wall, a night-stand with a tumbler and a plastic jug of water in which something grey- the wing of a fly it turns out- floats, an ordinary rectangular window with beige bars on the outside and a thick wooden door with a glass observation panel barricading me in. There's no sign of my bag or clothes.

That dead-dodo sleep after a speed-run has been interrupted forever. If I had known this was to be my last encounter with crystal meth, I would have paid more attention to detail, revelled in the splendid terrifying paranoia, the subsequent paralysis, the disavowal of food and drink. The strangest part for me, in all this miasma of hedonism, excess and drama that happened in LA, is that the 'grand finale' was to take place back in London.

My recollection of recent events is smudgy. I re-run and rewind the events while I inspect the cloudlike purplish stains covering my upper arms, calves, and ankles. Wedged between my legs is something rubbery and sticky with cold night sweat. Peeling my stick-thin thighs off it, I unravel what appears to be a wound up bathmat- a larger version of the type used to bathe infants. Then I remember how I'd awakened in terror and wanted the rubber mat with me in case 'the enemy' entered my room and tried to electrocute me.

My brain aches. An over-riding sensation of blurriness is constant. I sleep.

I wake up and it is daylight. The nurse has gone, at least temporarily. I bolt to the elevator which is almost in front of my door. It is a lock up ward but I am fast. I jump in the elevator and no one sees me. We are on the fourth floor and I get down to the ground floor where I see a glass exit door. I barrage through and no one stops me.

I am barefoot and wearing pale blue hospital pyjamas- not dissimilar to the jail uniform- and I am scared again. I race along a main road, Vauxhall Bridge Road and take a slip road, Wilton Place, into Victoria Station. I pass a Biguns Rib House Restaurant and inside I see the aforementioned MP and his blond daughter who are eating a meal and waiting for me to make my next move.

People turn to look as I zip past them. I head into the railway part of Victoria Station. I have no money. I have nothing on me, not even the keys to my father's house. I go to a pay phone and I make a call to my mother's friend, Jean, reversing the charges:

"Hello Clea, are you alright?" Jean asks in a light tone.

"No please, you have to help me! Someone is trying to kill me. I'm at the station and I don't know what to do!" I splutter.

Dead silence greets me for some moments. I detect whispering and now I know they are in on it too.

"I'm going to call your mother, Clea. Why don't you give me the phone number where you are and one of us will telephone you back in a few minutes-"

No way! I slam the receiver back on the hook. I turn and a female police officer approaches.

"Miss? Are you okay?" She looks kind.

I shake my head; tears start to roll like thunder down my face. I am woozy and before I know what is happening I am sitting in a police van with this woman who has poured me a cup of steamy tea from a thermos. Why is she being so nice to me?

"You fainted. So where have you come from?" She asks gently.

"Some place nearby."

"Is it a hospital?"

I nod, defeated. What is there to do but go back? They drive me back- in a normal van with regular seats and windows- and she escorts me back up to the fourth floor. No one says anything and a cordial male nurse offers me a cigarette. He sits down next to me on the worn lumpy sofa in the TV room.

"All the doctors are off till the 28th December so you might as well relax and watch some Christmas telly."

"I don't think I have much choice."

My poor father in his early 70s had not realised that I had left the coach until he'd almost arrived in Exeter; he'd assumed I was in the loo. When I question him about his evident lack of concern, he claims he believed I'd changed my mind and decided to go visit a friend.

Basically I had been too much for him to cope with.

When I am released from the hospital and return with

my father to his house in Fulham, I search everywhere for the Louis Vuitton suitcase and it is nowhere to be found. I know I had taken it with me to LAX airport and checked it in with two others (Mia had paid the excess baggage charge of $80), and I remember retrieving it from the carousel at Heathrow. Granted, back at the house I had been in a daze, throwing together my weekend bag for the xmas trip to Devon with all my suitcases thrown open haphazardly in an attempt to find and re-pack appropriate clothes and toiletries, but there were definitely three cases.

I am convinced that the missing suitcase had some thing hidden inside it that someone wanted and I had got it to them, unwittingly.

CHAPTER 27

Release and Recovery

You may shoot me down with your words,
You may cut me with your eyes.
You may kill me with your hatefulness,
 But still, like air, I'll rise.

Maya Angelou *Still I Rise*

Her wounds came from the same source as her power. . .
Adrienne Rich

Three and a half years later I receive an email from Marnie. I had had no contact with her since I'd left LA and that had made sense, although I wondered about her from time to time, and more than anything hoped that she had found the solace she so clearly craved.

Hi Clea,

I got your email address from Roxanne who was kind of weird about giving it to me. I managed to persuade her it was important because you'd want to hear the news that Gabe just got sentenced to 8 years jail time for child pornography. He'll get out in 4 or less, but at least they're onto him.
I'm okay. I moved to Sedona and now run a café/art gallery with my boyfriend. I met him in hospital when I broke my back, trying to escape the cops. I was stuck in there for over a year. Pretty serious stuff, but as Jeremiah used to say, 'You get arrested when you need a rest.' The whole thing was

really horrific, but we've got to look forward, not back, right!
I know you'll be okay.

With love and in my thoughts always,
Marniexox

PS: I understand if you don't reply.

Having travelled far with, and without, Marnie I find my reply difficult to compose and send. But most of all I am happy that she is alive and managing to put back the pieces of her own fractured life.

Maybe I'll go to Sedona someday; it's a place I've always wanted to visit. . .

EPILOGUE

Putting Back the Pieces. . .

I see the addict as a seeker, albeit a misguided one . . .
in quest of pleasure, perhaps even of a kind of
transcendent experience- . . .There's nothing to be
ashamed of in this impulse. On the contrary, it provides
a foundation for true hope and real transformation.
                                    Deepak Chopra

During visiting hours at the Gordon Hospital my father
recounts a conversation from when I was six years old. Belted
into the smelly leather passenger seat of his white convertible
MGB car, I declare:

"I don't want to live!"
"Why not?" My father asks.
"Because I don't."
"But you must have a reason?"
"I don't know why. I just know I hate living."

I doubt I will ever understand my own desire to self-
destruct, but it is undeniably part of my nature.

It is over ten years since I left LA for good. The truth is I
know this is my story but I do not recognise myself in it: I am
outside, looking in. Hindsight gives a clear and simple picture,
but nothing was like that at the time.

Once I am disgracefully thrown and flown out of Los
Angeles, arrested on my second day back in London, and
sectioned to a mental hospital, one might assume that I come
to some kind of life-changing decision. I do not. My mental
resources are limited and oftentimes scrambled. My belief that

253

I had been wanted dead holds fast- even without drugs in my system- and the reality of the chaos I'd left behind in LA- and indeed that which arrived in London with me- precludes any form of systematic recovery solution.

Some things are apparent: I am physically and mentally worn out. My sanity is bouncing between delusion and a shallow perception of reality. The mental, physical and spiritual damage I have caused myself needs to be repaired. I wade slowly- one pace forward, often two back.

Most people and families have experience, or know, of an addict who seemingly chooses to self-destruct, yet it is still one of the last taboos, like the mad aunt locked in the attic. In my own family alcoholism, depression and schizophrenia are prevalent, yet the subjects were never broached whilst I was growing up; indeed they are barely acknowledged today. I simply believe I have a responsibility to myself and other addicts, to stand up and own this reality. Addiction is a form of mental illness, and sweeping it under the carpet is not the answer. I know it's ugly, but it's not going away.

Recovery snail paces along- in fact, I reckon I have spent longer recovering, than I ever have on drugs, but that's just another aspect of the insanity of addiction. The solution: 'stay off drugs' is obvious, but never simple. The addictive cycle is hard to break; the aftermath is laborious, slow and messy because there are no 'quick fixes'.

Significantly, crystal meth is not available in the UK. Of course, there are other drugs and I seek those out, but never with the same obsessive greed and need that crystal meth engendered in me.

What I think is most important for anyone trying to get off drugs is a genuine belief in something tangible. Initially, for me, it was learning the craft of acting. I suspect that my experience on crystal meth was the catalyst I subconsciously chose to wake me up and fight to become happy: to make me conscious. On the plus side, I had the perverse good fortune to hit rock-bottom fast. Even when utterly deluded I could glimpse the evident dead end- I would either end up locked away in a mental hospital, in jail or dead. I was not ready to die so the only option was to quit and change. Part of me knew this was essential, but there was never a big moment of 'Aha! Now I get it' but instead increments of change that eventually bore fruit. And there were plenty of dark days in between.

Certainly I had lost my soul to crystal meth, but how do I go about restoring it? I know there is not one answer, but a combination of answers that start to teach me to respect my life rather than begrudge it, but like addiction it did not happen overnight. . .

Right before my release from the Gordon Hospital, a nurse takes me to register at the Stimulant Clinic in Earl's Court. Even though crystal meth has left my system, I cannot shake the idea that I'm being watched. I no longer fear being murdered, just that I will be kept an eye on. This obsession continues for at least nine months and I share it with anyone willing to listen. A couple of people suggest I write a book about my time in LA!

The day clinic is disappointing and nothing like the expensive, ordered and residential Promises, but an NHS drop-in centre on Earl's Court Road. They expect me to have motivation to face my drug problem, show up on time and attend groups. I pull it off the first week, but the energy and commitment never emerges and I attend in an uncommitted fashion. Getting out of bed, deciding what to wear, putting on my clothes and boarding the underground is hard enough, let alone attending an uninspired clinic five days a week. I never connect with the clinic, or the other patients, over the three month period, although I do get some order back into my life, as well as some much needed sleep. I decide not to try the NA fellowship in London and develop my own concept of recovery and regeneration.

The 'hole' returns with a vengeance. I am prescribed the same anti-depressant (Effexor) that Dr Rubinstein initially prescribed me and that helps to the point of getting me up before dark, in the wintertime, and progressively earlier while I become more acclimatised to my new life in London.

About a year after my return from America I start to fan some embers of my long-held dream of becoming an actress.

Inner resources spark into a low fire- a sensation similar to that which motivated my headstrong move to LA and subsequent spiral into drug addiction- that now propels me to enrol on a slew of acting classes in central London. I determine to transform my dream into reality. I take various part-time jobs to fund my plan. I live at home with my father who does not charge me rent while he also covers the household overheads, at least initially. I live like a student. This suits me well because in many ways that is what I am.

When I start to study acting I open a door into myself that is an important step for my own development as a human being, as well as my goal towards becoming a good actress. This extreme focus is what saves me because it gives me purpose, structure and a viable creative outlet. Classes require me to make commitments to other students, attend class regularly, learn lines, study, trips to the theatre and films, as well as further courses of study- connected to acting- like Alexander Technique, yoga and martial arts.

Before I'd become a tweaker I'd only had vague awareness of the power of the five senses- I was always in a frenzied rush from A to Z- and now it is required of me to investigate, understand and learn from them. In my acting classes I start to scrape away some of the defences I have developed- my personal armour- that I now carry with me, both mentally and physically, that create obstacles to the natural flow of emotion and movement. Through this process of sensory work (sense memory using sight, sound, taste, touch, smell) I become aware of myself as a physical and feeling person again. Having been out of sync with my body for so long, I had never questioned it, but now I start to experience what it is like to actually be conscious within my own body and to slow down and experience my own reality. This process of integration helps me to challenge my nervy speediness, and experience moments of stillness- not often granted- but a door has been pushed slightly ajar. I embark on a journey towards mindfulness.

Alongside the study of acting, I find a good therapist that I trust. When I first start therapy I am brittle, detached and unable to clearly identify emotions; an enormous rage brews inside me.

Fortunately, I have a couple of school friends who remain loyal and supportive, including Natasha and Vanessa. I also make new friends and keep quiet about my time in LA. If I go out to a party, or club- the tail-end of the rave scene is in declining swing- I take drugs if they are available- ecstasy usually, sometimes coke- but they never take me prisoner like my nemesis, crystal meth.

The jinxed black cloud over my head, that followed me from LA, starts to evaporate and my life is functional again, sort of. . .

The passage of time, alongside acting proves a healing tonic. Only when I venture into the competitive arena of talent agents, castings and auditions does my cracked base reappear in the way I start to doubt myself and take every rejection personally, even when logic suggests otherwise. My mind has cleared, but I start to binge drink alcohol in response to the situation. I have not forgotten what I learned at Promises about the cunning disease of Addiction, but because I am coping- superficially at least- I continue.

After about five years back in London, a sense of emptiness prevails: a desire for wholeness possesses me. Occasional acting jobs and a loving boyfriend do not relieve this inner emptiness. Will I always feel lost?

Prompted by my father- ever loyal- I suspect I need something tangible to get my teeth into- a philosophy to underpin and transform the core of my life.

My seeking spirit now heads out of the dark and into the sunny light of Buddhism. I attend some lectures and investigate the different schools of Buddhism available in London. I go to Turkey on a yoga holiday and while there I meet the practice of Nichiren Daishonin through my yoga teacher and her friend. What is truly incredible to me is the way this philosophy fits with what I have always believed about life, synchronicity and the ultimate power within humanity and the universe.

Most importantly, the Buddhism of Nichiren Daishonin

denies the existence of any omniscient, all-powerful deity. Hence, there is no one to judge, punish or forgive me for my past actions and behaviour. It is my sole responsibility, as an addict, to transform myself. My unhappiness is a result of cause and effect: from the karma I have made through my past causes during this life-time (as this book attests), and throughout eternity.

Through my Buddhist practice I set in motion a spiritual process of chipping away, dissolving and purifying the layers of negativity - guilt, shame, self-hatred, resentment, anxiety, fear- that I carry with me. When a strong emotion like anger, starts to monopolise my mood I chant to transform the anger into passion- from the negative into positive- and the revelation is that this actually starts to happen. What a relief to start dropping some of that heavy baggage!

Also, the joy I experience, through this process, alongside my involvement with Buddhist activities is above and beyond any form of drug-induced high.

Finally, I find the inner courage to sit down and make a stab at writing my story, something I have wanted to do ever since I returned from LA. By transforming my feelings of being a victim and an injured party, I venture back into my memories and re-live the people and events- and gradually my adventure and oftentimes painful experiences become a book: I create value through communicating my real-life story of addiction to others.

With Buddhism, I change myself in many ways, although my essence remains the same. Through this marked attempt at a balanced life-style my self-obsession and addictive tendencies head in a more creative direction. A cynic, understandably, might say I have 'grown up' whereas I feel it is all part of what I chose to challenge during this life-time.

Illegal drugs are no longer in my life, but alcohol still offers a challenge.

I had made a sick kind of bargain with myself: give up drugs, but drinking is okay. Undoubtedly, I craved the emotional blunting that alcohol gave me and I justified the occasional release that it afforded me. After all, alcohol is legal and in the UK, highly acceptable. In fact, being teetotal is viewed with disdain in my experience, especially as an aspiring thespian.

Then, seemingly out-of-nowhere, I experienced premature ovarian failure (early menopause) at the age of 35: a direct consequence of my drug abuse where I have irrevocably damaged my reproductive system. This unexpected and intense loss exacerbated my drinking. Through my Buddhist practice I could understand I needed to stop, or I would finally succeed in my self-destruction. But it was incredibly hard!

Part of me still believed that I had some kind of choice whether I drank, or not. In fact, as soon as I took an alcoholic drink, my illness was back in the driving seat and I could not stop. There were evenings I had a semblance of control and then more frequent binges where I stocked up and battened down the hatches to get drunk alone. On occasion I would be out socially and lose control, but my behaviour was always so bad that I consciously chose to drink alone rather than have to endure other people's recollections and call up friends and acquaintance, offering apologies.

I could stop drinking for a few months at a time, but invariably would return to the same pattern of use. The relapses were destroying me because of the recurrent theme of self-sabotage that I was unable to overcome.

After much soul-searching I enter rehab again for a month- Promis in Kent. I had become a binge drinker that got drunk between one and three evenings a week. My early menopause, or Premature Ovarian Failure, alongside my drinking had brought me to my knees. I was severely depressed, and exhausted physically and emotionally. I was very grateful to check-in to Promis. I had an entire month to focus entirely on myself and my emotional needs. What an incredible gift!

By the time I arrived I was bursting with unexpressed emotion- predominantly anger- and I was a challenging patient for most of my stay. But that time away- for recuperation, support, understanding, therapy and learning- enabled me to grapple with the reality that recovery from addiction is a life-long process. My first time in rehab, back in the late 1990's, was the introduction, and now I am entirely ready to accept I am an addict who has an illness that knows only destruction if left untreated. This was my journey; some addicts may understand their predicament more quickly than I was capable of. Some will never accept they even have an illness.

I still grapple with the 12-step philosophy- I am highly analytic by nature- but I have re-assessed my relationship and now see the AA Fellowship as a powerful tool in the battle against addiction. 12 Step Programs are spiritual and practical ways to nourish and develop the self, while staying free of alcohol and drugs. Attending an AA meeting is a dose of medicine for my addictive illness.

Thus far, I cherish the work I have done with my AA sponsor and I can sense the growth within me. Bill Wilson, the founder of Alcoholics Anonymous (1939) created the grassroots idea of one alcoholic/addict helping another- simple, powerful, egalitarian and non-elitist. The only requirement for membership is a desire to stop drinking alcohol, or using drugs. There is a worldwide support network in existence that I now feel part of. And attendance at meetings has become an antidote to the isolation I often feel as a recovering addict, as well as countering my denial. My wonderful sponsor, who is also a Buddhist, suggested I take my Gohonzon (Buddhist scroll) into rehab with me. I had it by my bed, on the widow-sill, and I chanted morning and evening.

As a Buddhist I found it very hard to admit complete and utter powerlessness over my addictive illness, but I have ultimately surrendered to this concept. I fought it for years and my illness re-surfaced as alcoholism. Basically my illness stayed with me, regardless of whatever chemical I favoured. And in the case of my addiction I believe I had to surrender to win. This is just one of the many paradoxes I have come across in recovery. Ultimately I consider myself a recovering human being because the most substantial loss to me was my humanness and compassion, for myself and others.

My hope is that society will accept addictive illness, as an illness, that can be treated- through abstinence, in my case, from all mood-altering substances- and a day-by-day recovery program. Historically, similar attitudes existed towards epilepsy, diabetes and other mental disorders like bi-polar and schizophrenia. I had to alter my own perceptions and understanding in order to make the correct adjustments in my own life. And I have had to accept that addictive illness needs consistent recognition in order to combat the negative aspects, so I combine my Program with Buddhism. It works for me. . .

Ideally, I strive to stay off all mood-altering chemicals, but I also accept that it is part of my nature to desire escape from reality. I still have occasional slips. Collecting a chip- awarded within Anonymous programs for years of 'sobriety' and a goal I aim for- does not equate happiness for me. True self-acceptance does. . .

~~~~~~~

I have been fortunate that my family- namely the Vronskys and my father- have remained constant and we have a good relationship again.

They are very special, compassionate people.

My relationship with my mother has improved, although I do not see her very often we speak over the phone from time to time.

Most of all, my relationship with my father has grown in extraordinary ways. I never expected to end up living with him and vice versa. He always gave me unconditional love and supports me, even when it is very difficult for him to understand what is going on in my life. We laugh a lot together now because harmony is restored, even though it arrived through total chaos. We enjoy each other's company and we talk on a level of honesty that was never hinted at before.

I am no longer a victim of my circumstances. I had always believed that there was an invisible web connecting us with everything; now I know nothing I experience is coincidental. I am the screenwriter, the director and producer of my own life and I write my own film every day with my thoughts, words and actions.

I can still be moody, morose and intense, but I remind myself that my life is not a problem to be solved. Life is to be lived right now and all I need to do is keep the door open, because it was never closed. It just looked that way from where I was standing.

Permissions

Grateful acknowledgement is made to the following for permission to reprint excerpts from previously published material:

Gather Together In My Name by Maya Angelou. New York: Random House (1974)

The Good Earth by Pearl S. Buck. New York: Washington Square Press (2004)

Great Women Writers: the lives and works of 135 of the world's most important women writers, from antiquity to the present by F.N Magill. A Henry Holt reference book. New York: Holt (1994)

The Doves of Finisterre by Julia Casterton. Norwich: The Rialto (2004)

Delta of Venus: erotica by Anais Nin New York: Harcourt Brace Jovanovich (1977)

Beyond good and evil: prelude to a philosophy of the future by F.W. Nietzsche. Penguin Classics. London, England: Penguin Books (1990)*Cocteau's World; an anthology of writings* by Jean Cocteau & M. Crosland. New York: Dodd, Mead Frost, R., & Lathem, E. C. (1969).

The Poetry of Robert Frost. New York: Holt, Rinehart and Winston (1974)

The Essential Jung, by Carl Jung, Anthony Storr. Princeton, N.J. Princeton University Press, ©1983.

The House of Fear: notes from Down Below by Leonora Carrington. New York: E.P. Dutton, ©1988.

Complete Works of Horace by Horace, J.C Kraemer. New York, The Modern library ©1936

Brilliant Traces, by Cindy Lou Johnson. New York, N.Y. (440 Park Ave South, New York 10016) Dramatists Play Service, ©1989

No Exit by Jean-Paul Sartre. New York: Vintage International. 1989

Seven Plays by George Bernard Shaw. New York, Dodd, Mead.1951

Chitty, Chitty, Bang, Bang by Dick Van Dyke, Ian Fleming, MGM Home Entertainment. Copyright Santa Monica, CA : MGM Home Entertainment, Inc., ©1998.

New York Times. 1993, PARS International Corp, Los Angeles Times, 1998, PARS International Corp

Acknowledgements

Special thanks to William Wykeham Basil Myers,
Lula Myers (RIP) Alice Green, the Joukowsky Family,
Pop Hayward, Dill Valaydon, Dean Gylten (RIP),
Rohanne Descy, Victoria Kanter, Robert Costanza,
Bene Naudin, Kiki Huygelin, Julia Casterton (RIP),
Stephen Morrison, Tanya Agathocleous, Andrew Hudson,
Simon Benham, Charlie Ward, Karen Ingman, Daisaku Ikeda,
the members of SGI-UK, in particular the members of
Pimlico District and the leaders in Kensington and Chelsea
HQ, the fellowship of Alcoholics Anonymous

About the Author

Clea Myers raises awareness in the UK about the dangers of crystal meth, the class 'A' drug that has become endemic in the US, parts of Asia and Australia. She joined forces with FRANK in 2006.

She has done various interviews for print and TV to maintain the high level of awareness around the potential chaos and damage that crystal meth will cause, in the UK, if it does manage to gain a foothold.

She lives in London where she works as an actress, writer and editor on www.thiswayupezine.com where she edits a section about addiction- *What's Your Poison*

She can be contacted at cleamyers@hotmail.com